THE DEVIL I LOVE
A CONTEMPORARY GOTHIC ROMANCE

THE DEVIL CHRONICLES
BOOK TWO

KAY FREEMAN

KAY FREEMAN LLC

The story, all names, characters, and incidents portrayed in this production are fictitious. No identification with actual persons (living or deceased), places, buildings, or products is intended or should be inferred.

Age 18+ Content:

This Gothic suspense romance novel contains power exchange dynamics and light BDSM activities. Both the hero and heroine are survivors of physical abuse. He's a victim of child abuse, and she is a domestic violence survivor. The hero's mother suffered from drug addiction, and his father used his religious fervor as a weapon. Her mother committed suicide. The book also contains graphic descriptions of sexual activities and scenes of violence. If you find any of this objectionable or triggering, stay clear. However, the book is healing and hopeful, ending with a positive, loving relationship.

A big thank you to my editor, Jason Pettus, who keeps me from making a fool of myself more times than I can count.

To my cover designer, Consuelo Parra, for creating such an outstanding cover.

To my husband, Barry, for always providing a sounding board and a shoulder to cry on.

To Ginny Hubbard, my best friend, who has always been there.

And lastly, to Sue Brown Moore, editor, coach, consultant, and teacher, for her guidance and generosity while working with me on this manuscript.

I

THE BREAKUP & HADES DOG

CRUZ

"We need to postpone the marriage." My words echo through the cavernous space, sounding harsher than I intended. The yellow flames from the candles reflect in River's eyes, and a tear slides down her cheek. It's like when you're passing a car wreck; I don't want to look, but I can't stop myself.

My bedroom is the quietest room in The Palace, which is the reason I brought River here. Everywhere else in the house is frenzied and boisterous as my employees get ready for work. They live here with me, and that's the way it's always been, and it seems it's going to remain that way.

River's shoulders slump. "I can't believe you're doing this, Cruz."

She collapses onto my throne, carved from ebony. I purchased the piece at auction. It was a steal. In the past, you had to come from royalty to sit on one, or kill someone who did. Most people today don't feel comfortable sitting on one unless it's in jest. You need a large ego to do it, which suits me fine. No one sits on it but me. River realizes she's made a mistake and gets up quickly.

Her face crumples. "Why must we?"

"I thought I could, but I can't. I've lived in The Palace since I was twelve and—"

River staggers toward me. "You promised. You said we'd be a family. You're going back on your word." Her forehead wrinkles.

"I can't give up a business I'm good at. I've done it a long time and—"

"You have Monsters now. It's a nightclub, and it's legal, not against the law like..."

She holds the rest of her words while holding her hands at the same time. She doesn't call it a whorehouse, a brothel, or any of the other nasty names people use to describe what I do.

"Be realistic, River. Monsters can't come close to earning enough money. It's just another Chicago nightclub. I make ten times the amount in receivables in a single day with The Palace. I'm sorry, River, but I can't give it up, or any of the others...yet. I've got too much overhead."

"But maybe someone else can run it and—"

"I can't; no one else can manage the women." Is it a coincidence that right at that moment, I see two of my workers leaving for the evening dressed like they're attending a sporting event? "Maya, Gino, step in here for a moment."

"What's up, boss?" Maya asks, spinning a baseball hat around her head and flashing her million-dollar smile, the one men three times her age can't say no to.

"Why are you wearing that?" I wave my hands over both of them.

"I like to be comfortable," Maya says. Gino, my new worker,

bobbed his head up and down. He's attractive with his dark hair, olive skin, and green eyes, and as long as he doesn't open his mouth, he remains that way; but as soon as he starts talking, it becomes apparent there's nothing upstairs, and his good looks fade away. That's why I pair him with Maya. She's the brainy one, and I've coached her to stick with him like glue and do the speaking for him.

"It's not about your comfort. Maya. It's about the client wanting to spend time and money on you. Go change. Lose the hat, take off the sneakers and the sweats, and wear a short skirt, a pair of stilettos, and a low-cut top. But leave something to the imagination. The idea is glamour and desirability. Gino—dress slacks, a blazer, and wingtips. We sell S. E X. Sneakers, and sweats don't cut it. Until that logo on your sneaker turns into a dildo and starts bringing in the dough, you aren't wearing them to see clients."

Maya bursts out laughing. "Cruz, you sound like my father when you said. 'It's not about my comfort, but not the rest of it. of course."

They both bounce out of the room, and I close the door. "Sorry, River. Gino's new, and he'd come back with nothing."

"When will you be ready to marry and give up the brothel?" River twists her engagement ring. The smell of burning sage is the only thing keeping me strong. I want to take back my words before I say them. Do anything to stop what's coming. But it has to be done. I need to make her go. I'd said several chants to build my strength earlier, but they won't protect us from what will happen when I say these next three words.

"I can't say."

River stares at me. "Joy and Alex can't live with sex workers. I'm sorry." She slips my skull-butterfly ring off her finger and places it in my open palm. "My children and I will have to move out, but at least you had the kindness to wait until after the holidays to tell me. Thank you for that." She rushes out of the room and closes the door behind her.

I release my breath and ease into my throne. The room spins and slips away. I run my fingers over the velvet seat. I didn't tell River everything. As soon as I learned in November that I didn't get the loan, I knew what I had to do. Without the money, I couldn't pursue my large-scale restaurant project, and since I needed to keep the brothel, I had to let River go.

Ring. Ring. Ring.

I jump out of the chair and grab the phone on my desk. "What...what do you want?" I growl, scattering the stones that form a circle on the floor, the sacred space I use to do my work in all directions.

"You've got three weeks to bring her to me," the voice on the phone says. "If you don't, I'll take her by force, and that will be a more unpleasant experience for her." The line goes dead. Should I call him back and tell him the engagement is off? This should end his hold on her and me, too.

I'm a fraud.

I close my eyes, remembering how easy I thought it would be; a few forms and I'd be on my way to owning a legitimate business, becoming a businessperson who people would respect.

"This shouldn't take long," I say before climbing out of the back seat of the SUV. "I just have to talk to the loan officer."

A few minutes later, after I'm inside the bank and have explained why I'm there, the greeter calls the loan manager and gives her my name. The greeter points. "Ms. Cranbrook's cubicle is there."

As soon as I enter the space, I feel something off. Ms. Cranbrook glares at me, her mouth a straight line. "Your paperwork, please," holding her hand out. I come closer and drop the loan application in her hand. Her eyes glaze over as she reads, and her face turns a redder shade the more time she spends.

"There's no way in hell I'd let this bank lend you a stinking dime," she finally says. I feel the floor shift under me. Something is very wrong. "You ruined my husband's and my family's life," she continues. "We almost lost our house, even our children's educational fund. We got close to a divorce. He's in counseling now for sex addiction."

"What are you talking about?" I ask, keeping my voice low.

"Don't lie. Your name's right here on the application. I looked you up. Bridgette worked for you. She took my husband for every dime he had. Coaxed him into spending thousands of dollars on her. Whatever he gave her, it was never enough. I'm sure you remember his name. Max Ryan."

I glance at her desk, and my eyes land on her nameplate, "Cranbrook," posted on wood and metal.

"That's my maiden name," she continues, her eyes sparking.

I remember Max Ryan, alright. He indeed spent thousands of dollars. I process credit cards for workers when clients don't pay in cash. Max Ryan maxed out all of his.

"I'm sorry..." I can't say I wasn't aware, because I was. I didn't know he was blowing the family's budget, though. I never asked if he was married or single. The truth is, at the time, I didn't care.

"I'm sorry too," she sneers. "Get out and don't come back." She wads my loan application into a ball and throws it in her trash can.

"Provided we can work something out, I can..." I hold out my hand, trying to suggest that I could give her husband's money back.

"You'd better leave before I call security." Her face is white now. She reaches for the phone, knocking her stapler off her desk, then a container of pens. I try to help her by picking them up, but she simply says, "Get out."

I do. What else can I do? I'm not a real businessperson. All I am is the owner of a sex business, a pimp. Real businesspeople don't get thrown out of banks. I come back to The Palace, realizing I can't move out or stop my brothel business. That's what's brought me to this moment, to reckon with what I've done and who I am.

Returning to the present moment, I notice the candle's wax oozing and dripping into the brass holder. I remove the small red velvet bag from my pocket and turn it upside down. The gold coin spills out, spinning around in a circle on my desk before falling flat with a clunk. Next, the tiny statue of Ganesh, a Hindu deity, lands feet-first. This magic had always assisted me before whenever I had any financial dealings. This time it's failed me, or most likely I failed myself. A witch knows your word is your worth, and I've already gone back on mine twice. I watch the candles burn. The last one smolders and goes out, and the stone walls turn as black as my thoughts.

ONE MONTH Later

RIVER

Chicago's gusts force me to button my coat collar and tighten my scarf. I scream back to my eight-year-old daughter, "Joy, keep up," only to have my instructions swallowed up by the wind. She dances her mittened hands along the wrought-iron fence, skips and sings, ignoring me.

Joy's been doing a lot of that, the ignoring part. She misses

The Palace and my fiancé, and holds me responsible for our breakup and having to move.

I catch my sunglasses before they blow away. My scarf whips from around my neck and rolls down the street, an emblem of my current condition. *Everything I care about leaves me.* A grizzly image of my mother's face still haunts me, and I push it away along with my memory of Cruz.

"Mommy, your scarf!" My daughter points as it lifts into the air like a red kite and vanishes over the fence into one of my neighbors' yards, marked with a sign that says "Beware of Dog."

In case people think it's just something to scare off would-be burglars, a beast appears behind the gate like something you'd find guarding Hades' underworld. He drags my knitted scarf, shakes it in his mouth, and drops it. When he does, he lifts his top lip, displaying his incisors and snarling. He's daring me to enter, drool dripping out of his mouth everywhere.

"Nope, keep it." I back away, trembling. Dogs are another one of my many phobias. I hear my mother's voice in my brain: *Go to the door, River, and ask your neighbor if you can have it back.* I ignore the voice and try to push the image away, too. I feel bad that I no longer look at photographs of my mother. The only way I can picture her now is the way I found her, hanging by her neck in her bedroom closet, body blue and eyes bulging. Why didn't I notice any of the signs beforehand? I couldn't, because I had my own problems—getting me and my children free of an abusive husband.

My daughter's giggles bring me back. "I guess he likes it." She points at the dog as he tosses it into the air, catches it, then drags it around the yard.

"I liked it too." My heart stutters. It was the last gift Cruz gave me before he broke the news and my heart.

Joy and I continue to move down the sidewalk, the pine scent overwhelming. Numerous discarded Christmas trees line the curb waiting for this week's trash pickup, a reminder that the best year of my life is behind me and the people I love are gone. In two weeks, it will be the anniversary of my mother's suicide, and today marks almost a month since I gave Cruz's ring back, but it seems like an eternity.

Our temporary house, a brownstone, is at the end of the block, but with the wind blowing in our faces, it feels like it's taking us forever to get there. It's a lovely neighborhood, one I could never afford without Cruz's help. The orange sun is disappearing behind the Victorian houses, taking the last bit of warmth with it. The Victorians are vanishing too, seemingly transforming overnight into the latest architectural rage: the Modern Farmhouse style. Roof towers, intricately designed woodwork, and cylindrical turrets in fanciful color schemes are being replaced by gable roofs with vaulted ceilings, numerous windows, larger covered porches, and carriage-style garage doors painted white with black accents.

The street feels more deserted than usual, but it's winter, and everyone's hunkered down inside, hibernating, trying to stay warm. A few chimneys have smoke billowing out of them, and I imagine the smell of popcorn. I push the thought of popcorn out of my mind. I overeat the stuff and don't allow myself to make it anymore.

"Why do we have to walk, Mommy?" Joy asks.

"Because we don't have a car and it's wonderful exercise."

"I don't need exercise. I do it at school. Cruz has a car." Joy bounces from foot to foot. "He could drive us."

"Cruz and I aren't a couple anymore. Don't you remember? We discussed it?"

"You said you were friends now. If that's true, he'd give us a ride." Joy stomps her feet and stares at me. The hair on the back of my neck stands up. My paranoia from the last year of living with Cruz is kicking in. Cruz said to always pay attention to my surroundings when I'm walking on the street. I swivel around, but the street is empty, except for a plastic bag dipping and dancing across the frozen sidewalk, and a calico cat that's skittered under a car.

Joy sees the cat too. "Can we get a cat, Mommy?" She grabs my sleeve. "Pleaaasse, mommy." Every time she sees one, she wants one.

"Maybe someday."

"You always say that," she huffs, rolling her eyes and stomping her feet again. If she keeps doing this, she's going to need new shoes again.

I've never told my daughter, but I'm scared of cats, too, and of hamsters, mice, guinea pigs, and the list goes on. I was getting better with Cruz in my life, but—

The goosebumps that cover my neck and arms aren't going away. Then I see him. He's tall and skinny, and a hoodie casts a shadow over his face, keeping me from seeing his features. He ducks behind a white Tesla on the opposite side of the street. The same thing happens to me as to my daughter whenever I see a Tesla: I want one.

"Come on, Joy, walk faster." *This is bad.*

"Why?" Joy asks, her feet frozen in place, refusing to walk.

I search in the other direction towards our house. Alex, my fourteen-year-old son, is already a half a block ahead, covering the sidewalk in long strides.

"Just move." My heart beats faster, and my stomach clenches as I reach for her hand. As I do, Joy snatches it away. I try again, capture her fingers and fold them into mine.

"Stop pulling," Joy says as I force her to catch up to me. I hear footsteps behind us, and the wind rattles the trees. The sky is blackening as I run, and I pull my daughter with me. I see the reddish house, and relief rushes through me. The rain and dust-streaked arched windows reflect the holiday twinkle lights surrounding them, welcoming us home. My son reaches the iron gate, walks down the entry path, and climbs the steps, facing the black double front doors, a glass window above them with the number "1409" in gold leaf.

The brownstone is huge, originally two separate residences. We only live in the part that's been renovated. The other part is a wreck and hasn't been touched yet. My children think it looks haunted, and I tend to agree, but I don't tell them that. *I'm supposed to be an adult.*

Alex punches the code into the lock, and we catch up just as he flings the door open wide, its hinges creaking. We follow him through. I pull Joy in and slam it shut behind us, turn the deadlock, and disarm and reset the alarm. "Lucy, we're home!" Alex bellows in a cartoonish Cuban accent.

"Why do you always say that?" Joy asks, placing her hands on her hips, facing her brother as she sloughs her coat off onto the floor.

"Because I want to," Alex says, smiling, and winks at me. He turns his back on his sister and heads for the steps, bounding up them two at a time, using the banister to propel himself until he disappears to the second floor. I hear his footsteps proceed down the hall to his bedroom, a secret sanctuary of teen-boy stuff I'm not privy to. At least we share the *I Love Lucy* reference.

"Pick your coat up and hang it on the hook, Joy." I flip on the porch light and look out the window, searching for the man, but he's nowhere in sight. This isn't the first time I've thought someone was following me. It started after Cruz, and I ended things, and in the last week, it's gotten worse.

I move to the couch and sit down, exhausted, and flip my sunglasses up on my head. The living room is my favorite room in the house. The walls are painted the color of butterscotch pudding, and there's a large white marble fireplace. A comforting *tick, tick, tick, tick, comes from the enormous clock on the mantel* that reads 6:35. I run my fingers over the upholstery, feeling the texture of the chunky bouche fabric beneath my fingertips. I feel each bump grounding me, reminding me I'm inside my home, safe. A rectangular light fixture of gold and glass hangs down into the room, casting a soft glow. The house is decorated handsomely and filled with beautiful furnishings.

I didn't do any of it, but I wouldn't change a thing. Cruz picked everything. He has money and taste. When I lived with him, I tried to get him to spend less because he seemed to work so hard for it.

"I grew up with nothing," Cruz would say with no emotion. "Now I have money, and I'm going to enjoy spending and buying what I please. Our people have to deal with assholes every night. Why shouldn't they have beautiful things too?" I couldn't give him a reason they shouldn't, and his employees adored him. Who was I to say anything to stop him?

If only Cruz could fill the hole in my heart as quickly as he transformed this house from an empty space into a showcase. He was never any Romeo, but I never wanted that. Still, I never wanted Frankenstein, someone who scared me silly, either, but Cruz is way too beautiful to be him. That's the problem. Cruz is too attractive for the likes of me.

I run my hands over my ample breasts. Why can't they be smaller? I look down at my stomach. I wish it were flatter. I hate the way it spills over the waistband of my pants. I stand up to escape from myself, but can't. I stare at the mirror over the fire-place. Cruz says I'm beautiful. I hold on to that thought and move my sunglasses. I see someone ugly. My nose is getting bigger daily, and my skin is too pink. Is it eczema? Before I can continue to tear myself apart, my phone shakes. I flip my sunglasses down again and cover my eyes to see less of my face reflected on my phone screen.

A text from Cruz:

Answer your phone tonight

Why?

I landed u interview 4 gallery job. They're going 2 call

Protean?

Y. That one

Am I good enough?

What r u talking about?

U know

No I don't.

My body

There's nothing wrong with it. It's in ur head. Land the job.

I'll try.

There is no trying, do it.

Ring. ring. ring.

I pick it up. "Hello?"

"Yes, this is the Protean Gallery. We've received your resume. We'd like to interview you for the assistant gallery manager position. Are you available tomorrow at eleven?"

I stumble, getting the words out, "Yes, def-def-initely."

"Fine, I penciled you in. The owner, Mr. Manchild, will see you at eleven."

I lean my head back on the couch and imagine my life if I got the job. Assistant gallery manager, salary plus commission. Perfect timing. I can pay the children's tuition. Since that damn attorney hasn't been able to get money from my husband's business partner, I need a job. I'd have one in my field again, without having to depend on a man.

As soon as I end the call, the phone rings again, but this time there's no one there, only heavy breathing. I hang up the phone, and it rings again. I let the phone ring and lift myself from the couch, heading upstairs and bringing the ringing phone with me. I can't handle any more hang-ups or heavy breathing today.

Knock, knock, knock.

I turn, take three steps down to the landing, and walk to the door. I don't want to answer it, but they keep knocking. I peek out the window at the front porch and see a man and woman standing there, whom I've never seen before. I notice they're holding a remnant of something in their hands and realize it's a piece of my scarf. I push my sunglasses on my head, open the door, and smile until I notice their faces. Both are wearing frowns and have angry eyes. The man sweeps his arms out, holding the torn scarf. "Is this yours?"

"Yes, how did you know?"

"We saw your name on the label." He points to my name, River Rogers, in black marker. "Our other neighbor said you moved in last month. Why did you give this to our dog?" He flings it in my face.

"I didn't, it blew off—"

"You should have done something. Our dog is at the vet because of your carelessness and—"

"It was an accident. I'm afraid of dogs and—"

"He needs surgery, and it's going to cost thousands of dollars to have the item removed from inside of him. We expect you to pay the vet bill."

"If our dog dies, we'll sue you," the woman adds, squinting her eyes and pointing her index finger at me.

"I understand, and I'm sorry. I didn't know my scarf blowing into your yard would cause this. Your yard had a sign posted to " Beware of the Dog. I took it seriously."

"Excuses," the wife says. "You should have come to our door and said something so we could have taken it away from him."

"Let's go," the husband huffs. "We'll be in touch about Buster when we find out more."

"Again, I'm sorry." I close and lock the door. My body trembles. I turn and climb the stairs, hung with framed pieces of my children's art, and stop and admire their creativity, hoping they'll provide some sunlight to this darkening day. There are photographs of Joy and Alex, and even one with Cruz and Joy on the wall. I hurry up the steps and push him out of my mind. *I have to stop thinking about him and move on. We aren't a couple anymore.*

"What's for dinner?" Alex yells from his room.

"I'll let you know when I figure it out!" I yell back.

I switch the light on when I reach my bedroom. It's not a large one, but it's special. I know if Cruz had considered the house for both of us, he would have found the bedroom lacking, but somehow, he knew the room was perfect for me. After I moved in, I realized Cruz must have known for some time he wouldn't marry me. He had the brownstone purchased and decorated, just waiting for the children and me to move into it.

The wallpaper in the paneled bedroom features all species of songbirds. There's thick crown molding top and bottom, painted a soft white, the kind you don't find in new homes. The room has two tall windows on either side of the bed that face the street, letting in plenty of light during the day.

All I want is a bath or a shower, but as soon as I enter, the phone rings again. *Ring, ring.* I pick it up, but as soon as I do, *click*. This is the fifth one today. Each day, I seem to get more and more.

I set the cell down on the dresser, walk into the bathroom, turn on the faucets, and watch the old-style clawfoot tub fill. After it does, I lower myself in the warm water and soak, but the angry neighbors, the calls, and the man following me are three things swirling around in my thoughts that I can't seem to wash away. *Creepers.*

2

NATIVITY

CRUZ

"Where is he?" The wiper blades squeak, squeal, and drag on the ice forming on the windshield. I scan the block where the brownstone sits, and search for Eddie.

"Over there." Liam points from the passenger's seat to a life-size nativity scene across the street. It's still up in the middle of January, and my new man, Eddie, is squatting in the straw between Mother Mary, Baby Jesus, and one of the Magi. "I didn't see him as the religious type," Liam chuckles.

"You've got to admit it, Cruz, it's a great disguise," my driver, Cork, says.

I wave my hand, dismissing the idea. "He'll never pass as a wise man."

Liam snorts, "You're right about that, mate," and settles back in his seat.

I exit the back of my SUV. Eddie lopes towards me, sliding

where fresh ice has formed, but catching himself. This time, he takes shorter steps at a snail's pace until he reaches me. I stare down at his pale face. The streetlight makes him appear more ghoul-like than he normally does. In that brief moment, he reminds me of someone from my past, but like many things I don't want to remember, I push it away.

"Why am I out here, Cruz?" Eddie wraps his arms around himself, shivering. He drops his hands by his side and shuffles on each foot. He isn't a large man, only five-eight and thin. He's got dark hair, almost black, and dark brown eyes, but there's something about him that women like. My men refer to him as "Billy the Bullshitter." He's got a story about everything, and my men and I seldom believe a word he says.

I stab my index finger into Eddie's chest. "I told you before what to do. Monitor the house, the woman, and the children who live there." I point to the four-million-dollar brownstone I purchased to absolve my guilt. "Report who comes and goes. It's very simple."

"I don't know if—"

"Do the job. I shouldn't have to come here." I've got a million other things to do to keep the money rolling in, but obviously I can't trust this guy with something as simple as this. My head throbs, and I do the only thing I can; I lash out at this moron, grabbing his too-thin collar with both hands and yanking him towards me, making him stumble.

Eddie's eyes bulge. "H-h-how, Cruz? It's huge!" I hurl him away from me. Eddie stumbles but somehow rights himself, straightens his shirt, and presents his case, palms open. "Boss, it's a lot of ground to cover for one person."

"I agree, but it's not as massive as The Palace. They'd need to be a superhero to get to the second floor, and all the windows have alarms. I've attached an extra surprise, electric charges, to the outside of the lower windows. Mostly you just ensure all is well, report what's going on, and call for backup if there's trouble."

"Who you keeping out, boss?"

"Anyone, everyone. The world's shit...dangerous. You can't be too careful." Who knows this better than me? I survived a drug addict mother and a father who—

"I got another question, boss."

"You seem to be full of them today." I roll my eyes.

"Why do they call you the Devil of LSD?" A smile slowly spreads, and he tilts his head to one side. "Is it because you sell drugs too?"

"Shut up. I'm no bagman." I wouldn't stoop to it. I shove my hands in my pockets, my fingers tightening. "LSD stands for Lake Shore Drive. And since The Palace is located on Hawthorne Place, only a few blocks away, the name stuck. Of course, the city council went and renamed it last year to DuSable Drive, so I guess I'll have to change my name to Devil of DSD. Don't see that happening, Eddie, do you? "

"Probably not," he shakes his head. "How did you get into the sex business?" Eddie's speed-talking and coming too close. *Is he a cop, working undercover?*

"Why are you asking so many questions?"

"I'm just wondering–"

I lean away. "People will always be interested in buying and selling sex, don't you think?"

"I guess so, but I've never paid. The ladies love me." Eddie runs his hand through his hair. "I bet the neighbors don't like you doing what you do in their neighborhood. Especially forcing women into the sex trade."

"Enough! They like me fine. I don't conduct business in The Palace. We go to the clients. And who told you I force them to do anything?"

"Ah, nobody, Cruz, I just thought—"

"You thought wrong. Stop thinking. People come to me to work. I don't make anyone do anything they don't want to do." *Or make them do anything I haven't done myself*, I wanted to say, but don't. I changed the subject. "What time did she arrive?"

"A little after 6:30 with the two kids, the teen boy and the little girl. Not a bad lookin' woman if she took off a couple of pounds and were younger." Eddie nods, rubbing his hands together. "I like 'em skinny." He winks and smirks.

I shoot Eddie a venomous look and loom over him. "Did I ask what you like? Your taste is abominable." Stifled snickers from Liam and Cork drift from the front seat through the open window of the vehicle. The fact is, River is thirteen years older than me, but age means nothing to me. I consider putting a curse on Eddie, but if I do, the neighbors might see or hear something they shouldn't, and who would take over Eddie's shift? Plus, I know I shouldn't. I don't use my magic to do negative things. I do wonder, though, if she's safe with someone this stupid guarding her.

"It's five degrees out," Eddie complains. His bitching draws me back. "Cruz, can't I get in the car with you to warm up?"

"Why didn't you wear a heavier coat? It's Chicago, and it's winter. Are you some clueless out-of-towner?"

"I dunno." He lifts his shoulder to half a shrug. "Please, Cruz—"

"No. Walk down the street, get a coffee, and come back." Do I have a spell that will increase this dummy's IQ? I climb back into the car to ponder other solutions.

"But Cruz—"

"You heard me. Go." I slide five dollars out the window and watch as he shoves the money and his hands in his pockets.

I should feel bad for him, but I don't. Some people might say I lack empathy, but that's not it. I have priorities, and people who work for me who don't try seldom become one of mine. He could be a hiring mistake, although thankfully, I haven't had many of those.

I glance back at my phone and watch Eddie walk briskly towards the convenience shop on the corner where a police car is parked. This is one time a police presence doesn't make me nervous. I glance up at the window again.

"River should have turned in by now," I say.

"Past her bedtime, is it?" Liam asks, turning around from the front seat.

"She's got insomnia, and it takes her forever to get to sleep, so she often checks in early, usually by nine, and reads in bed." If I were there, I could give her herbs and cast a spell.

"You've got it too, mate. I hear you pacing all hours of the night. Has it always been like that?"

"Since I was a kid." I don't tell him how it started.

"I sleep like a log," Liam says.

"I know. You sound like a chainsaw." My father snored too. I always wondered how he slept at night with all the evil he carried out. Watch any crime show on television, and it usually starts with the narrator saying, "He was a God-fearing man..." The story always continues with some atrocity that the God-fearing man carried out against his community. In my father's case, he never got caught. But like a body that floats to the surface in a swamp, the memory of what I saw that day won't stay down. I'm good at keeping it away during the day, but not at night.

Liam turns from the front seat again. "Is my snoring that bad?"

"Not bad enough to make me kill you. Yet," I joke.

Liam snorts. "Funny, mate."

A guy like me doesn't display weakness or share with others. If I don't have my shit together by now at thirty-two, it's too late. River is the only one I ever told about the beatings, but I never told her about anything else. Not a day goes by that I don't think about it or expect a knock at my door with questions about my father.

Tap tap. I jump, but it's only Eddie. I press the button and slide the window down. "Come on, Cruz, let me warm up." Eddie fidgets, as though chills are running up and down his legs. He clutches his cup in both hands and gives me sad puppy dog eyes.

Liam and Cork laugh and whisper to each other.

"Maybe for a few minutes, Cruz, before we leave," Liam says. "The wind chill's five below."

"Fine, for a few moments, Eddie, but next time dress for the weather," but I know Liam's exaggerating the wind chill. "Then back you go to your post."

Eddie climbs in the back seat and sits down next to me, kicking my foot. "I don't get why I have to watch this broad round the clock. Who the fuck is—"

"If you're going to whine about it, you can stand outside. And if you touch me or call her a broad again, you're dead." I close my eyes, lean my head against the window, and conjure up the memory of River when I first laid eyes on her.

"A man was hassling her," Clarissa, one of my workers, had said. "We couldn't leave her all alone in the bus station."

"Her husband's beating her," Marissa had whispered behind her hand when they brought her home. River's hair was the same color as mine, blonde, almost white, and like me, she doesn't dye it. Bones, my next-in-command at the time, thought we looked like brother and sister. I didn't turn her out like all the others, telling them that if they wanted to stay, they had to contribute, sell their bodies. I treated her like a friend instead, another thing I had never done before. We talked about art, books, and philosophy. I let her work in our kitchen and clean the house. River didn't stay, though. Her husband tricked her into going home, but a year later, she showed up at my door again, begging for my help, this time with two children in tow. This time, I changed the rules on her—

"It's just so cold out. Can't I—"

I grab Eddie's ear and twist it. His hoodie falls down. He screams out "Aaah!" and attempts to pry my fingers away from his lobe to no avail.

"I warned you. I let you in the car, and you're still whining and carrying on." I pinch his ear tight, overwhelming him. His coffee spills on his crotch, scorching him, and he wiggles back and forth in more pain.

"Cruz, leave him be." Liam jumps from the front seat and snatches the rear door open, allowing Eddie a way out. I let go of Eddie's ear, and he falls outside of the car onto the icy sidewalk. He jumps to his feet, slides on the ice, holds his ear, and shouts back as I follow him.

"You're crazy, man!" Eddie slips and slides all the way to the corner as I watch. He's right—I am.

Ring, ring.

I take out my phone and answer it without checking the caller ID. "What are you doing?" the voice asks.

I glance up to the second-floor window of the brownstone and see River's silhouette framed against it, holding her phone to her ear. Did River see the whole thing? I shouldn't be speaking to her and opening the wound again. It's not fair to her. I can't have her now or ever.

"Nothing." The smell of Eddie's spilt hazelnut coffee permeates the back seat as I climb back into the vehicle. I settle into the seat and glance up at the window.

"It doesn't look that way to me. Pushing people out of cars looks like something. Why are you sitting in a car in front of the house, anyway?"

I'd forgotten how much I love and miss River's musical voice. It's already calming me.

"Not *the* house. It's *your* house. I bought it for you," I remind her.

"I told you before, I can't accept it. I'm only staying until Jack's partner pays me for my half of the business, then I'll buy my own place."

"As you wish. But you could sell this home and buy another to your liking if you don't like this one." The more she resists doing what I want, the more I want to push her into doing things my way. It was that way when she was my slave, and it's that way now. It doesn't matter that she believes she's not mine anymore. She'll always belong to me until I leave this earth. If she leaves before me, then I'll have to join her immediately. Knowing she didn't exist would make my life meaningless.

"I can't take your money," River says. "We aren't together anymore."

"It's a gift." I don't care what she wants. I want her safe, and I want to provide for her.

"Thank you, but no. You didn't answer my question. Why are you here?"

"To check on you."

"A simple phone call or text is what normal people do. They don't stalk them. If you aren't coming up, please leave. You'll scare the neighbors."

The call ends, and she moves away from the window. River's orders surprise me and make me smile. River never had the nerve to order me about before. How my once slave has changed. Did I teach River to stand up to me? I don't know whether to slap myself on the back or in the face.

At one time, I tried to take everything from her...all her beliefs, her freedom. I wanted her to do only what I told her to do. What made me change my mind? "A simple phone call is what normal people do." River should know by now, I'm not normal.

I take off my coat and pass it up to Liam. "Take this to Eddie.

His clothes are wet, and his jacket is worthless in this weather. Tell him I'll send someone to relieve him in a couple of hours." Liam takes the coat and exits the car.

A few minutes later, Liam returns and settles back into the front seat. "I don't know about the new guy. He asks too many questions, complains too much, and has too many opinions."

"I agree. You checked him out, right?"

"Yes. Louie vouched for him. He said Eddie did three years for robbing homes, somewhere south."

"He'll catch on, eventually." My hand is on the door handle.

Liam nods and turns to face me in the back seat. The streetlight lands on his teeth, glistening with a smile. "He'd better, mate, or his balls will melt, and he'll be singing soprano."

"I'm going to go upstairs and check on River. I'll be back in thirty, but if I'm not, honk the horn." I exit the back seat, grab my other coat from the car's cargo area, and leave my men talking.

3
BEAUTY & SWAGGER

RIVER

"What are you doing here, Cruz? How did you get in?"
He's standing in the corner of my room, first in the shadows and then striding into the light. His beauty still stuns me. A man can be described as handsome, but when a man looks like Cruz MacKenzie, the word "handsome" doesn't do him justice.

"I'm making sure you're all right. What's with the sunglasses?" He stands at the end of my bed by the antique chest he gave me as an engagement gift. It's an antique Dutch Colonial, a campaign trunk with tapered baluster feet. It has an ebony star motif and a brass-hinged lock. I remember feeling special when I received the gift. My other two husbands, both deceased, had never given me anything so meaningful.

Cruz loves antiques. He goes to auctions every chance he gets. He collects fine things and keeps storage lockers full of them. What he doesn't keep in The Palace, he resells in a year or two for more than he paid for them. He studies the market and understands the value of various objects. Sometimes he'll take a chance on a piece he knows nothing about and does research for the fun of it. I don't remember him ever losing money on any of his purchases.

He's making me nervous, standing over me, making me lash out. "You didn't answer my question. How did you get in? I told you to call first." I jump off my bed. I don't want him to see me like this, half-naked. Cruz's good looks still disarm me. Why couldn't he have gone downhill after I gave his ring back? Gained a beer belly, gone bald, and gotten warts or pimples? Instead, he looks better than ever.

I always believed Cruz wasn't the type of man I could ever get, not with the way he looks...or the type of man I would ever want, either. A mobster? What was I thinking? How irresponsible of me. I have children. The thing is, he's more than his looks or his occupation. He's got a mind besides his beauty and his swagger. And besides, he's been nicer to my children and me than even their own father.

Cruz is like me in some ways. He loves to read, philosophize, and visit museums. The problem is that now he's the only man I desire, and I don't want to consider anyone else, even though he's dumped me. I pretend I don't care and don't want him anymore, but it's a lie. I compare every man I meet to Cruz, and not one of them comes close.

"How are you, River? You didn't answer me about the sunglasses." He points to my face.

"I'm fine. Oh, these things." I bring the frames closer to my face. "Umm, I just like wearing them." I bring my hands down and cross my arms in front of my chest.

Cruz circles me like a human lie detector, then comes closer and breathes me in. He comes back around and pauses in front of me, snatching the shades off my face like a striking mongoose. He looks at the glasses. "I don't fancy them."

"Give them back." I reach out, and Cruz flings them across the room. I hear them hit the wall with a loud crack.

"Don't hide from people, especially me. You're too lovely for that. I agree, though; you do look fine." His head bobs up and down, appraising me. His eyes grow large, like a starving man eyeing his favorite meal. "But too thin. Are you eating? I hope you aren't dieting again. I hate it when women do that, denying themselves. It's ridiculous and unhealthy."

No one's ever called me lovely except my mother and father, which is why I never believed a single word they said. I can promise you that no one's ever accused me of being thin, either. "My food choices are no longer your concern," I smartly tell him.

Cruz's eyes change in an instant, narrowing. His nostrils flare, and he moves closer still, his chest puffing out. He rolls up the sleeves of his white dress shirt. When he did this before, it was a warning. Sage and pine hit my nose like a truck. He likes to smudge his room every day to rid the space of negative energy, and the scent clings to him. I try to resist the sensation, but it's like trying to ward off a herd of stampeding rhinos with a toothbrush. My body is paying no attention to what my mind is telling it to do, and I feel my pussy throbbing and my face heating up.

"Are you sure you want to talk to me like this, with that tone, especially when I pulled strings and got you that interview you desperately wanted?"

The truth is, I'm not sure I do. Before we were engaged, Cruz was my master, and I was his slave. Talking back to him was not an option. It would lead to an unpleasant outcome: spanking, lockdown, loss of privileges, or something even more severe. "I'm not your slave anymore, Cruz, and we aren't a couple. Nor did I invite you up. You need to leave."

Cruz smirks, staring at me like I've lost my mind. And maybe I have. I've never spoken to him like this. I sense I'm teetering on a tightrope, awaiting a gust about to blow. He laughs, but his laughter has an edge. He stands close. "Careful, River," he whispers. "Nothing's changed for me." His breath blows a shiver up my neck.

I don't back down. "Let me remind you, you left me." I thump his chest with my fingers.

"Did I say you could touch me, River?" Cruz cocks his head and narrows his eyes.

"Ahh...no, but this is your fault."

"Really? You've rewritten history to suit yourself. I postponed the marriage, but it was your decision to return my ring." He drags it out from under his shirt. "See? I have it right here, next to my heart." He's wearing it around his neck on a silver chain. "The marriage is delayed, not off."

"It's over." I flip my hand in the air.

Cruz captures my hand in midair and brings it to his heart. "Not for me. You'll always be mine."

I pull my hand away and clasp my hands together. "I belong to me."

"You'd better stop reading those romance books of yours. They're giving you a false sense of love. Our love isn't sweet, it's passionate and on my terms."

"It better be on my terms, too," I respond, staring him down.

He takes hold of my shoulders and backs me up, pinning me against the wall. "Something's gotten into you. I'm not sure if I like it. What is it?" When I don't answer him, he continues, "Don't forget, I know what you like." He lets go and runs his finger along my lips, his voice taking on a wistful tone. "I know I fucked up and never explained things fully." He rubs his palm over his heart. "And it's killing me." He licks my neck, then bites it softly.

I push him back. "We aren't right for each other."

He lowers his head, his shoulders slump, then he lifts them.

"Please don't say that. You're the best thing that's ever happened to me."

The truth is, Cruz is the best thing to happen to me, too, but in my heart, I wonder why he chose me. He could have any woman he wants. I'm too old for him. Then there are all the other differences. When he walks into a room, he demands attention. When I enter, people don't even notice me, or worse, don't even realize I've entered. He's a witch, and I'm Catholic, and his lifestyle—

Cruz's eyebrows draw together, and he asks, "What are you thinking?" But he doesn't let me answer; instead, he presses his lips against mine, kissing me, dispelling any doubts I may have had. It works. After a few seconds, I'm a goner and his again. He lets his hand travel down to my waist and then to my ass. He slides his hands inside my panties, placing one hand on each ass cheek and squeezing, making every part of me heat. "Who owns you, River?"

"You do."

"That's my girl." Cruz grinds into me, his eyes connecting with mine. He threads his fingers through my hair, happy with my answer, and nuzzles my neck.

Beep beep. The car sounds from outside. "I'm sorry, I have to go," Cruz says, pulling away. He picks up his long, black wool coat and slides into it. "I'll call later." He draws out a coral-colored rose from inside his coat and presents it to me like a magician. "A beautiful rose, for my beautiful flower." He bows.

I bring it to my nose. It gives off the odor of a hundred roses. "Thank you, it's lovely." I stare up at him like a silly schoolgirl.

"Like you, perfect the way you are. You're going to do great at the interview. It's in the bag."

"You didn't threaten the owner or anything, did you?"

"Don't be silly, of course not. I got you an interview, that's it. I have confidence in you." He brushes his fingers across my lips. He leaves the way he came in, without me seeing how, but that's not the only thing that remains a mystery concerning Cruz MacKenzie. *Why do I still love him so, when I try so hard not to?*

I walk to one of the long windows that frames my bed. The branches on the trees in the yard are heavy with snow and ice. The glass has condensation on it, and I clear it away with my fingers. I watch Cruz cross the icy street, now sprinkled with new snow. He seems to float over to his SUV like a god, while anyone else would be sliding and slipping. He gracefully climbs into his vehicle, and the dark car moves away down the street, disappearing into a grey moon.

4
BEAT DOWNS & CONSEQUENCES

CRUZ

"I checked receivables from yesterday. Davey was short," Liam says.

Cork stares at the road.

"Again? How short?" I ask.

"Two hundred." Liam shakes his head and doesn't look at me.

I smash my hand with my fist. "I warned him last time what would happen."

"What do you want to do?" Liam taps his fingers on his legs.

"It's not what I want to do, it's what I have to. This is the second time."

"Could be he's using again." Liam opens and closes his mouth, like he's trying to find the right words to say to make me change my mind.

"He should have come to me for help and been honest. Since he didn't, a beating, and after that, he's gone." I slice the air with my hand. "I'll do it in front of the others at our morning meeting. It sends a message to the others, not to make the same mistake."

"Why don't you just...you know, give him the evil eye or cast a spell or something?"

Liam's suggestion is ludicrous. He doesn't even believe in witchcraft. "I don't use spells for anything negative. You take a chance if you do. There's a saying: 'Cast an evil spell, receive evil back.' And I'm not using my religion to collect two hundred bucks."

"Perhaps you could cure him of his addiction with your magic," Cork suggests.

"It's not a parlor trick. And besides, a person has to swim for the raft. My magic can't fix him if he doesn't want to save himself. As I said, he gets the beating, then he's gone."

Liam grunts. "Are you sure you want to do this in front of the others?"

"I've earned the right to do what I want, when I want." I slam my fist against the back of his seat. Why is Liam second-guessing my decisions?

"Take it easy, boss, I'm just helping you think things through. Isn't that my job?" Liam asks.

"I suppose." I check my drip account. "Yes!" I pump my fist in the air. Liam stares at me, confused. "I made a hundred thousand dollars in the stock market today on a trade."

I saw a house in Guatemala that I'd like to buy. I could move River and her children. I could visit every few months. Protect her from Conti. *Yeah, like she's going to go for that.*

"On second thought, you're right, Liam. It's starting the day on a negative note, with a beatdown first thing in the morning in front of the others. Where's Davey now?"

"He's at the Blue with a client." Liam checks his watch. "Should be in the hotel bar by now. You know he likes to worm drinks out of the customer afterward. We can pick him up if you want to."

"Let's do it. I want this over with." My stomach twists in

knots. The silence in the SUV envelops me. I watch as Cork, my driver, and Liam exchange brief glances with each other as we get nearer to the hotel. They're wired too. As we approach the motel entrance, I give them instructions. "Liam, make sure you don't spook him. Just say I need a word with him. And Cork, start driving as soon as he's in, and lock the doors. We'll take him under the bridge. It's deserted, but with all the noise from the traffic above, no one will hear any sounds he might make."

"Got it," Liam says, and Cork nods his head.

As soon as we pull in front of the hotel, a valet tries to take the car, but Cork waves him off. Liam gets out of the car and sprints inside. A few minutes later, Liam comes out laughing with Davey. Davey's only 5'8"; I'm taller at 6'2". We're both in decent shape. As far as I know, Davey isn't a fighter, but you never know how people will react when they're having to defend themselves.

Liam settles in the front seat, and Davey sits in the back with me. The sound of the locks snapping down seems louder than normal. My adrenaline is already speeding through my body, and I have to clasp my hands to keep from grabbing his neck and choking him out. "How's it going, Cruz?" Davey slaps my shoulder.

I look at his half-open eyes. He's high on something. I grab and tear his white dress shirt sleeve open, checking the inside of his elbow. "What's this?" I point to five fresh needle marks that make me want to play Connect The Dots.

"Nothing, Cruz, nothin'." Davey pulls away. He brushes the back of his neck.

"Where's the money you earned?"

"Right here, Cruz. I got it all." He removes the cash from his leather jacket pocket and passes it to me. I can tell by his lopsided smile that he's hoping the money will change the mood in the car. "Here's sixteen hundred. The guy tipped me five hundred. He was happy with me."

"I'm glad someone is. Tell me the rules of the house, Davey." I hand the wad to Liam. I don't want blood on the money. It makes for a messy deposit, with too many questions from the teller.

"Uh, what do you mean?"

"Don't be stupid. You had to memorize them when you first started working for me. Repeat them, Davey."

"Let me think.... No lying, no stealing, respect each other's personal space, share and contribute, and no drugs." His lips close in a grimace.

"Correct. Very good, Davey. Obviously, you didn't do that, did you?"

"Ahh, no, I screwed up."

"What did you do?"

"I lied and shot up." Davey's rocking back and forth in the small space of the car, coming close to bumping into me, and he's refusing to look at my eyes.

"What else?" I sneer at him.

"I stole." Drops of sweat are rolling down his fake-tanned face.

"You did. The problem is, this is the second time you've stolen."

"Please, Cruz, I promise—"

"Your promises are worthless."

Cork slows down and brings the vehicle to a halt under the bridge. The doors unlock, and Davey hears them too. He flings the door open and jumps out, but doesn't go far. I'm holding on to his jacket, and it rips. "Where do you think you're going?" His arms start to come out of his sleeves. I yank him back hard, and he spins around. He's unbalanced, but he's still standing up, a few feet in front of the car. There's a quiet under the bridge. Just our breathing and the *clunk, clunk, clunk* of tires hitting the road on the bridge above us. The sky is fighting with itself, clouds bruised with night and bleeding with light from a hopeful moon.

"Please, Cruz, give me another chance. I won't do it again."

Davey's mouth is open, and the car's parking lights shine on his bleached teeth.

"No, you won't. I can promise you that." I create a space between Davey and me. I pull my right fist back and fire forward, landing it on his face, opening a gash above his left eye. He bends down, shaking his head, blood beginning to dribble. I drag him up to face me. "You fucked up this time, Davey, and you've got to pay."

Davey wheezes, "Please, Cruz...don't."

"Why did you steal?" I plant my feet more firmly in place this time. My right foot is back, and my right fist flies faster this time, a one-two punch to the nose and mouth. One of his teeth flies out into the black night, and another one lands in the dirt in front of me. Should I pick it up as a trophy? What a fucked-up thought. What do I want with this junkie's tooth? If Davey still worked for me, he wouldn't be able to earn without dental work, and he'd need implants, and they cost four thousand dollars a pop. I'd have to give him the money and take it out of his pay. How many jobs would he have to take to pay for his implants?

Davey hits the ground. He's making this too easy for me. He's not fighting back. All he's doing is begging and sniveling. I'm not enjoying this as I should be. When someone steals from me, and I'm getting even, I'm relishing every second, but not this time. I realize my knuckles are cut and burning. This begins to infuriate me and provides me with the fire I need. I stand him up again.

"Please, Cruz, I'm sorry, I shouldn't have, but I couldn't help myself. I'm sick...I have a problem..."

"Shut up. I don't want to hear about your fucking problems. You had a choice, and you made it." I think about my mother and all the bad choices she made. The times I went without food in my belly, the gnawing hunger pains. The times she fed me nothing but donuts and candy bars. The toothaches I had because she didn't take me to the fuckin' dentist, and all the dental work I have to get now because of her. My teeth look great, but most of them aren't real. Between the caps, crowns, and all the rest, I've spent thousands.

Liam grabs my shoulder. "Boss, it could be overkill."

I push him away. "I'm not asking your opinion. This isn't a democracy. If you don't like it, work somewhere else." Liam sucks in a quick breath. A look of pity appears on his face, but it's at me, not Davey. He heads back to the car.

I pick Davey up and place him against the pillar of the bridge. He opens his mouth. He looks like a jack-o'-lantern. Blood is coming out of several places on his face, and his eyes are closed. I grab Davey's shoulders and bring them towards me as I tuck my chin and, using the hardest part of my head, aim for the flat of Davey's forehead. *Whack.* Davey goes down, splayed on the ground. He's barely conscious when I crouch next to him. "You're a worthless excuse for a human being, a lying, scumbag drug addict." Blood splatters are on my white two-hundred-dollar organic cotton shirt.

Dave regains consciousness, groaning and reaching out to me. "Can I come back?"

"You're kidding me? If you do, I'll kill you. I don't want to see you ever again. I'll have the others pack your shit and leave it on the front porch of The Palace." I walk away and enter the car.

"Should we go?" Liam calls back from the passenger's seat in a hushed tone.

"Unless you want me to administer first aid to that worthless junkie."

"Don't be snappy. He's still a human being, Cruz."

"Is he? How much was his date?"

"Twelve hundred," Liam says.

"Give him fifty percent of that. He got a tip of five, but he owes us two for shorting us, so only pay him three. Make sure he knows why. I don't want this freak thinking I'm stealing from him. Go pay him his money."

"I'll tell him, mate." Liam climbs out, walks over to Davey, bends down, hands him his money, and shakes hands with him.

"It's good you're giving him anything at all," Cork says. "He's going to sink it all in his arm. Or is that what you're hoping for, that he kills himself?" Cork reads me too well.

Liam twists back to look at me when he returns to his seat. "You're bleeding, Cruz."

"It's just a nosebleed. It happens when I head-butt."

"Davey said to thank you for the money. He wanted me to tell you he's sorry." Liam passes me his handkerchief.

I stare out into the frosty night and wipe my nose. Cork flicks the vehicle's driving lights on again, fully lighting Davey's huddling form, and I watch as he counts his money. Cork starts the ignition, moving our car from the bridge, and we drive away through never-ending darkness.

I run my fingers over my cut knuckles. I couldn't come back from killing a man over two hundred dollars. One of these days, I'm going to go too far. I wrap my fingers around the silver skull and butterfly ring on the silver chain around my neck and trace the skull with my fingertips, knowing River's finger once wore it. I wear it now. I let the ring go.

Liam interrupts my thoughts. "I'm sorry about interfering back there, mate. I didn't want you to kill the guy. He's not worth it."

"You did the right thing, Liam, calling me off." I fish the ring out again and bring my thoughts back to the woman I can't and shouldn't marry.

Liam notices what I'm doing in the rearview window with the ring. "What happened between you and yer woman?" He takes out his bag of tobacco, balances it on his knee, and opens it. A sweet, smoky, cherry scent fills the car.

"It's personal," I say.

Liam turns back and says, "Is she worried about sharing ya with the ladies because you run women?" He winks, his dark brown eyes sparkling from the overhead light. He returns to what he's doing, reaching into his pocket and fishing out his rolling papers. I don't answer questions like this, but I've gotten closer to Liam than most of my other employees. After I hired him, his brother died in a motorcycle accident, and he confided then that two years prior, he'd lost his mother to breast cancer. Plus, I treated Liam rather badly when dealing with Davey.

I clear my throat before answering him. "River has children, and she's concerned about their well-being, how it may influence them. I promised I'd sell the brothels, and we'd live in The Palace with the children. And then—"

"Yer changed yer mind?" He gives me an understanding nod.

"Yes, and I told her it wasn't a good idea for us to marry right then. Earnings were down and—"

"Whoa, breaking off an engagement. That explains why she's raging," Liam says. "Plus, you can't tell yer woman yer going to do one thing and then go do another." Liam places the rolling paper on his leg and, with two fingers, pinches some tobacco out of the bag, putting it on the paper, rolling the shag up, and placing it between his lips, like he does several times every day. "Want one, mate?"

"No thanks. I didn't break off the engagement; she did. I just said we needed to wait. She took it wrong and gave back the ring."

Cork chimes in, "You're lucky she didn't shoot you. My old lady would have."

"So your woman knows you drive girls for a brothel?" I ask.

"Hell no." Cork swallows down a laugh. "She'd kill me. I told her I'm your bodyguard and that you traffic drugs and guns."

"So she's okay with guns and drugs but not sex workers?"

"Yeah. She's good with guns and has one herself. As far as

drugs go, she mows the grass, so she's cool with that and happy with the pay, cause she likes her kicks."

"Why did you want to postpone marrying?" Liam asks. "It seems like you—"

"That's a story for another day." I'm not ready to tell Liam that River was once my slave. If Liam and Cork knew that mobster Angelo Conti, who runs this town, has a vendetta against me, I wonder how eager they'd be to work for me. At the very least, they'd both want a bump in pay. I ponder the ethics of not telling them.

"See if anyone needs a ride. If they do, we can swing by before we head back to The Palace," I say.

"Barkley's on standby. He can do it," Liam says.

"I told you to do it."

Liam checks his phone. "Everyone's still on calls, Cruz. I don't understand why Barkley can't—"

"I can't establish sound relationships with the women if I have others do the work. They need to know I'm involved and care about them."

"I understand," Liam says.

"Do you?"

"Yeah. You care about the girls."

"I care about receivables. If you treat your people well, they treat you well, which means they earn. I saw how things worked the other way with the madame who owned The Palace before me. She ruled by threats and brute strength. Women ran away; they didn't earn anywhere near what our people do, and there were nothing but problems. I'm not going down that road. Therefore, we keep everyone happy if we can. It's simpler and easier. There are times to get rough, but I try to keep people happy if I can."

I don't tell Liam everything. If he knew I'd once been a slave too, what would he think? And that bitch thought she could get away with selling me? Gloria was the one who ended up in the purgatory she tried to create for me.

"How was Jessica today? Her anxiety any better?" I ask.

"Much better. Having her meditate twice a day seems to have helped her moods. And the yoga regime, too," Liam says.

"Stay on top of her. Book a massage appointment for her next week. Remember, if one person is unhappy in the house, that unhappiness spreads to the others. It's a herd mentality."

"Seems you *can* put a price on happiness," Cork nods his head.

"Is that why you do the energy work and all the other mumbo jumbo?" Liam asks.

"I don't consider it mumbo jumbo. Keeping a positive work environment is important, whether you work in a coffee shop, a department store, or an office. People need to be taken care of."

"Yeah, you're right, mate. Businesspeople gotta motivate their workforce."

"Part of Wicca has to do with interconnectivity, and since I believe we're all connected and they're my family, it's important that they're happy."

"You never cease to amaze me, mate."

"I don't understand how they never bitch at you," Cork says. "I can't even handle one woman, and you handle living with twenty-three in The Palace. Plus, you got the other brothel in Evanston with fifteen there, and you got the one in Peoria too, right?"

"I don't have that one anymore. I gave it to someone. I'm going to open another in Chicago soon. I'm looking for the right location."

"He's not Mr. Nice Guy," Liam says to Cork. "I mean no disrespect. You're fair, but you're very clear about the rules, and when people break them, you lower the boom, as you did with Davey."

"You can't let people get away with things. Consequences are important. If you don't enforce those consequences, you'll have problems. You'll have challenges hiring people."

"They know they'll be safe here, that you'll take care of them. That isn't any different from how other businesspeople attract workers to come and stay, mate."

"I never thought about it that way, but I'm still not like real businesspeople. Real ones graduate from college."

"Not always, mate. Look at Steve Jobs and Steve Wozniak. Neither one of them graduated from college. They started Apple out of their garage."

"That was back in the '70s. You could have been a college dropout back then, and no one would have cared. It's different now. You need a piece of paper to do anything worthwhile. Even the greeter at the bank wanted to know where I earned my business degree. She made a face when I informed her I didn't have one."

"What about that guy Jan Koum?" Liam says. "He's the guy who invented WhatsApp, that everyone chats on. He's an emigre from Ukraine and started out poor, like us. He didn't begin his business until 2009. Facebook bought the app for billions of dollars. Not bad for some geek with a good idea."

"What I want to know, Cruz, is how come you didn't give the woman at the bank a harder time?" Cork asks.

"The two security guards with guns she had standing at either side of the door. And the truth is that we wrangled a shitload of cash out of her addict husband. She had a right to be angry." *I can't be wrong about the college degree, can I?*

"What are you going to tell our people about Davey?" Liam asks.

"The truth. He used drugs, he stole, he lied, and he faced the consequences. But I'll remind them that if they need help with drug use, I'll pay for it if they come to me."

"That's a good idea, Cruz. And as far as the loan, I don't see why you can't try other banks."

"That's a thought."

Cork looks in his mirror, "Hey, Cruz, a cherry top's following us," and sure enough, when I look over my shoulder, there's a cop in the rear window. Then another one joins him.

"Could be someone saw us beating Davey and called in our plates," Cork keeps his hold on the wheel, relaxed, but his eyes in the mirror, dart back and forth.

"Maybe the neighbors complained about the noise Eddie made when you visited River," Liam says.

The cop turns on its lights and sirens. Is it possible my past has caught up with me, or am I just being paranoid?

"Pull over, Cork." Cork signals and slows to the curb.

We stay in the car, and within minutes, more police show up. Cork rolls down his window, and as I look around, I see more police officers running towards our vehicle from every direction with their weapons drawn. I warn my men, "Keep your hands where they can see them. We don't want to end up as a tragic morning news story."

The police officer at Cork's side asks, "Is a Cruz MacKenzie in the vehicle?"

Before Cork can answer, I yell, "I'm in the back seat."

"Step out of the car with your hands raised," an officer says.

After they search me, take my identification, and handcuff me, they place me in a police vehicle. "What am I being arrested for?"

"Sexual battery," the officer says, pushing me in a police car.

"What?" That can't be right. I bounce my foot nervously and rock in my seat. Surely it's a case of mistaken identity.

5
THE INTERVIEW

RIVER

I see my reflection in the plate-glass window. Oh my God, I look like hell. I'm fat, and my hair is flying in all directions. Why did I wear this flowery dress? I circle the street. I'm early anyway, so I go to the coffeeshop one street over.

I order my drink and sit down next to a longer table where six people are gathered, five men and one woman. They have laptops open, and the woman sitting at the head of the table seems to be running the meeting. She's like me in that she has a large chest, but not like me in that she's confident and in control. The others are hanging on her every word and taking notes. I listen to what she has to say too, and have to pull myself away when I realize it's almost eleven and time for my interview.

The first thing I notice when I arrive at the gallery and push the doors open is the walls. They're arctic white and splashed with color. An artist has created an installation and painted on the walls. The floors are made of bleached bamboo, and someone has randomly thrown additional strips of canvas onto them. The bright lights create a space I would love to work in. There's a long counter in the gallery's rear and another long, skinny one up front along the glass window.

I notice a large group of women standing and chatting. They all stop and stare at me. They're all dressed in blazers, most of them in black, with slacks or skirts. Christ, I should've worn my black blazer and pencil skirt. The dress makes me look less professional than them. My neckline is too low, and my breasts are pushing out of it. What was I thinking? I'm filled with shame.

I approach the desk, sign in, and, sure enough, discover the women are all here for interviews, a group one at eleven o'clock. My eyes fall over each one. They're younger, thinner, and prettier than I am. I realize I won't get the job. My head hurts, and I'm sweating. Damp circles form under my armpits. I see my rear end reflected in the glass of a painting as I stand waiting. It's huge, too big to work here. I'll knock into things.

The other women's eyes stare, judging me. They think I'm here to clean. I need to get out of this place before they hand me a broom and I embarrass myself. *Shut up, shut up, my brain screams.*

One woman makes eye contact and smiles. "Hi, I'm Lia."

"Umm, hi, I'm River Rogers. Been waiting long?"

"No, maybe five minutes," Lia says. "He'd better get out of here soon, I've got another interview at twelve."

"I didn't know this would be a group interview. I've never done one of those."

"Yeah. They're strange, but it's a way for them to meet a bunch of people at one time and then bring back the two or three people they like. Positions like this don't come along every day. That's the only reason I came," Lia says.

"I'm pretty nervous."

"Don't be. Think of it like speed dating," Lia says.

"I've never done that either."

"Speed dating is fun. All you gotta do is speak up," Lia says.

"I think I'm going to be ill."

"Are you sure?"

"Yes. I'm not well. I'm going to leave my updated resume on the desk with a note. It was nice meeting you, Lia."

"You're just going to leave?" another woman asks.

"She doesn't feel well," Lia says.

"It doesn't matter. If she wants the job, she should stick it out."

"Why don't you mind your own business?" Lia points her finger at the woman.

"It's okay, Lia. She's right. I don't want to make anyone else sick and—"

"You should stay and sit right next to her and cough all over her," and Lia smiles.

My stomach churns, and I move to the door as fast as I can. Now I've started a fight between two women. I see them shaking their fingers at each other and hear them exchanging angry words as I open the door.

The entire way home, I'm filled with dread. What will Cruz think when I tell him I bailed on this interview after he pulled strings to get it for me? I don't know how he managed it, but he did. Imagine, Protean, the best gallery in Chicago. Not just a salary, but a commission on each sale too. Plus, if I wanted to transfer to their Manhattan gallery, I could. That's if I hadn't given up and run away. Once more, I've failed, but this time I've failed my children, too. I was so excited to work in a gallery. I knew it was too good to be true.

I unlock the door and enter the house. It's quiet, and I've got a few hours before I have to go to school and meet the children. There's a whistling sound. I walk closer to the fireplace. It's the wind coming in the chimney. Banging sounds make me jump. Are they from outside? I open the door, check the front of the house, and see that one of the shutters is loose and banging. That's the problem. I come back in. More noises, this time pounding from next door, but no one lives there. Is someone working on the house? I didn't see any vans or work trucks parked outside. I ignore the sounds for now and walk upstairs to my bedroom.

I'm drawn to the hope chest Cruz gave me as a wedding chest. I still have my wedding dress tucked inside. I never noticed it before, but a piece of wood appears loose on the front. I should tell Cruz; perhaps he'll want it fixed. I touch the section, and it comes free in my hand. A yellowed piece of paper with worn edges drops to the floor. The ink is barely legible in places.

> To whoever finds this letter,
> This trunk is magic and will hold your dreams
> But it is up to you
> To follow them

It is up to me to follow them. I chant to myself several times.

All night, I fixate on how I'm going to explain to Cruz how I didn't interview for the job, how I ran instead. Or should I lie to him? I pray he doesn't call. How am I going to get the children's tuition money? I lie in bed, unable to sleep until two a.m., when I decide to return to the gallery in the morning, when they open, and beg for another chance to interview.

I can't find my black pencil skirt in the morning, so I wear the pleated cranberry one, a black blazer, and a flower print shirt. I created a note card with bullet points listing all the contributions I made while working at the museum. After I drop the children off at school, I go to Protean Gallery and peek through the window. It's just after nine. The doors are locked, so I tap on the glass. I see a man's bald head pop up from the desk. He walks from the back of the gallery to the front and unlocks the door. He's scowling, and his mustache twitches. "We're closed. Come back at eleven."

"Yes, I know. I'm River Rogers. I was sick yesterday, but I left my resume. Can we chat?"

His eyes take me in, "River Rogers, the Barnard graduate with MoMA experience?" I nod."What happened yesterday, again?"

"I didn't feel well."

"I see. I suppose I could give you a few minutes. I'm Henry, Henry Manchild. Follow me. We can talk at the desk in the back. I wouldn't bother, but your experience piqued my interest. So, what have you been doing with yourself since then?"

"Umm, raising my children. I did some docent work and—"

"Tell me more about MoMA."

"I helped with marketing activities, contacted artists, whatever needed to be done in the new works gallery."

"Perfect. You've got the academic and museum experience I'm looking for. Let me look at you."

He backs away from me and gives me the once-over.

"Don't take this the wrong way, but you'll need to step up your game. Since we sell fine art, we deal with wealthy people, so it's all about appearances. Start with your hair, something a bit more stylish, and the same with your clothing, something more sophisticated. Some of my managers get a few nips and tucks here and there." He opens his desk drawer and hands me three business cards. "These should help."

One's for a beauty shop, another for a clothing boutique, and the last for a plastic surgeon.

"You have two months to get yourself in order. Any problem with that?" He asks.

On the one hand, I'm pleased to have landed the job, but on the other, I've just been told to my face what I've always suspected about myself—I'm not good enough.

"No, no problem. Thank you, Mr. Manchild. I appreciate the opportunity. Thank you for giving me a second chance."

He hands me the employee contract and another form to complete.

I prattle on. I'm nervous, and I drop the forms on the floor. I need to get out of there before he changes his mind and realizes he's made a mistake in hiring me.

"Can you start tomorrow?"

"Yes." I have a dentist appointment, but I'll cancel it. No way can I say no.

"Can you fill the forms out now? You can use the desk over there. I'll see you at nine tomorrow morning."

Like that, he dismisses me. I walk to where Mr. Manchild pointed and fill them out. Meanwhile, an artist comes in to drop off her work, and I see her talking to another worker who's just entered through the back door and to Mr. Manchild. I take the completed forms to the counter to leave them. On the way there, I drop one and bend down to pick it up, and that's when the unthinkable happens...I bump a pedestal, hitting it with my rear end.

"Oh, my God!" I hear the artist call out, then the sound of something wobbling. Another employee runs behind me, and there's the clatter of the object hitting the floor and glass shattering. When I pick up the paper and turn around, the ceramic piece is on the bamboo floor, broken into pieces, and the artist and Mr. Manchild are glaring at me.

The other employee whispers, "Sorry," shrugs, and gives me a wry smile.

"It was an accident," I say meekly.

"Just go." Mr. Manchild flips his hand. "Come back in the morning." The artist glances back at the floor and lets Mr. Manchild lead her away.

I take the forms to the counter and then walk towards the door as fast as I can.

The employee follows me. "Don't worry about it. Everyone

damages something when they start. You simply got it out of the way early. I'll tell you what I destroyed when you come back tomorrow." He winks and opens the door for me. "And by the way, my name's Tony. Welcome aboard."

As soon as I reach the sidewalk, my cell shakes in my pocket. "Hello?"

"It's me."

"Cruz, I got the job."

My face is hot, and my hand trembles. I'm still reeling from knocking over the piece of ceramics.

"Why wouldn't you?"

"Because I chickened out yesterday. I practically had to beg Mr. Manchild for another chance to interview."

"The only person you ever beg is me, your master."

"You aren't my master, Cruz. You aren't even my boyfriend."

"That may be, but don't you ever beg that guy, or any other man, for anything. You understand me? You're too good for that. He should get down on his knees and thank God you're willing to work there. You have a degree from Barnard. You worked at MoMA."

"That was years ago, and I was an assistant to an assistant at MoMA. Now I'm just some middle-aged woman with two children who hasn't worked in decades."

"I don't care. He'd be lucky to have you. You know more about art than that moron ever will. Plus, you have taste. The things I've seen that guy do..."

"You've seen him what?"

"Never mind. Just don't beg him for anything."

"Alright, Cruz. Thank you for helping me get the job. But I need to let you know, I just knocked a ceramic piece off a pedestal with my butt that cost twenty thousand dollars."

"I would have paid twenty thousand dollars to see that."

"Cruz, this is serious. I'm surprised he didn't fire me on the spot. The artist was standing there when it happened. He's most likely going to take it out of my pay."

"They have insurance for this sort of thing, so he'd better not."

"They do?"

"Of course. Didn't MoMA have insurance? Look, I gotta go, I can't talk at the moment."

"Where are you? It sounds like some kind of factory."

"I'll call you back later."

Suddenly, an automated recording says, "Your five minutes are up," and the line goes dead. That was weird. Where is he?

ANGELO CONTI

"She doesn't live at The Palace anymore," Ricardo says. "According to the bartender at Monsters, she's not his slave either, or even engaged to him. The bartender says River gave the ring back. She lives at 1409 N. Dearborn with her children. I checked it out. Cruz still lives in The Palace with the women who work for him."

"Good work, Ricardo." Angelo takes another sip of his latte, licking his dry lips as the aroma of coffee wafts through his luxury automobile, and he begins driving towards the address.

He feels comfortable in his heated seats as people outside his window clear sidewalks and fight winds and weather. Angelo pulled many strings and paid a lot of money to get Cruz arrested the other night. He didn't think the police roughed him up enough. If the girl sticks to her story, Cruz will do ten to fifteen years and learn an important lesson: to stand by the agreements he makes. Angelo has made sure Cruz won't get bail for at least a couple of days, if not longer. It all depends on which judge he draws. This is his first step in getting revenge. Angelo had also wanted to take River that night, but he couldn't find her.

"Did you learn anything else, Ricardo?"

"Cruz is buying another bar, opening another brothel in Chicago too, and starting some other enormous project, but no one seems to know much about that one."

"I'll have to squash it. Anything else?"

"Yes, boss..." Ricardo pauses.

"What is it?"

"I followed River yesterday, and after she took her children to the St. Cloud School, she went to the gallery district to a place called Protean. It's located at 702 North Wells Street. My under-standing is that she got a job and starts today."

"Why didn't you tell me this at the beginning of our conversation?"

"I tried—"

Angelo ends the call, turns the vehicle, and heads towards North Wells. Angelo will purchase The Palace in foreclosure, bring River Rogers to his dungeon and make her his slave, and poor Cruz will go to jail after his conviction on rape charges.

As Angelo drives towards the gallery, he listens to the jazz channel on his satellite radio. Frozen rain plays havoc with traffic. It's still early enough that he lands street parking and watches River through the lit glass window. Her light rose dress clings to her voluptuous figure, and she appears to be dancing as she moves through the white gallery space, decorated with colorful paintings.

Angelo hasn't seen River in person since the dinner with Cruz almost a year and a half ago. He hasn't been able to forget about her, even though he's tried. Her hair has grown longer, and she's lost a few pounds. He's not sure he likes it. He uses his binoculars and notices the sprinkling of freckles on her pale skin. When she bends over to pick up a paper that drops on the floor, it's as if she's bowing only to him. He snickers. He'd planned to have her wear a collar and kneel before him in his dungeon, but Cruz didn't keep his word and backed out of their deal. *Bastard!* Rage crashes through Angelo, but from around the corner, a younger man wearing a wool cap appears, distracting him, and his anger lessens. He watches as the man enters the gallery door. River and the man greet each other and shake hands. The man takes off his hat, and she hands him a cup of coffee. She says something to the young man, and he laughs.

Angelo places the binoculars on his lap, and his face heats again. He unbuttons his collar and rolls down the window. "You won't be laughing the next time you see her," he says out loud to himself. You won't be able to walk, motherfucker."

He picks up the binoculars off his lap and aims them back at the plate window. River climbs a ladder and steadies herself as the man hands her a smaller painting to hang on top of a larger one. They seem to go together. The man holds the ladder and looks at her legs in her knee-high grey suede boots as she hangs and straightens the work on the wall. "I might have to blacken your eyes, too." Angelo sighs. The man catches River's hand to help her down. "I'll break your fingers as well." River smiles, takes down notes, walks around the gallery, and places Post-it notes by each painting on the wall.

Angelo picks up his phone and makes a call. "Aho, there's a younger man who works in the gallery with River. Short brown hair, late twenties or early thirties, about six feet. Send a message. Give him a beating."

"What you want me to say?"

"Nothing, just take care of him. And Ricardo, don't wait. Do it today."

"I thought you said to send a message."

"The beating is the message." Angelo hangs up and watches River. She turns to look at her desk, then walks over and picks up her phone. Her face changes after she listens to her cell. River's smile slides downwards, and then her mouth opens wide. After she hangs up, she snatches her purse and puts her cell inside. She pulls on her gray sweater and long charcoal wool coat and rushes outside. The wind blows at her hair, knocking pieces loose from her ponytail, and her cheeks flush. Her coat opens, revealing the dress's V-neck, her breasts' fullness, and the paleness of her flesh pushing against the fabric of her dress. Angelo sees a hint of her white lace bra peeking out.

He yearns to touch the creaminess of her breasts, but since he can't, he slides his hand inside his pants, touching himself instead. His cock hardens, and he wonders about the size of her nipples and what shade pink they are. Is it the shade of the inside of a conch shell, or a deeper pink like the dress she wears? He grips harder, bringing his hand up and down as River leans against the outside of the building and hugs herself. He holds his breath with frustration. When she breathes, her breath swirls into the cold air. He wishes he could wrap his arms around her, too, instead of holding his cock and balls. "You're pitiful," he says to himself.

Angelo releases his cock and honks the horn. River opens her eyes and runs towards his car, climbing into the back of it. Angelo smiles. She thinks he's the driver she's called. His car must be the same color as the car she's supposed to receive.

He signals and leaves the curb. He knows who she wants to see and where to take her.

6

IT'S COMPLICATED

RIVER

Beep, beep. A wave of nausea washes over me. The smell of car exhaust hits my nose. It can't be true. Cruz would never take a woman without her consent, would he? I tuck myself into the back seat of the Blue Acura, relieved to be out of the cold and moving, doing something. I take out my phone and text a woman named Jo-Jo, another mother I'm friendly with at the same school that Alex and Joy attend. *I have a family emergency. Could you take Alex and Joy to your house when you pick up yours?*

Jo-Jo—*I'd be happy to help.*

I'll call the school later from the police station and let them know about Jo-Jo. I call Mr. Manchild and pray he doesn't pick up, and I can just leave a message.

"Hello, Protean Gallery, Henry Manchild speaking. How may I help you today?" *Crap.*

"Hi, this is River. Ah, I had to leave early for a family emergency...I apologize."

"We aren't starting off too well if you're leaving work early already. Will you be back today?"

"I'm not sure. I'll try. If not, I'll be back tomorrow."

"This better not happen again for a long while. Don't make me regret hiring you." He hangs up.

"Boss giving you trouble?" the driver calls from the front seat.

"It's my first day. He's not pleased with me leaving early."

"You don't remember me, do you?"

"Excuse me?"

"Always so polite. I can assure you, we've met before."

I look up at the mirror. I only see his eyes reflected there, not the rest of his face.

"Have we?"

Before I can say more or he can answer, he pulls in front of the police station, and car horns start beeping, forcing me to leave the car. As I climb out of the back seat, someone calls out to me, "River, over here."

I close the door; the car pulls away, and I notice the badging. It's not an Acura like the car service said it would be; it's a BMW. Who was the driver I just rode with? He's already halfway down the street, too late to call him back and question him.

A man I've seen a few times, who called to me and works with Cruz, rushes towards me.

"Liam," he says in an Irish accent, holding out his hand. His hair is golden brown, and it comes down to his shoulders. He sports a goatee, too. We walk up the steps together and stand inside the vestibule, out of the cold. Liam's not as tall as Cruz, only six feet, but he's very handsome.

"Nice to meet you, Liam. Cruz talks about you all the time. Is it true?"

"It's true that they arrested him, but it's a setup, luv."

"I hope he can fight it." My voice wavers. "He called me yesterday, but he didn't say anything about it."

"He didn't want to worry ya. He's waiting for his attorney to show up, and they won't let you in to see him before then, but I thought you should know. They've been stalling with booking him, letting him call his attorney and all the rest."

"Thank you. It was kind of you to call."

"Best not to let him know I did. He'll be angry, I worried ya." Liam lowers his gaze.

I nod my head. "I don't like keeping things from him, but I understand. You're a good friend, Liam, and he needs one right now."

"I try, but he doesn't let people close. I'm sure I'm not telling you anything you don't know, though. From the little he's disclosed about you, the man's crazy about ya. Hang in there, River." Liam's hand lands on my shoulder, and his fingers provide a gentle squeeze before he walks away.

After they search my purse and push it through the X-ray machine, I talk to an officer. She sends me to the second floor, where I sit in a room painted pale yellow with dirty walls covered with stains and scrapes. We sit in chairs, some covered with torn plastic, others metal folding chairs. There are no windows, and the only lighting is fluorescent. The floors are tiled with faded, dirty, and chipped mustard and brown-colored linoleum squares. I call the school and let them know Jo-Jo will take my children at 3:00, then check my phone for messages and notice the driver reported I wasn't there when she showed up to pick me up. Whose car did I climb into?

After an hour and a half, I'm still waiting to see Cruz. I find a machine that dispenses coffee, and I purchase a cup of the worst coffee I've ever tasted. It's like someone ground up old cigars and made them into an elixir. I drink it anyway. I go into the hall for a few minutes and reach out to Jo-Jo.

"What's going on?" she asks.

"My ex-fiancé got arrested."

"The one who canceled the engagement? I'm surprised you're still close enough to want to help him. I'd let a guy like that rot in jail forever."

"He just wanted to wait."

Luckily, Jo-Jo doesn't know that I was a slave for Cruz, or I'm sure she'd have even more to say about him.

"He's loyal," I say.

"He dumped you. That doesn't sound loyal to me. You're the loyal one."

"I know...but he had a reason, I'm sure."

"He dumped you," Jo-Jo repeats.

"It's complicated."

"It always is, honey." She laughs.

I never expected to fall in love with Cruz when I became his slave. I became his slave because he promised to protect me and my children from my husband.

"He must be good in the sack. That makes it even more complicated."

She's right about that. Cruz changed me in that way, too. No other man is ever going to equal him in the bedroom. Unfortunately, where before I could go months without it, now a day without sex seems impossible. *Damn, Cruz MacKenzie.*

"Thank you, Jo-Jo, for taking the children."

"Don't worry about a thing. Talk later." She ends the call.

I walk back into the waiting area. Another hour passes when a guard finally comes into the room.

"You're here for Cruz MacKenzie?" She asks.

I nod.

"I'm sorry, but he said for you to go home."

"Please, I've waited all day," I say.

She sighs, closes her eyes, and motions at me. "Follow me." I follow her down the hallway before she can change her mind and go into an interrogation room, she indicates. Minutes later, Cruz is brought in, and his handcuffs are reattached to a metal ring on the table bolted to the floor. He's wearing a grave expression.

"I told you to go home," he says, his voice devoid of emotion.

"I'm sorry. I couldn't. I'm worried. I had to come."

"This isn't the place for you. Go home, River."

"I love you, Cruz," I say, but he only shakes his head and indicates to the uniformed officer in the corner of the room that he's ready to go back to the holding cell.

I left my new job and waited all day here for this? All I hear is the buzzing of the overhead fluorescent lights in my ears, and the words go home, go home, go home in my head.

I walk outside the police station. Traffic is whizzing by, and cars are honking. The early night is misty, and there's a layer of pink glittery snow on the sidewalk. I wanted acceptance from the one person in the world who matters most to me. In a small way, I suppose I got it.

Since Jo-Jo has my children, I decided to take the bus to the boutique Mr. Manchild recommended. When I enter the shop, I head to my size, large, and pull out some T-shirts. Someone is hovering behind me. "Can I help you?"

"Umm, I'm looking for Jeanette?"

"You've found her."

"I need some help with my wardrobe. I just got a new job at Protean Gallery, and my boss told me he wants me to improve my clothing choices."

"Manchild? Yeah, he's kind of a dick, isn't he?"

I let out a loud laugh without meaning to. "Wow, I didn't expect you to say that."

"Why not? That's what he is, if he's telling you to dress better." She looks me up and down. "I rather like your outfit. The color looks good on you, and I like the sweater with it. One tip I'd give you is that blazers are more businesslike than sweaters. I'd keep sweaters for Fridays. I'd build your wardrobe around skirts, blouses, T-shirts, and blazers. Nice and simple. Let me pull a few outfits for you. You have great coloring, beautiful skin."

"Really? I think my skin is too pink."

"I'd like to dress you in charcoal rather than black because of your rosy skin. Black will wash you out, but pink agrees with you."

"I have a problem with my stomach and my breasts."

"I take it from a statement like that that you have a habit of buying clothes too big for you?" Her eyes were questioning. "That ironically makes you appear even bigger. Try this on. Let me see it on you." She pulls some other items and sets them aside.

I test out the shirt and come out of the dressing room. "Opinion?"

"Your perspective is more important than mine," Jeanette says.

"It's okay, I guess."

Jeanette comes over and touches her fingers to her lips. "It's too large, especially on the shoulders. Try the medium. If it's too tight, we can alter the other one."

I tug the medium on, and it isn't as tight as I thought it would be. I pull it down over my torso. Yes, it forms to my breasts, but it clings to my curves, and it's like Jeanette says, it fits my shoulders. I walk out of the dressing room.

"Ah, now this one fits you," she exclaims happily. "When you put a blazer over this, it'll rock."

She helps me slide my arm into the blazer. I appear more put together when I examine myself in the mirror. Jeanette's right; I'm a medium, at least in this case.

"Do you like the blazer?"

"Should I be able to button it?"

"Do you plan to?"

"I'm not sure."

"Try to."

I do. "I can."

"The sleeves are too long. We should hem them." Jeanette folds them up and pins them. "Try this blouse and these two skirts. Between them, they'll give you an entire week's worth of outfits."

I could never have done this by myself. Jeanette has a talent for selecting things that look stylish on me and create a casual sense of ease. She understands which fabrics have some give and will close over my boobs and stomach.

When I glance at my reflection in the clothing, my stomach and breasts appear normal-sized, like those of other women. I change back into my street clothes, and I purchase it all. The blazer and skirts need to be altered, but they'll be ready next week. I thank Jeanette for her help and leave the store.

Ring, ring. I answer it before checking. An automated voice tells me it's a collect call, and I accept it. "I'm sorry," Cruz says, a bit of panic in his voice. "I didn't mean to be harsh back there. I didn't want you to see me locked up like that...and you to be exposed to...God knows what. Can you understand?" Is Cruz crying?

"Yes, but I'm certain you didn't do it."

"Thank you for having faith in me, River."

"I'll always have faith in you, always."

"I only have a minute, River. I just wanted to apologize and explain myself to the only person whose opinion matters to me."

"Oh, Cruz...be safe."

"You as well, River." The phone goes dead.

ANGELO CONTI

Ring. Ring. "Hello."

"When are you coming home, Angelo?"

"Soon, Poppa. Twenty minutes."

"It's Marco's birthday today."

"Marco's dead, Poppa."

"One o'clock." His father hangs up. He believes he's lost the wrong son. Angelo will never be as good as his brother Marco, no matter what he does.

Marco would laugh at Angelo's predicament, at not being able to please their parents. His parents had never gotten over his brother's death. Angelo had to feign tears at the funeral fifteen years ago, and this afternoon he'll have to pretend he still mourns.

His parents' house is neat and not ostentatious. His father, Enzo, always lectured, "Do not spend in ways that call attention to yourself. " They would argue about this. "You're doing this wrong, Angelo, " his father would say. "The way you live is going to bring the law to your doorstep."

"Angelo, my baby, you're home," his mother says when he walks in. The kitchen smells like basil, parmesan, and fresh bread.

"Good to see you too, Mama. Where's Poppa?"

"Out back in the garden, talking to Marco."

"Momma, Marco has passed."

"His spirit is here. Your poppa talks to him all the time. He hears his voice in the wind."

"It's cold outside. Poppa's too old to be out in this weather. Tell him to come in. I thought he wanted to celebrate Marco's birthday."

"You might persuade him to come inside."

"I will." Angelo makes his way through the house. His parents recently had the house re-painted. He makes his way towards the back patio as his father's favorite opera, *Rigoletto*, plays. He opens the French doors and climbs down the stone steps covered with spots of ice and sand. The garden, of course, is desolate in winter. Everything appears frozen. His father is huddled over what remains of several of his favorite rose bushes, ones he propagated. One is called the Marco rose.

"Poppa, Poppa, what are you doing?" Angelo asks. His father doesn't respond. He stares down at his rose bushes and whispers something. Angelo walks closer, hoping to get his father's attention or to hear what his father is saying. Snowflakes fall and blow sideways around them.

"I'll seek revenge for what your brother did," his father whispers. What he hears shocks Angelo, causing him to turn and run back up the stairs.

"Did you talk to dear Poppa?" his mother asks. Angelo doesn't answer, just passes her silently and exits the house, while she follows him out to the car. "Where are you going? Aren't you staying to celebrate your brother's birthday?" He ignores her and gets in the vehicle. "Come back!" his mother calls out. Angelo drives away. He knows now that his father somehow learned the truth. Angelo can never return to his parents' house.

"Why did you kill me?" Marco's voice booms.

Where is it coming from? Angelo looks towards the passenger seat and brakes too hard, spinning the steering wheel to the right and almost hitting a car in the right lane. The other driver blasts his horn at him. Angelo slows down, puts his flashers on, pulls into a fast-food place, and parks his BMW.

He closes his eyes and breathes, trying to will his brother away, but when he opens his eyes again, Marco still sits in the passenger seat. He has a bruise on the side of his head where Angelo had hit him. They had gone riding together as they often did, and Marco, as usual, had been teasing him.

"I can take Joanna from you. It'd be easy. I'm better looking than you and better in bed."

Angelo wasn't about to let his brother take his fiancée, as Marco had done with all his previous girlfriends. He had clenched his teeth and kept quiet, waiting for the right time, then he had snuck up on Marco when his back was turned and struck him on the side of his head with a log. Angelo had set the scene up to make it seem like Marco's horse had balked at taking a jump.

Angelo glances at the passenger seat again. A ghostly Marco smiles at him. "So, little brother, you got away with it and all this time has passed, but now you have other problems, yes?"

"Shut up."

"I can help you." The ghost of his brother says.

"I don't need your help. I fucked Cruz good."

Once more, all this because of a woman. I could fuck River too."

"You can't. You're dead."

"You had something to do with that, but you can't stop me. I can still touch her, even now."

"No, no one touches her." Angelo reaches out, and his hand slides right through his brother's body as Marco laughs.

"Why the problem with Cruz MacKenzie? You were friends. Of course, I'm your brother, but it didn't stop you from killing me."

"Cruz and I had a deal. He didn't follow through."

"Got it. A deal is a deal. No doubt about that."

"Because of Cruz, my marriage to Joanna ended. She divorced me, and my children are mad, too. I can't concentrate on anything. I even invested in the art gallery where the new woman works. I had one of my shell corporations invest under a phony name."

"Wow, you have it bad. An art gallery's a money pit."

"Even my father-in-law in Miami is pissed, too."

"All it takes is a few pokes with your cock to free yourself from her."

"Do you suppose that having her will eradicate Cruz from my system, too?"

"You need to kill him," Marco says, "as you did me."

When Angelo shifts his focus back to his brother, he's gone. He takes out his phone to make sure the tracker software on River's phone is working. Yesterday, he had his men place trackers in the lining of several purses and a laptop carrier they'd found hanging on a coatrack by her front door. Dressed as a repairman for the phone company, his men tricked her son into letting them in while she'd been upstairs taking a bath.

Angelo turns the car on and pulls out of the fast-food place. He's shaken from what took place at his parents' house and seeing his dead brother, but not deterred from stalking River Rogers.

7

PRINCIPLES

CRUZ

The bailiff announces, "Please rise. The court of the Second Judicial Circuit, Criminal Division, is now in session, the Honorable Judge James Flannigan presiding." Everyone in the room stands as the judge, a man of about fifty years old with silver hair, enters the courtroom.

"Good afternoon, and please be seated," the judge says. "Are we ready to begin?"

My attorney, Marjorie Dallas, smiles. "Yes, your honor." The prosecutor simply scowls at me and silently nods to the judge.

The judge looks back at the prosecutor. "You're on."

The man jumps to his feet and points at me accusingly. "The state intends to show that the defendant traffics women and has now attacked Malory Jenkins. He's a menace to females everywhere. He should remain in custody until the trial without the possibility of bail." I notice the prosecutor's suit jacket is too small to button, and he's got dark stains on his maroon tie. You can see all of this because fluorescent lighting covers the whole ceiling.

"Defense?" the judge says.

"Where's the evidence?" she says. "It's all hearsay. The defendant's record is spotless. He has no arrests or convictions, not even a traffic violation. He is not a threat to the safety of the people of Chicago, but rather a respectable and successful businessperson. Your honor, I request that you release my client on his own recognizance until the trial."

"I agree, Ms. Dallas," replies the judge. "The defendant has no prior convictions. Cash bail is no longer required for crimes of this nature in Illinois. Therefore, the defendant is released until—"

"There shouldn't be any trial at all," I say. "The case should be dismissed."

The judge frowns and says, "I'm just about to send you home, Mr. MacKenzie. Do you really want to flirt with contempt of court at this point?"

"This whole thing is ridiculous," I continue. "There's no proof. This should never have gotten to this point in the first place."

The judge's mouth twists downward. "Okay. Defendant is found in contempt of court and is remanded to Metropolitan Correctional Center until he is ready to apologize to the court. Next case." He bangs his gavel.

Marjorie gathers her notes and legal pad and places it back in her case. She smiles at the judge, then turns to me and whispers. "What's your problem?"

"It's the principle of the thing."

"You're willing to stay locked up just on principle?

"Yes."

"Be my guest. I'll return tomorrow to discuss these charges and how you wish to proceed." Then she pauses. "Your girlfriend, River..."

"What about her?" I ask.

"Call her and get her off my back. She's called me three times today about what I'm doing about getting you out, and I think she's hurt that you won't talk with her."

"I'm trying to protect her. I don't want her exposed to a place like this."

"I understand, but from her vantage point, it's one more rejection, and it seems she's having a problem with her daughter. Joy blames her mother for you leaving."

I nod my head. "I'll handle it." My head is killing me.

"Good. We all have things we don't want to do, but sometimes we have to put other people's interests before our own. It's called being an adult." She scoops up her case and marches out of court.

The truth is, I can't let River get closer. It can only harm her. You mean it can only hurt you, I say to myself. You're afraid to let anyone get close.

MONTEL MACKENZIE

Montel clutches his cell and presses it to his ear. This is River Rogers," the recording plays. "I'm sorry I missed your call. Please leave your contact info, and I'll get back to you." His cock stiffens and rubs against his corduroy pants. Her voice always has this effect on him. He coughs, out of breath after carrying boxes through the ice and snow. He hasn't even reached the third-floor apartment yet, or could this be another effect of hearing her voice? He ends the call and shoves the phone deep in the pocket of his waxed canvas jacket. A gust of wind whips across the small landing where he's rested. He looks out at a cobalt sky with streaks of fluorescent pink as day turns to night and flakes of snow blow in his face.

He climbs ten more steps to the top landing and unlocks the door. A blast of frigid air pushes him into the dark cavern of his rented space. Montel considers the message he could have left and sings it out: "I'm stalking youuuuu." The words echo throughout the empty room. "I'm your new neighbor. I love watching you in downward dog." *Thump, thump.* Montel forgot about the other one. She's kicking the walls again. Thank God they made the place of thick plaster, and no one is living in the second-floor unit. This one will learn soon enough.

He dumps his duffel and boxes on the honey-colored hardwood floor. The binoculars, stun gun, and computer come out first. The taser makes things easier. He's quiet, entering the bedroom. Little Mouse scares easily, and even though she can't see him, because of the blindfold, she has other senses. He tasers her once. She flops her body around like a fish out of water, but can't move her arms because he's tied her up. "Stop making noise, please," he says politely. She'll be like all the others soon. In the past, the fear of pain and the desire for food would convince his victims to do whatever he demanded soon enough. He tried the taser on himself once—a mistake. He had to purchase a new couch because he couldn't eliminate the unpleasant odor of urine from the cushions. Unfortunately, it only disables the victim for a brief period. He smells urine. "Bad girl. You wet yourself. I'll punish you later." She tries to speak, but he can't make out her words through the gag.

Montel returns to the living room but leaves the bedroom door ajar. He doesn't like people, but the irony is that he also doesn't enjoy being alone. He couldn't believe his luck when Little Mouse and her friend knocked on his apartment door the day before last. It was only Christian to invite them in for coffee when they brought him news about the end of the world. They discussed Armageddon. It came sooner for her friend than she'd expected. Funny how things work: God was sending them to him so he didn't have to go hunting for victims to satisfy his need.

Montel had come to Chicago last November to make amends with his son, but as soon as he set eyes on River, he put his plan aside. What is it about his son's fiancée? He concluded it's her pale, luminous skin, with a hint of pink. He'd seen nothing like it outside of Renoir paintings. Luckily, the relationship between his son and River fizzled within weeks of Montel setting eyes on her. Then she moved out of Cruz's house into her current one, and Montel found it easier than he expected to secure a rental across the street.

He takes a seat on a gray milk crate, his knees pushed up to his chin. It makes him feel like a child when sitting on it. He calls out to Little Mouse, "Sitting here reminds me of how my father used to force me to wait for punishment when I'd done something wrong. Would you believe, Little Mouse, that I was always doing something wrong? My son Cruz is just like me. If my father were here right now, he'd repeat a quote from the Bible: 'So is he who goes in to his neighbor's wife; none who touches her will go unpunished. Proverbs 6:29.' My father was a preacher, too. That's why you don't need to worry. When you die, I'll prepare you for heaven, just like I did your friend."

Montel presses the binoculars' frame against his eyes and aims them at where River lives. He hopes the shades are still up. "Yes," he mutters when he discovers them so. Too bad the windows are dark. He doesn't know where she is. She should be home by now. He lays the binoculars down and sighs. His eyes wander around his empty room. River's home is different. It has comfortable couches, a fireplace, photographs, and paintings.

He stole River's mail first. After that, it got easy. He found her number and email address. The lazy man's way of stalking. You can find out a lot about a person from their social media, but

River's different. She doesn't share much. Montel admits River's more a fixation than any of the others. Usually by this time, he's already taken, killed, and sent them to heaven or hell, and disposed of the body. Things are just getting started with River.

He's been tailing River to her children's school and even following her while she shops. He didn't today because he wanted to do more research. "Guess what I did today, Little Mouse?" he calls to the other room. Of course, she can't respond. She talked little even before Montel gagged her. Her friend did all the talking before he ended her life. "I made a visit across the street to the neighbor I told you about." Besides not speaking much, Little Mouse wore thick glasses. The first thing Montel did was take them away and break them.

Montel walks over to his captive, looming over her. He drags her to the wall and leans her against it, removing her blindfold. Her eyes grow large, then she squeezes them shut, shaking her head and mumbling, the gag impeding her speech. "Stay still when I speak to you," he says, stunning her again. She topples over on her side, and her body rocks back and forth. He goes back to the main room.

People today think security systems are foolproof. If Montel hadn't worked for an alarm company for ten years in Syracuse, maybe River's would be. River's house proved to be different from what he expected, too. He couldn't explain it, but the house made him feel uneasy, which is why he inspected every part of it. He found a secret staircase hidden behind a bookcase that framed her living room fireplace. It brought him to her bedroom. The hidden panel there blended in with her wall. He'd seen bookcases like these before and knew that, based on the thickness of the book-cases, there was more to it. He wondered if River knew about it. The only room he felt like himself in was River's bedroom.

Montel lay on her mattress and inhaled her scent. Exotic. Rose, jasmine, and citrus smells swirled around him. Montel left his own smell on her pillow. She might even catch a whiff of him later. He left something even more important behind, spy cameras, motion- and light-activated. Whenever she enters the room and turns on the light, the camera will record everything she does, and Montel can watch it all.

He also discovered the second bookcase in the living room had another secret walkway to the house next door. No one appears to be living there. He unlocked one of the windows in that house on the ground floor, so he now has a way to get in and out of her house without involving River's security system at all.

Montel knows renting an apartment across from hers is risky. He's seen his son and his son's men several times, surveilling River's house from an SUV. Last night, he saw River undress through the window, and afterward, he had to take Little Mouse out and play with her harder than he'd planned. He'll have to do more soon; that's how it works. It was one reason he'd left Syracuse.

When some of the windows of River's house glow gold, Montel scrambles for the binoculars. His breath quickens when he sees what he desires in the circles of the lenses. He checks the time. It's after seven. He writes it all down—January 21, 2023, 7:00 p.m.—in a log under her name. He keeps all his victims' comings and goings there. He imagines what he'll discover under River's skin when he peels it back with his blade. Is this what it means to get under someone's skin? He giggles but stops when the sound ricochets through the space and makes him sound like a girl.

Montel has to wait another hour before River finally arrives in her room. The light comes on on the second floor, and he calls out, "Action," carrying his computer into the room and plopping it down next to his latest victim. "This is River, the woman I told you about," he says. "Look." Little Mouse's frantic eyes swim through the room, searching for a way out. He takes hold of her chin and forces it to the screen. "I won't tell you again. Check it out or else." He lays the gun by his side. Mouse's chin quivers.

"She's a complicated and sensitive woman, and pours her emotions out on paper. She loves my son, an unfortunate thing. My son is like me, incapable of empathy for other humans."

Little Mouse nods her head. They stare as River seems to become more upset and looks around the room, seemingly realizing someone has lain on her bed. She covers her eyes with her fingers and cries, like the woman now sitting next to him, but this one has her hands tied together.

Montel can't relate to either woman's sadness. He gets excited by pain, his own and others', but he celebrates his ability to torture River when he hasn't laid a finger on her. It's been a long time since he's screwed with a victim's head. He'd forgotten about the fun that ensues. Many years ago, he switched to only torturing their physical bodies instead.

River doesn't seem to know what to do. She picks up her phone, then puts it down again, arguing with herself. She finally rises, grabs her cell, and exits the room.

"What do you think, Mouse, should I call her?" he asks. Little Mouse freezes in place. Montel leaves the room, returns with his scalpels, and strides towards Little Mouse. "I have a new game for us." He removes her gag. "First, you need to be punished."

"It was an accident. I couldn't help it—"

"You're not blaming me, are you?"

He watches her eyes. She knows it's a trick and there's no way out. If she says yes, Montel will punish her; if she says no, he'll punish her for wetting herself. "It was a mistake," she says.

True. "So you deserve punishment because you made a mistake. Answer me."

"Yes," Little Mouse says.

Montel hasn't let her sleep since she's been here, but neither has he. He has a radio on a timer that goes off sporadically at a loud volume, dialed to a heavy metal music radio station. Soon, he'll have to feed and bathe her, too. Toys can be played with but must be cared for; eventually, they break, and he can't play with them anymore.

After Montel is done correcting Little Mouse, the rattling windows in the old Victorian home are quiet, and the rage inside of Montel tames. For the first time in four days, Montel rests. Little Mouse can rest now, too.

8

BROKEN PART

RIVER

"What's this doing out?" I'd left my journal in the nightstand drawer, but now it's lying on top of the nightstand, open. Oh my God, it's bent back at the page where I wrote about the first orgasm I had with Cruz! The room smells different, too, like dirty sneakers or towels left in the washer too long without drying. I walk to my bed. I made it this morning, but now the spread is uneven, and my pillow has a slight dent, like someone has lain their head on it. My heart beats faster.

I race around my room, looking for more proof that someone has been in my room. I take my phone. Should I call the police? Should I call Cruz? I'll sound like someone desperate for attention. I call no one. I light some candles in my bedroom, go downstairs, open a bottle of my favorite pinot noir, return to the room, drink half the bottle, sit in bed, and read until...

"No, get away, stop!" I wake up with a jerk and look around the shadowy room. Where am I? I'm in my house. "I'm safe."

I check the clock. It's two a.m. It's just another nightmare. Why am I having them again after so long? I'm far away from Prince Edward's, Canada, and the school where they hated me. Should I go down and consume my favorite thing? Mint ice cream with hot fudge and whipped cream? No, I'd only do that if I didn't gain a pound. I wish I could stop thinking about food, fat, and my body for once. When Cruz and I were together, I did. He evoked a sense of well-being and desirability. My insomnia now is worse than before. I shake my head and squeeze my eyes shut, holding back my tears. I go to the window and look out. Cruz's car isn't here tonight because he's in jail. If he were here, he could help me. He used all his witchy magic, and it often worked. He said things work if you believe they do.

I take out my journal and read back my thoughts from two weeks ago, the last time I wrote in it.

I SHOULD HAVE KNOWN BETTER. I'M NO MATCH FOR CRUZ'S PERFECT FACE, HIS FIRM JAW, GRAY-BLUE EYES, AND TALL, MUSCULAR BODY. I'M NOT PRETTY ENOUGH FOR SOMEONE LIKE HIM. I'M MUCH TOO TRADITIONAL FOR SOMEONE LIKE HIM. NONE OF THIS STOPPED ME FROM FALLING IN LOVE WITH HIM. I KEPT TELLING MYSELF NO, AND HE KEPT PUSHING ME TO SAY YES. HE'S A CRIMINAL, BUT IN THE END, NONE OF IT MATTERED OR STOPPED ME.

WHEN HE ASKED ME TO MARRY HIM, HE PROMISED SO MUCH, INCLUDING TO GIVE UP HIS BUSINESS FOR THE SAKE OF MY CHILDREN. I BELIEVED HIM. I GUESS THAT MAKES ME TOO STUPID TO LIVE, LIKE THE WOMEN I READ ABOUT IN MY ROMANCE NOVELS.

THAT'S WHY ALL OF THIS IS DIFFICULT. NOW I'M

FORTY-FIVE, ALMOST FORTY-SIX. I HAVE TO START OVER AGAIN AND

Ring, ring. I reach for the phone on my nightstand.

"Hello?" I hear nothing but heavy breathing again. "Who are you? Stop it!" *Click.*

This is the sixth call today.

Ring, ring, ring, ring. I heave the phone, and it hits the wall across the room, making a loud banging noise, and then becomes quiet.

Dark shadows dance around the room, except for the yellow flickers from a candle. I'm irresponsible to fall asleep with candles lit. I've been drinking. I could burn the house down and harm my children. I'm drinking too much these days, trying to forget that I'm alone again. Add this to the growing list of things I need to stop doing. How am I going to improve my looks if I drink so much?

I turn on the light by my bedside, blow the candles out, and rise from my bed. I locate the phone on the other side of the bedroom and retrieve it from the wool rug, its final landing place. Despite the cracked screen, it turns on and lights up. I go to my messages and scroll to the last one, discovering it's from Cruz. His sexy voice rumbles in the darkness.

"I'm sorry about the other night and not seeing you in jail. I shouldn't be bothering you. I'll stay away. I want you to be happy."

I don't delete it. I listen to it again and then again. "I want you to be happy."

The truth is, I don't want him to stay away. I want him to know that I'm happier when I'm with him. I power off the phone, lie down on the mattress, stare out the window at the stars in the distance above my neighbor's house, and remember how things used to be. My mind shifts again. I write in the journal:

I NEED TO CONCENTRATE ON BUILDING MY CAREER AND RAISING MY CHILDREN. I CAN'T LET CRUZ BACK INTO MY LIFE. I CAN'T GET INVOLVED WITH ANYONE AGAIN.

I push my face into the deepness of my pillow, and my body heaves. I smell something strange. I throw the pillow on the floor. I cry until Joy bursts into my room.

"Mommy, Mommy, I can't sleep! I had a nightmare. I heard someone crying. Someone's chasing me, and they won't leave me alone." She wraps herself in my arms and snuggles next to me.

I stroke her head and pat her back.

"Shh, it's alright," I say to her. "It's just a dream, you're safe here. I'll take you back to your room and lie down with you."

I walk her back and squeeze into her twin bed with her. I run my hand through her hair, and in a few minutes, she falls asleep in my arms. Her breathing is slow and even as my mind races, replaying the past.

I crawl from Joy's bed to keep from waking her up. When I get back to my room, I scrawl in my journal again. I had perfect parents. A chill comes through my body.

I write:

I REMEMBER MY BUTTERY BODY AND ALL THE BRUISES THAT GATHERED ON IT THAT THE OTHER CHILDREN GAVE ME. I HID MY CLOTHING FROM MY MOTHER SO SHE WOULDN'T ASK ABOUT THE RIPS AND TEARS AND HOW THEY GOT THERE.

Why am I dredging this up now? I need to get over it. I pace around the room. I'm a grown woman. Before I met Cruz, I hid myself and tried not to get noticed.

"All you're doing is making people think you're weak. You're not, so stop acting that way," Cruz had said.

I pad to my bathroom. I know I hid one in the vanity. I paw through it, removing the beauty supplies, piling them in the sink, the cotton balls, my tweezers, and all the other things I seldom use, then the paper lining, until I find what I've hidden but haven't forgotten. I haven't used it in years, but here it is waiting for me, shiny, silver, and sharp. I pick it up by its protective cardboard cover and take a piece of tissue from the dispenser. I go back to my bedroom and sit on the bed.

"Don't do this. You're fat..." I want to stuff myself with cookies. Thank goodness I didn't buy any. I feel guilty about not buying them for my children. But I know if I do, I'll eat them. My mind is a hurricane. I shut my eyes and try to move the memory away. I need the pain gone so my brain can rest and I can sleep. I need the release. The therapist advised to wait for the emotion to pass...but I'm unable to.

I hold the blade between my thumb and forefinger and bring it across my upper thigh, leaving a long, thin line. I exhale, and the blood oozes out. I experience the release with each cut I make. Following the five cuts, my emotions flatten. I soak up the blood with the tissue. The blood leaves a shape on the tissue that resembles a monster's face. Sensing the physical discomfort diminishes the mental anguish. I return to the bathroom, rinse the blade, bury it back in the drawer, find the antiseptic, and apply it to the cuts. Eucalyptus hits my nose and makes me think of Canada again. I cover the marks with a large flesh-colored bandage. I turn off the light and creep back to bed. If anyone asks, I'll say I ran into a broken window.

The truth? I ran into the broken part of me.

CRUZ

"Open twenty-three," the guard says. Once it opens, a massive, bald individual saunters in. The gate clangs closed on both of us.

"What we got here?" the man sneers, his eyes half-closed. "I'm your new cellmate."

He fills the entire room, but I've taken down larger foes. He looks like he's been taking gym candy, and some of those types turn out to be nothing but pumped-up pussies.

"I want that bunk," and he points up at me.

I don't give him a chance to say more. I kick him. A crunching sound emits from his nose, and it moves sideways. Blood spurts and splashes on the floor. I jump off my bunk and pin him against the beige-painted cinder blocks before sweeping my foot under his huge clodhoppers and bringing him to the brown speckled linoleum floor. Once he's down, I stomp on his face three times in the middle of his forehead. I bend down and punch him in the mouth twice. He's not moving. I stand up and examine my previously bruised knuckles.

"What's going on in here?" A guard looks inside.

"Nothing."

"Why's he on the floor?"

"He slipped."

"He'd better be in a bed the next time I come back," the officer says.

I drag my cellmate to the bottom bunk and get him partially on it. His legs hang off the mattress. Drool spills out of his open mouth, and he makes some gurgling sounds. One of the people who worked for me told me it's important to send a message that you're not someone to be messed with. The first time anyone tries to do anything to you, you come back full force. If you do that, others will know you're not someone to toy with, and word gets out.

"I'm glad you changed your mind and chose the bottom bed. Most people prefer it."

I climb back up to the top and lay my head against the flattened pillow. I conjure up an image of River's face, and it calms me. I'm going to need magic to raise and direct my energy to center myself. I'm going to need a spell of protection, too. I take three breaths and chant the spell three times:

> Elements of the sun,
> Elements of the day,
> please come this way.
> Powers of the Night and Day, I summon thee.
> I call upon thee to protect me! So may it be.

River is the only woman I've been intimate with. I'm not talking about fucking. I've lost count of them. I'm connected to her. I've shared something with her beyond the physical. There's no one else I've ever let close to me, that's why I had to let her go. I'll only hurt her if I keep her, but the truth is, she could hurt me, too. She's too close...But I haven't let her go. I keep going back.

I discovered early that you can't trust anyone. I mean, if you can't trust your parents, who can you trust?

River made me believe it might be possible to have a genuine family. Before she came into my life, the only family I had were the women who worked for me... and the truth is, they have their own families, so they can never be my real family. But that's as close as I ever got before River walked into my life with Joy and Alex.

An hour later, the bell rings, the gates clang open, and men flood out into the open area, headed for the dining hall for dinner. I jump down and shake my bunkmate's shoulder. I don't need any trouble in here. I need to wake him up and get him to the chow hall. He groans. "Let's go. It's chow time."

The guy opens one eye. "Come on, get up. We'll both get busted for fighting if we don't show for dinner."

He stumbles from the bed, holding onto the cinderblock wall. I hand him a washcloth. "Wipe your face. What are you going to tell them?"

"I tripped." He shakes his head back and forth.

"Good. What's your name?"

"Stupid."

"Your real name," I chuckle.

"Joey."

"I'm Cruz. Let's go eat, Joey."

"What you in here for?" Joey asks me, moving through the doorway.

"Sexual battery."

"What's that?"

"Rape."

"Sexual battery sounds better."

"How about you?"

"Not paying alimony and child support."

I stop moving. "Do you want your children to go without?"

"I lost my job and—"

"Bullshit. Get another."

"My wife has a job. She also had a more talented attorney, and I had a crappy one. I don't even think one kid is mine."

"It doesn't matter. The kids need a father, clothing, food, and a home. Your wife can't do it alone. Do the right thing."

"You're right. As soon as I get out, I'll try to get another job. I've always been a failure, a bum. This is just one more thing I've failed at, being a husband, a father, and a provider."

"Stop whining and do something about it. When you get out, you can work for me."

"Really." He looks skeptical.

"Yeah. But I'm taking your child support out and giving it to your wife. And if you fuck up, I'm firing you. Then I'll beat what you owe me out of you. Got it?"

"Thanks, Cruz. What do I gotta do? It's not illegal, is it?"

"Does it matter?"

"Not really. Just wondering."

"I have to find out what you're good at. You aren't much of a fighter. You have a scary presence, so that's something."

"Thanks, I think. I can't believe you're going to help me."

"Why?"

"Because of the way I acted when I first met you."

"I knew it was an act."

"How did you know?"

"Because I've done it myself, acted like I'm a big man to hide that I'm a little shit. Now shut up and let's go."

"Thanks, Cruz."

We enter the dining hall. There's nothing to eat but unidentifiable food items. I don't consume any of it. I spend my time watching everyone to figure out who's an actual threat and who's a fake.

"Can I have your food if you don't eat it?" Joey asks.

"Take anything you want."

"Thanks."

Following our return to our cell, I find myself on the top bunk, chanting, while Joey occupies the bottom. I begin to drift off. Joey asks, "You didn't do it, did you?"

"No, I didn't."

"Bummer," Joey says.

"Yeah, bummer."

A sudden sadness pulls at me, and I sink lower and lower, even though I'm not even in the lower bunk. Ironic. Fuck. This isn't where business people are supposed to spend their time.

9

SECRETS & UNICORNS

MAXKSIM OBERLIN & DAVID SHIRE

"What are we going to do?" Maxksim Oberlin says to his attorney, David Shire, as he surveys Central Park. "It's been a year and a half, and we still can't get access to my money." He stops talking when David's assistant-paralegal enters carrying a silver tray filled with steaming cups of black coffee, sugar, cream, and spoons.

The assistant-paralegal is in his mid-twenties and handsome. He sets everything down on the credenza. Maxksim notices David appears younger and happier than he has in some time. He has never had a male paralegal before.

"Thank you, Bruce," David says. David's more than Maxksim's legal counsel; they've been friends since elementary school. They all came up the hard way, David, Jack, and he, growing up in Brooklyn and working their way through college together. Maxksim can smell notes of cinnamon and vanilla, but can't be sure whether they came from the coffee or from Bruce's cologne as he walked by. David's office is on the top floor of this skyscraper, and he can afford the best of everything. He should; he charges by the minute.

"I need the funds to buy that building we want to turn into condos," Maxksim says, taking a sip of his coffee and burning his lip. "I've got to have the money for closing in two months. You've tried all of your legal maneuvering, and Jack's bitch, River, has us tied up in court." The success of this condo will shore up his other properties. At least that's what his accountant has led him to believe.

"I told you a year ago to make arrangements with the widow." David fingers the yellow legal pad on the spacious wood table. "Some money is better than none."

"Settle with her? How can I do that when the grieving widow wants to take half of everything? We've done it your way. Now we're going to do it mine." Maxksim notices the shelves of books behind his friend, the Yale Law School graduate who was first in his class, but finds no answers in them to Maxksim's problem.

"No, Maxksim, don't. Chicago is not your town, and it's your partner's wife we're talking about."

"He's not my partner anymore. Pearson is dead, and I'm not so sure this bitch didn't have something to do with making him that way. Jack was not a drug user and never sold them either, but the police claim he died from an overdose. The newspapers reported the room filled with drugs and cash. Why would Pearson sell drugs when he could make all the money he would ever need dealing in real estate? Jack was a real estate savant."

Maxksim is in the predicament he's in now because he doesn't have Jack's real estate savvy. He reaches for the cup of coffee again and takes another sip. "The whole thing smelled rotten from the get-go. I told the lead detective in Chicago before they closed the case, but they didn't want to listen."

David shakes his head. "That might be, but you can't prove

anything. Frankly, it might have had mob ties. One body was missing its hands, and you can't just—"

"My intention is to show River Rogers what I can do. That should be enough to get her attention. I don't need permission from the big boys to come into their town for that. But since you're anxious, I'll inform you I've already reached out to the person in charge, and everything's been arranged. Now I'm going to call my two men."

David nods his head, and Maxksim reaches for his phone inside his pocket, next to his gun. David excuses himself from his office. He probably doesn't want to overhear anything he'd have to testify about later. After Maxksim makes his call, he sips his coffee and stares out the window at the skyline before him. In another week, his life will be perfect; he'll get his way, have his money, close on the condominium, and start the renovation project.

As Maxksim leaves the room, he looks through the glass door. David is with his paralegal, bending down over the desk and nuzzling Bruce's neck. Maxksim has known David for over twenty years. Until last year, David was married with three children. When David sees Maxksim, he pulls away and says, "I'll walk you down."

Maxksim and David enter the elevator together. "I'm dating him." A flush creeps across his cheeks. "I've never dated a man before, but...I like this one. I can't explain it. I hope it doesn't offend you. Rest assured, it won't affect our business relationship or our friendship."

"Of course not. As long as you can continue to do your job, I don't have a problem," Maxksim says, stepping out of the elevator. "And as far as friendships go, we've been friends forever, and I can't see how that will change, unless you decide to fall in love with me."

David laughs. "No chance of that. You aren't lovable."

"I'll keep in touch about the other situation."

"Be smart about it." David straightens his tie.

"Of course. You too." *Ding*. Maxksim steps off the elevator. Maxksim realizes he's going to need a new attorney when this is over. He can't have a faggot for a lawyer. *Your knowledge of anyone is not as extensive as you perceive.*

CRUZ

"Are you out?" Marjorie Dallas asks over the phone.

"Yes. Thanks for handling things with the judge."

"You should have behaved yourself, Cruz."

"I understand."

"Why do you do some of these things you do?"

"I don't like being told what to do." I pull out the greeting card I got from Parkway Drugs. I'd come here first. I'd already decided what to write on it, so it didn't take me long to put the words down. I put the gift inside while Marjorie lectures me. I check the notebook Liam's given me of The Palace's earnings for the last few days. Not bad, but nothing to crow about either. I'm multitasking, which means I'm getting things done, but not very well.

Liam makes a face. "The girls were upset you weren't around. They were worried."

"The judge accepted your handwritten apology," Marjorie says. "He wanted to keep you in there another two days, but after a little extra convincing from me, he came around. In the future, can you trust me to do my job? Either I'm your legal counsel, or I'm not. Do you want to hire someone else?"

"No, of course not, or I wouldn't have paid you enough of a retainer to last a year."

"Then you need to trust me. You're paying me for my advice and expertise. Believe me, I'm going to put your interests first. I got a partial background check back on the woman who brought charges against you."

"And?"

"Like you heard in court, her name's Malory Jenkins. She's got a record, but a minor thing, a shoplifting charge from three years ago, dropped. She works at a boutique. Interestingly, she quit a day before she filed charges. Her bank account increased by twenty thousand dollars the day after, too. It wouldn't surprise me if someone gives her another increase in funds. I'm monitoring the account. The deposit was from a company called AT LLC. I have a private investigator looking at the formation papers to see who the owner is."

"Who's the woman?"

"I told you."

"No, beyond that. Where did she go to school? Where was she born? Who are her friends?"

"We're still checking into that."

"Can I have a copy of the report?"

"Why?"

"I just want it."

"I suppose. I'll send you a copy when I make one."

"Thank you, Marjorie. How about Joe Goldstone, my cellmate? Did you take care of things?"

"Yes, but I still think this is a mistake. Cruz, what's his background? I don't think—"

"Don't worry. Let me worry about him."

"As you wish. But make sure if you go out anywhere, you have someone with you besides this Joe Goldstone."

"I promise I'll take one of my bodyguards. Can we talk later? I need to go."

"I suppose," she says. "Be careful." I end the call.

"Is this the bank you want to stop at?" Cork asks, pointing at Choice Savings & Loan.

"Yes, that's the one. Pull over. This shouldn't take long. I just have to submit this paperwork to the loan officer."

I enter the bank and sit down at the loan officer's desk, one Mr. Rickstraw. After introductions, he takes several minutes to thumb through my application and other paperwork. Finally, he lifts his head and says, "I'm sorry, Mr. MacKenzie, but you don't have enough collateral for a loan this size. You don't have a history of paying back large loans, either."

I can't strong-arm him or shoot him, as I would with anyone else who would dare to say no to me. Things don't work this way in the business world.

"Come back in nine months and show us what you've accomplished with Monsters, and we'll see what we can do." He smiles and sticks out his hand. All I can do is take it and try not to crush his fingers as I exit.

"How did it go?" Liam asks.

"Strike two."

"Might be easier to rob a bank than get a loan from one," Cork smirks.

"Drop me off at Dolls. It's two blocks over." I pull down my shades. Once we arrive, I get out.

"You want me to come?" Liam asks. I shake my head no. "No bodyguard? I thought you told your attorney you'd always bring one while you're out."

"I'm not expecting trouble at Doll's, and there are plenty of witnesses. Come back in thirty minutes."

"Check out all the college students waiting out front," Liam says.

"How do you know they're students?"

"The clothes they're wearing, mate."

"I don't get it. When did slippers and pajamas become public attire?"

"Watch what you say, Cruz. It makes you sound old," Cork chuckles.

"I *am* old. You and Cork go over to Monster's, get last night's earnings, and make the bank deposit. By then, it'll be time to return, and then we can go get the new guy."

Cork loses his smile and lowers his window. "What new guy? What's he going to do?"

"I met him in prison. I don't know yet. He could be muscle for the new brothel." They give me the look, the one I love, one of worry. "Don't concern yourself," I continue. "You're not being replaced." I walk into the cafe.

The whiff of roasting beans and brewing coffee fills my nose. There's a woman waiting for her coffee who's bundled up and has a toddler in tow. The toddler is trying to reach for a pastry on the counter, but the mother is telling her no. The mother pulls her hard, making the child fall on the floor. The toddler turns red and starts wailing.

"Carla, Americano with skim milk," the barista calls out. The mother snatches her child off the floor, drags her over, picks up her order, and leaves the shop with her child. I grab the pastry, throw some money at the register, then follow them out and around the corner. I plan to slap the woman around where no one's watching.

Once I catch up with her, I push the woman against the side of the brick building. Her eyes grow huge, and she drops both her coffee and the child's hand. I whisper, "What's wrong with you?" I seethe. "Why are you so rough with her?" I point to the toddler.

"I didn't mean to." The woman's eyes water. "I lost my job. My rent's due. Everything is too much this morning."

"Those are all bullshit excuses."

"I know. You're right."

"You can't take it out on her. She doesn't deserve it."

"You're right. I'm sorry." Tears slide down her face.

"You need to tell your daughter."

The woman bends her head down to her child. "Mummy's sorry she was mean."

"Here, take this and give it to your child." I hand the woman the pastry, and she gives it to her little one. The child rips the paper off, smiles up at me, and dives into it.

I pull my wallet out and hand Carla some cash. "Here's some money for your rent. You'd better pay it, not spend it on booze, drugs, or anything else. You touch her again as you did inside there, and I find out, I'll come back. You hear me?"

She takes the cash out of my hand. "I won't, I promise." She counts the money. "Thank you. Again, I apologize for my actions."

"I'll be watching." I head across the street, towards the school, and wait by the fence. My chest hurts. Am I turning soft?

I pull the envelope out of my pocket, the one with the unicorn on it. It's purple, her favorite color. I hope she likes it. Of course, I can't see it now because it's hidden inside a white envelope. Joy loves unicorns, so the chances are she'll love the card. I bend the envelope back and forth before stopping myself. I don't want to knock all the glitter off. I hope I can talk to Joy and explain. Kids need to know that when bad things happen to adults, it's not their fault. Not River's either.

The metal and glass doors spring open, and hundreds of children stream out into the fenced yard. How will I locate Joy among all these children? How will she find me? After five minutes of searching, I still can't locate her. Has something happened to Joy?

The doors open again, and I spot her; she's on the grey steps. I exhale, relieved. I notice how small and alone she appears.

That's how it was for me when I was in school. I was always

the loner. I had to keep my family's secrets. The other children thought I was weird, and I was. My clothes were always dirty, didn't fit me because they were from thrift shops, and I smelled. My mother never washed them; she was always too busy getting high.

Joy hesitates to come down. I watch as a few kids walk towards her. Joy seems afraid of them, and she's not smiling, like she used to. Someone pushes her, but luckily, she catches the metal railing. I want to climb the fence and grab the boy, but I hold myself back. *They're just children. I know what's going on. I've seen it before, from both sides. You can be the hunted or the hunter. I'm the hunter now.*

"Joy, Joy! Over here!" I wave my hands in the air. At first, she's unsure. Then she runs towards me, pushes her fingers through the fence, and touches mine with hers. "Were they bothering you?"

"Not really." Her eyes look back at them. "Why did you leave us, Cruz? Don't you love us anymore?"

Her question breaks me. I don't blame her for changing the subject. It's hard to admit you're a victim, just as it's difficult to admit to myself that I've hurt her. The feelings I always push down now rise, choking me. It hurts to know how much pain I've caused her and the rest of them by leaving. Joy's eyes are questioning and wet.

I bend down and slide my gift under the wire fence. "I bought you something. Can you read it?"

"Yes, I can read almost anything, even books for seventh graders." Joy rips the envelope open. "My favorite—a unicorn." Joy's lips turn up.

It doesn't surprise me that she can read anything, because her mother is off-the-charts smart, so her daughter and son will be too.

"Careful, there's something inside. I made it for you. I most definitely love you, Alex, and your mummy, too. Can you keep a secret, Joy?"

"Yes." She nods her head, her hair sliding into her face.

"I had to leave to keep you safe. Bad people were after us, and in order to protect you, I had to move away. Do you understand?"

She smiles and discovers the gift inside. "It's a necklace!" she exclaims, putting it over her head. "With a tiny bottle hanging off it."

"Keep it under your shirt and place it under your pillow when you don't wear it. The bottle contains magic that will make you happy. Whenever you feel sad, bring your hand to it and rub it. The gift and the card are a secret. Someday, we can all be together again. Both are a reminder that I'll come back for all of you, but I don't want you to blame your mother anymore. It isn't her fault or yours that I had to leave. Are we good?"

"Yes." She sticks her lips up to the fence, waiting for a kiss. What can I do? I kiss her. She smells like watermelons and strawberries. As she pulls away, the school bell rings and all the children head for the double doors.

"Hide the card and the necklace. It's our secret."

"Our secret," she repeats, heading towards the steps with the others.

I wobble, feeling dizzy, and hold on to the wire, remembering the day I discovered my father's secret, but he threatened me to keep his secret. Joy lines up at the bottom of the steps. I wait until she's inside.

I walk towards Doll's, and my sickness passes just as my men pull up in front of the shop.

Should I tell River what I saw happen to Joy at the school? I could have made her a different bottle to wear, one offering more protection. Fear pulses through me; not for myself, but for Joy. Sirens blare in the distance.

"Let's go pick up Joey," I say when I get in the car.

My men are quiet until Liam finally says, turning around, "Are you sure about this guy?" He wrinkles his brow.

"Not yet. I'm still getting to know him, but I'm willing to give him a chance." We drive until I see him. "There he is." I point at him.

"He's a huge dude," Cork says.

"It's going to cost more to feed him," Liam sighs.

"He's on time. Off to a good start." I open my door.

"Hey, Cruz," Joey says.

"Get in. Joey, that's Cork driving, and Liam next to him." Liam and Cork nod.

"Hi," Joey says.

"It took some maneuvering and quite a bit of money to get all your back alimony and child support paid. I'm giving you a chance, so don't blow it. "

"I promise I'll do the best I can."

I pass him a notebook. "Take notes. Write stuff down. If you haven't figured it out yet, we sell sex, men and women, but high-end. Please show them respect. Don't talk down to them ever. You're not the boss of them. You're here for one reason: to keep them safe so they can do their jobs. Understand?"

"Yes, Cruz."

"Next rule, no one owes you anything. If you want something from me, you earn it, just like the rest of them do. If you want to be part of my family, contribute. I've decided your contribution will be security for my workers. We'll try something else if that doesn't work out. Everyone makes mistakes, me included. Apologize if you make one and move on. If I do something you don't like, don't stew about it. Come to me and say something, and we'll discuss it. The most important thing you must do is listen to our people. Mastering the art of attentive listening is a skill. Watch their body language, make eye contact, sense how they're feeling, not just what they are saying with words, although that's important too. Don't be afraid to ask them questions and repeat back what they say. You'll get more information, and you'll remember what they say better. Lower your speaking voice. It makes people listen to you better. Never raise your voice to them, ever. This is important with my people, especially, because many of them are submissive."

"Got it."

"Every day, I want you to write notes on your perception of each person you interact with; how you think they're feeling, what they say, things like that. Understand?"

"Yes, I'll do it."

"Another thing. There's a school, St. Cloud, a few blocks from here. I want you to go over there at 12:15 and watch for this little girl," and I hand him a picture of Joy, "Watch what happens at lunch recess and write it down in your notebook."

Joey takes the picture, "Got it, Cruz."

"You can start tonight at The Palace at seven pm. The directions are in your notebook."

"Do you have any questions, Joey?"

"No. Thank you, Cruz, for the opportunity. Nice meeting you guys." He waves to Cork and Liam, who nod back. Then Joey climbs out of the vehicle at the light.

"He's quiet, mate," Liam says after Joey gets out of the car.

"Overwhelmed," Cork offers.

"I mean, do you think he's smart enough for what you're asking him to do?" Liam pulls at his collar.

"I think people have treated him as dumb his whole life. I believe there's more to him. And if there's not, I'll find out."

Liam smiles. "I'm sure you will."

10

PICKING LILIES

RIVER

"We don't want to alarm you," Sister Eleanor says at our meeting. "We thought you would appreciate being informed. I saw your daughter speaking to a strange man during early recess."

My heart pounds. There's a large arch-shaped painting behind Sister Eleanor's desk. It's of a nun in a garden picking lilies, and you can catch the bottom of the model's reflection cast in a pond as other flowers grow on top of the water. The lilies are shaped like trumpets, which sound the message that Jesus has risen. Why the hell am I distracted by this piece when my daughter is talking to strange men?

"We have a video, just in case—"

"Just in case of what?" I ask.

"In many of these cases, the child knows the person. Perhaps it's a family member we haven't met before, or a babysitter. Here, look. It's on my computer screen." Sister Eleanor spins the monitor around for me to see.

All the hang-ups I'm getting at home and at work, could he be part of that? The old monitor looks like some ancient relic. How does it even function? How can this school charge its exorbitant tuition fees and have monitors this old?

The man in the video is stooped over Joy, dressed all in black. There's delight in Joy's eyes as she looks up at him. His long fingers reach through the fence and touch Joy's hand. I've felt those hands brush my body many times, and I've stared at him in much the same way. I recognize them before the camera captures his stunning face.

"That's my former fiancé."

Sister Eleanor's mouth opens wide, then closes. "I see," her lips forming a grimace.

"Joy had a very tough time when we broke off the engagement. He's trying to fix things." I gulp down air.

"You might tell him to try a different way. There are protocols at the school, and he needs to request permission to interact with any of the children." She narrows her eyes and taps her foot.

"We're experiencing a challenging period. I hope you can empathize with what our family is going through," I say.

Sister Eleanor brings her hands together. "The sisters will pray for you." She bends her head and closes her eyes. After a minute of silence, she leaves her seat and comes by my side. She takes my hand and walks me to the door. "Please talk with him. God bless you both." She opens the door, escorting me out.

I decide to say nothing to Joy about the incident. My relationship with her is fragile already. I'm hopeful whatever Cruz said will help. He always has a way of making others feel better when he wants to. He's powerful in a way only a witch can be.

Joy is sitting on the bench and, as soon as she sees me, for the first time in a long time, she smiles. She runs towards me and wraps her arms around my waist. I can't remember the last time she hugged me like this. Joy steps back, a wide smile spreading on her face, and takes my hand.

"About time," my son Alex says, coming off the bench too. "It's four o'clock. What did you do wrong that you got called into the principal's office?" he asks.

"Ordered pizza for dinner one too many times. Let's go home." I motion to him.

"That isn't possible, is it?" my daughter asks, cocking her head to one side.

We head down the hall, and I can see snow falling through the double doors. "See, Mommy?" Joy points. "It's snowing."

It's a short walk from St. Cloud to our brownstone, but I'm getting the same vibe as before, like we're being followed. There's a blue sedan behind us. The vehicle circles the block and comes back again. The car's tinted windows make it difficult for me to see who's inside. I notice another man with dark hair on the corner by the convenience store. Is he the man with the hoodie from yesterday? No hoodie today.

I reach the door with my anxiety at an all-time high. I unlock the door for the children, motion them inside, and close it. I go back outside to fish the mail out of the box by the front door and look behind me. Two men are sitting in a white SUV on the opposite side of the street. I hurry and lock the door, searching out the window and watching the blue sedan drive by again.

"Mom, what are you looking at?" Joy asks.

"What are we having for dinner?" Alex asks as I lower the shades.

"Can we have pizza?" Joy grabs hold of my arm.

"Not tonight." If Joy had her way, she'd have pizza for dinner every night of the week, and for lunch, too.

"Hot dogs, then?" She pokes me.

"How about soup and toasted cheese?" I offer.

"Yeah!" Joy screams as I scan the mail. The standard amount of junk, a letter for Cruz, and a manilla envelope addressed to me with no return address. When I open it, I slide a large, unfolded sheet of paper out, with cutout letters that form words. It reads:

SOON WE MEET AGAIN.

I clutch the paper, and my hands tremble. Who would send me something like this?

"Cool," Joy says as she hovers over my shoulder, freezing me and keeping me from wadding it into a ball. "Did Cruz send it?"

"Maybe. Let me start dinner." I head for the refrigerator, pretending it means nothing. Could Joy be right?

"I need to do a book report. What's 'age-appropriate' mean?" Joy bites her lip.

"It means something an eight-year-old would read." I take the bread and place cheese on it.

"You mean something boring and for babies."

"Joy, you know that's not true." I cover the cheese with the top piece of bread and butter it. "We'll go to the library, and you'll find a good book."

I place a frying pan on the stove and turn the burner on. I locate a can of tomato soup in the pantry, pour it into the soup pan, add the milk, and stir. When the sandwiches are done, I cut them in half, put them on a plate, pour the soup into cups, take them to the island, pour glasses of water, and put out another plate of carrots and celery. The smell of butter and melted cheese fills the kitchen.

"When can we go?" Joy sits down and munches on her toasted cheese.

"On the way back from school this week, or maybe this weekend. When's the project due?"

"I don't know," Joy says.

"I'll check the teacher's website and find out. Let me call your brother." I walk to the stairs and call out that dinner's ready, and a minute later, he enters the room. Lately, it astonishes me every time he comes into view. He doesn't look like a kid anymore. But then again, he isn't. He's a teenager, almost fourteen years old. Plus, he's one of those children born with an old soul. He has more common sense than I'll ever have.

Alex picks up the soup first, takes a sip to check the temperature, then gulps the rest down and places the empty mug back on the island. He eats one half of the sandwich, breathes in the other half without saying a word, and stares at mine. I pass my plate to him.

"Thanks, Mom, I'm starving," he says through a mouth full of food. "Did you know a python snake can eat something as big around as they are?"

"I hope you aren't trying to do the same thing."

"I bet I can."

"That's not a bet I'm making with you."

"I can eat as much too," Joy says.

"I don't think you can even finish that sandwich." I wink at her just as my phone begins to ring. I answer it, walking out of the kitchen. "Hello?"

"Did you get my note?"

"Who is this?"

"You first. Did you get my note?"

"I don't know. What did it say?"

"About our meeting."

"That was you?"

"Listen. Soon you'll be doing this for me too..."

There are some kind of slurping and sucking noises. "Ahhh, I have to—"

"Do you know what she's doing?"

"Not really."

"Keep listening and see if you can figure it out..."

I spend ten seconds listening to weird sounds, until finally saying, "I have something on the stove, and it's burning." I end the call, and I'm so creeped out, I turn off my phone.

"ALEX, shut the computer off and go to bed." *Thump thump thump* goes the overwhelming bass pounding from his speakers.

"It's a new song," Alex says.

"You have school tomorrow. Turn it off and brush your teeth."

"Okay, Mom." Alex rises from the computer and heads to the bathroom. My favorite part of the day is when my children are safely tucked in bed, and I kiss each of their foreheads.

Joy's door is ajar, and the light is off. I step inside, and she's resting on her side, curled in a ball with her eyes closed. Her hair is a bird's nest with pieces sticking out everywhere. One piece spills into her mouth, and I push it away. There's a smile on her lips. There's something clutched in one hand, a card. Something shiny is hanging off her neck. I touch it in disbelief. An amulet. Did Cruz make it? I flash back on the ones he made for me for my anxiety and insomnia.

I move the card away, and she shifts, but I lift it without waking her. I move towards the light in the hall. The outside is a purple unicorn, covered with glitter, and some of it sticks to my hand. I open it and recognize the print, because it's so distinctive. It's from Cruz. I can tell because every letter is perfect and uniform. I want to put the card back in Joy's hand, but I can't; the need to know what he's written is overwhelming. I read it instead, and the words go straight to my heart, taking my breath away. Could what he wrote be true? Cruz seldom lies, but would he do so to protect my child's feelings? Yes, he might. He loves Joy and respects children's feelings. He has a softness for them that he doesn't display for adults.

I return the card, placing it between her pink fingers. She lets out a sigh and folds her fingers around it protectively. A tear rolls down my cheek, but I wipe it away and tuck his words in my heart. I press my lips onto Joy's forehead. My eyes water, thinking about the man who wanted to repair things between my daughter and me. I turn the light off, close the door after me, and head down the hallway to my bedroom.

I've brought my phone upstairs, and now I turn it on again, placing it on my dresser. It immediately rings. I don't want it to wake my children, so I answer. "Hello."

"You shouldn't have left before I finished."

"What are you talking about?"

"I didn't dismiss you, yet you hung up."

"Who are you? Stop calling."

"If you'd have stayed, you might have learned something from her. She's good at her job. Very good. But I imagined your lips on my cock, not hers."

"Stop. I'm hanging up."

"If you do, I promise I'll hurt someone dear to you."

"What?"

"You heard me."

"Who are you?"

"You'll learn soon enough." The call ends. Will he hurt the children? I go back in and check on Joy again. She's where I left her, with a smile on her face. I go to Alex's room. His light is out now, and he's also sound asleep. I take the stairs downstairs. The pictures of my children still line the steps. I secure all the doors and check the windows too. I make sure the alarm is still set. I climb back upstairs and enter my room, my hands trembling.

My bedroom is dark, and I smell him, the aroma of burning

leaves and sage. "How did you get in?" I say out into the darkness. "Tell me the truth." My eyes acclimate to the dark and search for him. The foil birds on the wallpaper look like gold coins in the room's blackness.

"I've told you I can appear and disappear at will. Witches don't need keys, but still, you continue to doubt me." Cruz is leaning back in my chair. He's much too large for it, and it doesn't accommodate his long frame. His blonde hair is loose, and the moonlight catches his angular face when he moves. I turn the lamp on to enjoy him more. There's a sprinkling of light hairs on his face. It looks like he hasn't shaved for a couple of days.

"You also told me once you have experience with breaking and entering, and can break into any house with a bobby pin or a paper clip." I sit down on the bed.

"Keep that up, and you might get what you seem to desire." He rises from the chair.

"And what's that?" I ask.

"A spanking, of course." He removes his coat and lays it back on my chair. "You must desire one, with your tone and ordering me about the other day."

"Lost your clairvoyant powers? I'll remind you again, I'm not your slave, we aren't engaged, and like before, I didn't invite you here."

"That's true, but—"

"Therefore, I do not want or agree to any spanking. Could you please leave, Cruz?" I head for my closet, dismissing him. "My day has been trying." Should I tell him about the phone call?

Cruz laughs. "You're interrupting me now when speaking, too?"

"I don't want to go into it, but...I'm glad you got bail."

"Changing the subject? It didn't take that long. I could have gotten out yesterday, but I had words with the judge."

"That was stupid."

"Now you're calling me stupid?" Cruz jumps out of the chair and stands over me, scowling.

"All I'm saying is it seems silly to stay in jail extra days when you could have—"

"Be quiet. Marjorie says you were worried." He tips my chin up and stares into my eyes, as if trying to figure out what's going on with me.

"Of course I'm worried. Anything can happen in there. And when you wouldn't see me, I..."

"Couldn't live without me? Is that what you're saying?" he smirks, stroking my hair.

"Stop teasing me, please." I back away. His touch brings my body alive, and I don't want him to start me up again.

"I can handle myself. Have no fear. No person or thing will ever impede me coming back to you, except maybe you."

"I don't know..."

"What don't you know? If you can forgive me? I know you don't understand, but I had to put off the marriage. I came tonight because I was worried and..." He looks around. "Tell me why it's so cold in here. Is the heater broken?"

"To save money, I turn the heat down at night. We're all in bed then, anyway."

"You don't need to be frugal. Let me pay the heating bill. I'd pay for everything if you'd let me. I have a man watching the house, and he claims there's a strange car that keeps circling, coming and going. Have you seen anyone?"

"Sometimes I feel someone's watching me." When I say the words, a shiver goes up my spine.

"Tell me about it." Cruz sits down on the side of my bed, covered with a crazy quilt made from pieces of velvet, one of my favorite finds purchased at the Lincoln Antique Mall before we broke up.

"The other day, when I was coming home with the children, a

man followed us and ducked behind a car. I think I saw him today, too. Then there's a blue sedan with tinted windows. I saw him—"

"Cork can drive you and the children."

"No, we aren't your concern anymore." I pick my blouse up from the floor and walk to my closet to hang it up. Cruz watches me and smiles. He's trained me well. Cruz is a neat freak, but I don't live with him anymore.

"Think about the safety of your children."

"Let's not argue." I move towards the bed. "There's something else. Weird phone calls, hard to explain. The last one was creepy. He said we were going to meet, and he was going to punish me because I hung up on him."

"Change your number."

"I don't want to. It's a hassle."

"Now you balk at any suggestion I make, instead of doing what I say."

"Because you don't suggest. You bark orders. Please go, Cruz. As I said, I'm having a tough day."

"Yes, I hear you. Tell me why."

I can't. The truth is, this is hard because I love him. When he's near me, I'm reminded of the day he told me he didn't want me.

II

SURVIVAL

CRUZ

River turns and stares. Her eyes are the color of a public swimming pool on opening day, aqua blue and crystal clear. They penetrate mine. I'm cognizant of her thoughts—I've broken her trust. From her perspective, I have. She also thinks she's not good enough for me, and that's why I wouldn't marry her. She couldn't be more wrong. Where River's self-doubt comes from, I've never understood. Unlike mine and most of the other women who live in my house, her childhood was idyllic. The reality is I'm not good enough for someone like her—I'm damaged goods.

"What's going through your mind?" River asks. Her eyes study me as she speaks.

"What's going through yours?"

"Why do you do that? Every time I ask a question you don't want to answer, you ask me a question back. It's rude." She strides to the closet and removes her yoga top, presenting me with her naked back. "Oh, I forgot, you don't share your emotions, you'd rather hold them in check and brood."

Her accusations and tone shock me. River is usually courteous to a fault. She doesn't like to hurt anyone's feelings, so she agrees with people most of the time. When she stayed in The Palace, I even saw her laugh off slights from some of the other women to de-escalate conflicts. For her to act like this is out of character. She's like most of the women who work for me, submissive.

"I'm not brooding. I have something else in mind." I move closer to her. "I still love—"

She puts her hand up, "Don't say it, Cruz." River continues to dress, putting her arm through the sleeve of the kimono I purchased for her, the orange silk one with streaks of black. "Don't say you love me."

I reach out and take her hand to calm her. "Perhaps tonight we just worry about what we each need."

"Do you always have to be like this?"

"Like what?"

"Controlling and manipulative?" She moves her hand away.

"Yes. It's called survival. You might want to try it. Be careful with love. It gives people power over you."

"Must I?"

In two steps, I'm on top of her. I press my body into hers. I bring my lips to her mouth. She struggles at first, but I slide my hand down the side of her body to her waist, then her ass. I bring my arms around her. My embrace calms her, just like a cobra does with its prey. After a minute, she breaks away, moves towards the bed, removes her yoga shorts, and sits at the foot of the bed. When I walk towards her, she touches the bulge in my pants and tilts her chin up.

"I'm not like you, Cruz. I'm able to give of myself, and I don't control anyone but myself. I believe love gives one power; it doesn't take it away. If there were more love in the world, things would be better. Is this what you want?" She unzips my pants and reaches in.

My eyes widen. I try to hide my shock. This isn't her way. She always waits for me to direct her.

"You must have read my mind," and I stroke her head. The silkiness of her hair still amazes me. River pulls my cock out of my pants. She's in the perfect position to open her mouth and run her tongue around the head. "Beautiful..." I sigh. I don't know what's going on, but it's hard to argue with it. A submissive wouldn't do this unless I directed her to. She brings her hands under my balls and begins squeezing as she slides her tongue down the length of my cock. Then she puts her entire mouth over it and sucks harder. She squeezes my balls harder, too. "Ease up, River," I murmur with a bit of alarm. It occurs to me she might be trying to hurt me. I need to control this and get her hands off me.

"Get on your knees." I pull on her hair, gently, and guide her. "Take me deep, River. I want to feel the back of your throat. Make me believe you want this. Stop using your hands. Let me fuck your sweet mouth."

She drops her hands to her side and moves her mouth up and down over my shaft, over and over, then comes up to the head and swirls her tongue around it.

I whisper, "Touch yourself. Go ahead. I don't care which you pick, your clit or your nipples. I want to see you enjoy yourself."

Her robe is open, and she places her hand on her nipples and flicks them back and forth.

"You look so damn beautiful, River. Keep going. A couple more strokes and I'm going to—"

Ring, ring, ring, ring, ring.

Fuck. I can't believe this...

She stops sucking me and reaches for her phone on the nightstand.

"Hello?" She looks confused for a moment, then turns to me. "They hung up," she searches the screen for the caller ID.

"Are you kidding me?" I assert mental restraint to keep myself from grabbing the phone and breaking it. Seconds later, her cell rings again. I snatch the phone out of her hand. I'm pissed and eager to find out who this caller might be. Does River have a boyfriend?

"Who is this?" But there's nothing but breathing for a few seconds, then a click. "How long has this been going on?" I ask, staring at her.

"A few weeks." River stands up and holds her hand out, waiting for me to give her phone back, but I don't.

"As I said, you need to get a new number."

"I'd have to tell everyone."

"So what? Have you tried calling the person back?"

"No, but—"

"I will. I've memorized it. I'm going to find out who it belongs to." This time, all I have to do is push the button. The phone rings and rings.

"You need to go." River grabs the phone back out of my hand and walks towards the door.

"Is there anything you want to tell me about?"

"Are you accusing me of something? If I were in a relationship, I would tell you." Her eyes challenge mine.

I should know better. River is the most honest person in my life.

"I'm sorry. I apologize. But there's no question you should get a new number." I see the vibrator and, under it, the latest romance novel she's reading in the open drawer of her nightstand. This one has a vampire on the cover. River seems to have a thing for vampires. I pick them both up and hand them to her. "I suggest you use my replacements more. You need a release. I've never seen you this worked up before."

"What gives you the impression that I'm agitated?"

"The fact that you initiated the blow job, you're arguing with me, raising your voice, and that you think getting a new phone number is overwhelming."

Her face turns red. "You mean I'm acting like you? Oh, whatever will you do? But you work in a brothel so you can fuck whoever—"

Before she can get the rest of her words out, I move, giving her no time to react. I grab her waist and pull her into my lap as I sit on her bed and flip her over. Her head dips towards the floor, and her hair falls there too, causing the vibrator and the book to drop from her hand. Her kimono lifts and spreads open, revealing the pale skin of her glorious, plump ass.

"Stop it, Cruz," she says. "Let me up, right now."

The thing about River is that even though she's submissive and seeks approval, she somehow manages to regularly put her foot in her mouth. She did it all the time when she was my slave. Tonight, however, is different. She's talking back to me. But then again, as she pointed out, she's no longer my slave, and we aren't even dating.

"You've been asking for this all night. I'd say you need it." I bring my hand down. *Slap.*

"Ouch!"

"Do you want to reconsider what you said about me fucking my employees?"

"I didn't mean it."

"Do you want more, River?" She's right; I have no standing to spank her, and certainly no right to do so without permission.

"Yes, I want more."

"Say 'please.'"

"Please, Cruz."

"How many?"

"Four more, please," she exhales.

"Good girl. Five seems right. How hard?"

"Hard. Please."

Slap, slap, slap, slap.

She'll have some lovely bruises to remember me by this week. After I finish, I keep her bent over my knee and knead the skin on her ass. I slide my finger into her pussy, and she groans.

"Cruz, please," she moans, moving against it.

"Do you want me to make you cum?"

"Don't fuck me."

"That's not what I asked."

"Yes, I want to cum." She sighs.

"There's no shame in it."

"We aren't supposed to be seeing each other." River's body tenses.

"Who says? You need this. I need this." I lean over and pick up her vibrator from the floor and roll her onto the bed, and that's when I see them. "What's this?" I point to River's thigh.

"Nothing, just a cut." She covers it with her hand and then tries to get off the bed.

I grab her wrist, push her down, and examine her thigh more closely."How did it happen?"

"It's not your concern." She tries to escape, but I push River down again and lean on her, holding her arms and pinning her to the bed.

"Shush. Look at me and tell me when it happened."

"A couple of days ago, maybe."

"I don't like it." My pulse quickens, and I watch her more closely, searching for other clues about what she isn't telling me.

"It's not your business anymore." River refuses to meet my eyes.

"You'll always be my business." I touch the cuts. What did she use? "Don't do it again. Understand? If you do, I'll..."

"You'll what?" She peers into my eyes, challenging me.

"I don't think you want the answer to that." Then I lower my voice, "Are you going to tell me why?" How can I fix this?

"No." She looks away, staring at the ceiling, her eyes watering. This time, I let her up from the bed, and she moves towards the door. I follow, spin her around, and pin her against the wall. I place my fingers under her jaw and tilt her face to look at me. Her eyes are blue and full of confusion.

"Tell me the truth and don't lie." She has nowhere to go. I can detect her fragrance, oranges tonight.

"I don't want to talk about it. Please, Cruz." She touches my hand with one of hers.

"You've turned into a coward."

"I'm not. You don't know." She closes her eyes.

"If pain is what you seek, that's my jam. I'll give you all the pain you can handle and then some. I won't leave scars either. Anytime you need a dose, call me. If you won't talk to me, turn the light off and lie back down on the bed. Move." I grab her shoulder and shove her hard. She almost lands on the floor instead of the bed, but catches herself.

My anger is getting the better of me. That River is mutilating her body, which is driving me insane. I want to punish her for hurting herself. The absurdity of the situation makes me lash out. I punch the wall.

Now there's a hole in the plaster, and white dust drifts down to the floor.

I sent her away to keep her safe, and now she's leaving deep cuts on her lovely skin. I know why she's doing it, to release the pressure, and for a while it may work, but she'll eventually be right back to where she started.

River's eyes waver back and forth. "What are you laughing at?" River bites her lips and twists a piece of her hair around her finger. "Please tell me." She's nervous, and she should be, because I've used my crazy laugh.

"You don't want to find out."

I want to frighten River and put the fear of God into her. If I hurt her too, will she stop hurting herself? That's ironic. I'd rather hurt myself than hurt River.

I've got a massive migraine. I turn the light off myself. River lies on the mattress in front of me like a baroque banquet, ripe for me to feast upon. I lay down beside her.

"Spread your legs and bend them."

I turn on the vibrator and bring it to her clit. The problem with vibrators is that they bring a woman off too quickly. I circumvent this by turning it on and off in short bursts, keeping her on the edge. We're a minute in, and she's already writhing all over the bed. I place an arm on top of her to keep her still. Restraint heightens sexual pleasure. Tonight, I need to make it last as long as possible, especially after seeing those cuts. She needs an extra-long session to deal with what's bothering her. Who am I kidding? I do, too.

"Where are your dildos?"

"I don't have any." She clenches the sheet.

"What? Why not?"

"You kept the sex toys, remember?" Her hands tremble.

"I am a bastard, aren't I?"

"Yes, you are." River gives me a half smile.

"I should punish you for agreeing."

"But if I disagreed, you'd punish me too," she snickers.

"You're right." I hold up my hand and wriggle my fingers back and forth. "I don't need dildos. I have these." I bring them to her pussy, sliding in the first one and then another with no problem. I can hear how wet she is as I thrust my two fingers in and out. I go faster, stretching her wider as I go. I spread her legs wider, too.

"Do you want more?" I ask.

She nods her head. River was always a quiet one. It had taken me a long time to get her to talk to me and express her wishes. Even now, I have to drag things out of her.

"You've forgotten, nodding doesn't work with me."

"Yes, please," she says, her eyes glowing.

"Good girl," I add another finger, filling her, and let the vibrator do its magic.

"Cruz, oh Cruz, please, let me cum." I can feel her pushing down on my fingers.

"Don't cum yet."

"Please, Cruz..." I remove the vibrator, attempting to make the scene last longer. I pull my fingers from her, too. "Cruz, please." Her body trembles, and she reaches for my hand.

"Do you want to cum for me, River?" It's a game we've played many times before.

"Yes, I want to cum, please, Cruz." River's face is pink, and her body rocks back and forth.

"First beg, and then I'll think about it."

"Please, Cruz, please, please, let me cum."

"Will you call me 'sir'"

"I'm not wearing the collar."

"I know that, but...as a favor. Then I'll grant you a favor."

"Sir, please, let me cum."

"I will, River. In fact, I'm going to help you. First, I want you to touch yourself. Go ahead. I want to watch you."

She props herself on her elbows, then brings one hand down to her clit and circles it several times.

"I'll help." I place my two fingers back into her tight pussy. "How do my fingers feel?"

"They feel wonderful." Her face shines, full of awe.

"Describe it for me, River."

"I'm on fire, I'm so wet."

"You've missed me, haven't you?"

"Mmm."

"Words, River. Tell me about it with words." Our eyes lock, and her cunt squeezes my fingers. "That's one way of telling me, but tell me with words."

"I dream about you almost every night, and I wake up on fire."

With my other hand, I take hold of her nipple and flick it, causing her to gasp. "How do you put out the fire, River?"

"Umm, I touch myself and use the vibrator. I can't sleep." River's other hand clutches at the sheets.

"Do you dream I'm a vampire, like the man on the cover of your book?"

"How did you know? I bought the book because he looks like you."

"Sweet. Should I go faster, slower? Order me about."

"Harder, rougher. Make it hurt, sir," She bites her lips.

"That's my girl. Is that why you cut yourself? Did you miss the pain I provided? The outlet I gave you?"

"I don't know. Sir."

"Tell me the truth, River."

"Uh, that is the truth, sir." She swallows and fumbles as she rubs her clit.

I've made her nervous, browbeating her with all my questions. "Are you sure you want pain now?"

"Yes, I need it."

"I'm not forcing you?"

"No, I want it, please, sir." I believe River needs the pain.

"Tell me what you want."

"Pinch me."

"Where?"

"Don't make me tell you. You know where. You know all my secrets."

"I want to hear you say the words, River. Say the words."

"Please, Cruz, please, don't make me."

"Why not? Why don't you want to say those words?"

"It makes me sound—"

"Sound what?" I pinch her nipple harder, too, and watch as her eyes roll. A couple more strokes of my finger in her pussy and she's gone. There's no stopping her orgasm now, and I watch it race towards her. She reaches up with one hand and clutches the collar of my shirt. Her blue eyes close. "Don't close me out. Let me in."

Her eyes snap open, her bosom heaves, and waves of pleasure wash over her. River's so beautiful when she's coming. Her cunt squeezes around my fingers, attempting to hold them.

"Wish for something, River," I whisper. "Send your wish and use your sexual energy to power the universe."

I kiss River's lips, and she bites me back hard and says, "I wish for..." But she gets lost in her orgasm, and I taste my blood.

When she's done with her orgasm, I cover her with a sheet to keep her warm. I sit next to her. I let her watch as I lick my fingers clean of her essence. She's the most delicious thing I've ever tasted. I wonder if the Greeks were thinking of pussy juice when they wrote about the nectar of the gods.

The house is cold. I should get the HVAC checked or purchase some space heaters for the bedrooms. I go to the bathroom, get a warm washcloth and a towel, then return to the bedroom to clean and dry her, and afterward cover her with the crazy quilt. I thread my fingers through her hair.

"What did you wish for, River?"

She clutches the sheet and quilt. "I wished for you and something else, but it won't solve anything. Besides, haven't you heard that you shouldn't say your wishes out loud?"

"I thought that was just for candles on birthday cakes. Just tell me," I say.

Her eyes land on me. "I wished that you'd tell me the truth about why you left me, and stop using the business as an excuse."

I sit back down on the bed beside her, gather her up in my arms, and kiss her. "I left because I love you. To keep you safe."

She nods but turns away like she doesn't believe me. "Cruz, don't come over here anymore."

"I won't if you promise not to cut or harm yourself. But if I see any more cuts on you, then I'll make you my slave again. I won't care what you say. I understand why you're doing it. It's easier to hurt yourself because you can't handle big emotions. Like right now, I'm in pain too. I'm tired of being a monster. I don't want to wear this mask anymore. I want to be Cruz MacKenzie, the restaurant owner, but they won't let me."

"Who won't?"

"All the regular people who get to go to college and have families. Who sit behind desks and judge me. They don't think I'm good enough. What will happen if I take off the monster mask?"

"You can with me, Cruz. You know that."

"How can I, when my angel wants to destroy herself? Don't you see that cutting yourself is just another way the demons try to get in and take over? Don't let them. I can't lose you. If I lose you, I'll—"

"You won't lose me, Cruz. I'll stop. I will." She reaches for my hand.

"You're the only good thing I have. You, Joy, and Alex." I take River in my arms and squeeze her, infusing her with all my strength. Before she came to The Palace, my life was all black and white, but River gave it color.

I've frightened her, though, and she's pulled away. I touch River's face, hoping to bring her back to me.

"You don't have to hide from me. You can say the words, whatever they are, and it won't make me think or feel differently. You can ask me to do anything, and I'll do it for you. You can be whoever you want to be in this bedroom."

"Alright, Cruz. Will you show me who you are?" She touches my face.

I hesitate to tell River about Joy, especially after seeing what River's doing to herself. Still, it's her daughter, and River needs to know. I let go of River. I pull myself together. Burden or not, I put the mask back on. I pretend I'm not afraid.

"Soon. First, we need to talk about Joy."

Fear washes across River's face. River doesn't believe what I tell her at first. When I tell her I sent my man, Joey, back and that he saw Joy being pushed around by the same group of children, River breaks down in tears. As we talk, everything falls into place about why River's so unsure about herself these days, and why humiliation brought her to her knees when she was my slave. She reveals she was also a victim of bullying during her childhood in Canada. "How do I talk to Joy about bullying when I couldn't keep from being bullied myself?" River asks.

"You don't have to say anything, just listen."

Then River changes the subject. "You've got mail. I left it on the island in the kitchen." That's her cue for me to leave. She and I use the same techniques when we want to avoid things. "Thank you for...whatever."

"Whatever? It's called an orgasm, River." I move towards my coat.

"Yes, right, um, thank you for my orgasm." She blushes. "What about you? I can do something for you."

She touches my cock, and I respond to her touch, but I stand up. "Not tonight. Next time." I don't know when I'll see her again, but I've got to check on things at the club. I bite her lip and inhale her. Her blue eyes meet mine, and for this one second in time, she's mine.

"I'll see you later," I say and pick up my coat, leave the room, and head down the steps. I step over the three that squeak. That's how you can get in and out of old houses without the owners knowing. There's nothing magical about that. River doesn't know how I appeared in her bedroom without her seeing, but there's a secret staircase behind the bookcase in the living room that goes directly into her bedroom. There's also a hidden trapdoor outside, concealed behind some bushes and covered with debris and dirt, that leads into the cellar. This provides another way into the home, one that River knows nothing about. I prefer homes that have secret entrances and hiding places. They aren't so easy to find anymore.

I made a note to myself to contact the number that was calling her phone. It's most likely a burner phone; if it is, it will make it almost impossible to find out who's calling her. I also need to contact a heating company about the lack of heat.

The mail addressed to me on the island is junk. The same bank that won't loan me money now wants me to apply for a high-interest credit card. I see a piece of paper lying next to it, with cut-out letters taken from a magazine. SOON WE MEET. Is this for River? Did Joy make it? I think about going upstairs and finding out more, but my men are waiting, and there's money to be made. I leave it on the island and walk out the front door into the chilly night.

12

SPECIAL DELIVERY

MONTEL MACKENZIE

River's hand trembles as she makes the first cut, and her eyes display fear. A buzzing, throbbing, electrical sensation courses through Montel's body as he watches her mark her flesh with the razor blade. It's all he can do to resist the urge to go over there right now and cut her himself, but Montel would need to send the children away first, or it would get quite messy.

Her hand is swift and confident on the second cut, and her eyes show determination. The one after that, her eyes display anger, but by the fifth one, there's only peace. Or are her eyes displaying resignation? Montel isn't sure. It's hard to keep from watching the video again and again. It's mesmerizing, addictive, almost more so than when River did it live. She won't need to harm herself next time. He'll do it for her. Montel wonders how far River would let him go if she weren't restrained, in terms of depth and number of cuts? His tools are much more precise. He has a set of scalpels that could make her body beautiful.

If Montel restrains her, though, he could take her even further. When you exert power over a victim, they're under your control. You own every part of them—their mind, their body—at least until they leave this earth. Did his son do this with her, too? Montel has fantasies and questions. He wishes he were there to make cuts to her throat. He'd suck the blood from her and wipe it on her body and on his cock, fucking her using her blood as lubricant.

The video ends too soon when River turns off the light, and the picture goes dead. Damn. He gets up from the computer. He looks out the window and sees her light on in her bedroom. Montel becomes excited and checks the feed. The cameras are live. He pushes a button on his computer, and the cameras are recording. Cruz is in the room with River, and what Montel watches fills him with rage and jealousy.

"Look at her." He drags Little Mouse out of the bedroom and points at the computer screen. "She's a whore. She's sucking his cock." River is giving Cruz a blowjob, the kind he warns his male parishioners about. He tells them not to watch or read magazines that show pornography. It's smut. River takes Cruz in her mouth a little at a time, playing with him, running her tongue up the shaft, then down again, changing the tempo. Cruz's cock is bigger than his. Montel wishes River were licking his cock. She tilts her head down and swirls her tongue around the head. "She wants to do it. She's a whore, just like Jezebel." He wants to go over there, burn her house down, cut her tongue out, and kill his son. Did his son teach her this?

"Her mouth belongs around my cock," he angrily murmurs. Despite Montel's rage, his cock swells and longs for River, pushing against the fabric of his pants. He can't stop watching the show across the street as it continues until River reaches for her phone. "Do you believe that? She's answering her goddamn cell?" Will Cruz allow this? If it were him, he would take the phone away and stuff it up her ass. Seconds later, his son finally snatches the cell from River. Montel smiles.

Cruz flips River over his lap and starts spanking her. Montel watches the screen enthralled. The only thing that would make it better would be if she were bound and if Cruz used a cane and drew blood. After he's done, he flips River onto the bed. For whatever reason, after a few words, the lights go off. Even with the binoculars, it's too dark for Montel to see much.

"Fuck, this shouldn't happen. I want to watch." Montel slams the laptop shut and turns to Little Mouse. His face is hot. He clenches his fists and opens them, then clutches onto Little Mouse. He sits on the milk crate and bends her over his lap. Her hands and feet are bound. He strips her leggings and panties down to her ankles and exposes her white ass. He slaps her, again and again, and keeps going as she thrashes against him. His cock stiffens as she fights him. Montel knows where he wants to have her, on the kitchen island. He drags her, but she tries to resist him. She hasn't before. Little Mouse is a petite girl, no taller than five-two, and there's no way she can fight off someone his size. He's six-foot. Does she think he's going to kill her? He spins her around and bends her over the granite.

She's ready for him—her pussy's wet. He rams into her hard. The spanking made her receptive. As he fucks her, he pinches her nipples, and she grunts through her gag. He takes his stun gun off the counter and shoots her, but misses. Little Mouse screams through her gag and tries to throw him off. Montel holds her down and keeps fucking her. Little Mouse's pussy clutches and milks his cock, keeping his orgasm going for a long time.

"Next time you go where I want you to, or you'll get this up the ass," he says, breathing heavily and shoving the taser in front of her eyes.

RIVER

Knock, knock. A man outside the glass door is holding a box. I hurry to the front of the gallery. "Delivery for River Rogers," he says.

Why would somebody address something to me here at the gallery? I unlock the double lock. "I'm her."

The delivery person hands her the box. "I have another one out in the truck. It's much larger. I'll get it." I hold the door for the delivery person and examine the return address on the package. *The Palace.* The shipping person returns, carrying an unwieldy wooden crate with black letters stamped on the side. "Someone likes you. You must be planning one hell of a party." He brings the box in and leaves it on the floor by my desk.

"What is it?"

"Champagne. This crate holds twelve bottles."

"Who's it from?"

"You'll have to call the shipper. There's a number on the label. I'm sure they can look it up." I search for my wallet and hand the man a tip. "Enjoy," he says, going out the door.

I rip open the smaller box. What did Cruz send me? Oh my God! There are four of them—a pink one, a large purple one, a glass one, and a stainless steel one with balls on it. I slam the cover back on and hide it under my desk. What was Cruz thinking, sending the package here?

I fire off a text asking him. A few minutes later, a response comes back from Cruz.

I didn't think you'd want it stolen off your
front porch by porch pirates.

How am I going to get them home?

Put them in your purse.

My bag isn't big enough to carry four
dildos.

I'm sure you'll figure something out.

Did you send me champagne 2?

No. Why?

I PICK up the shipping label from the champagne just as the gallery phone rings. "Hello, Protean Gallery, River Rogers speaking," I say in my best River North Art Gallery voice.

"River, it's Tony. I won't be in today. I got beat up last night leaving."

"Oh, no. What happened?"

"Two thugs jumped out of the back of an SUV when I was walking home last night, a couple of blocks from the gallery."

"How bad is it?"

"I have a broken leg, rib, fingers, and toe. Bruises all over, and two black eyes. I'm getting released this afternoon, but for obvious reasons I'm just going straight home."

"Feel better, Tony."

After I hang up the phone, the bell hits against the glass. I didn't have time to lock the door again after the deliveryman left. "I'm sorry, sir, we don't open until eleven," I call to him from my desk. I don't recognize him at first, but then he smiles, and every-thing rushes back. The night at the restaurant with Cruz. My face heats, and my stomach churns.

"You got the gift." The man points at the crate on my desk. He's the man Cruz wanted me to fuck, who thought champagne and money were aphrodisiacs—Angelo Conti.

"We're not open yet," I repeat. What is he doing here?

"Sit down." Tony isn't here, so I'm all alone with Angelo Conti. I don't have a choice, so I take my seat. Angelo Conti brings the other chair in front of mine and plops down, blocking me in. "It's good to see you again, River. You remember me this time."

"What do you mean?"

"You don't recall the other day, when I was your hired driver?" he chuckles. He holds on to my knee and keeps me from running. "There's no reason to leave. I'd never hurt you, or at least not without your consent, of course. Besides, even if you got by me, I have two men outside the door who won't let you get far."

"I don't want to be rude, but I work here, and I'm not supposed to have visitors."

He reaches over and takes my hand, stroking my palm and looking into my eyes. "Consider me a new client."

"I don't know you." I try to take my hand back.

"True, you don't. We never got the opportunity, thanks to Cruz. He didn't keep his side of the agreement." His eyes flash with anger.

"I know nothing about that, and I'm not with Cruz anymore."

"I do believe you're not with Cruz anymore, but I don't believe the other part. You were all over me in the restaurant. You sat on my lap like a good little—"

"Stop it."

"He drove you to my house and—"

"I don't want to talk about it."

"There's no reason to be embarrassed. Since you aren't Cruz's slave anymore, you're free to become mine."

"I won't do that."

"I imagined you'd say something like that. I'm more than willing to accept you as my submissive instead."

"What about your wife? Cruz said you were married."

"Don't concern yourself. We're divorced. And even if we weren't, we had an open marriage. I'll give you a day or two to make any arrangements you need to make to move in with me. We can work out the terms and—"

"I have children."

"So do I, but it's a large enough house to accommodate all of us."

"What will my children make of me living with a man who's not my husband?"

"You lived with Cruz MacKenzie."

"Yes, but we were engaged, and once we weren't, I moved out."

"I wondered about that. Which one of you broke off the engagement?"

"That's none of your business."

"Yes, it is. Since you're going to be my submissive, I deserve to know everything about you. Frankly, I'm a bit surprised by your demeanor. Having been with Cruz, I expected you'd be much more obedient."

"That might be why I'm not with Cruz anymore."

Angelo chuckles. "You're amusing. I won't argue with you about this. It's going to happen. If you insist and you're concerned about appearances, I'll propose and give you a ring. The children can either stay with us, or I'll send them to boarding schools, your choice. We can work out everything, your monthly allowance and—"

"I can't."

"You can and you will. And we can celebrate with this." He points at the champagne. He stands up and walks around the space, eventually stopping in front of the Boudicca painting. "I like this piece. It reminds me of someone. I must have it."

"It's not for sale."

"Don't be silly. Here's the price tag. $22,000. Reasonable for a piece of art. Put it on my black card."

Mr. Manchild walks through the door. "Good morning, River." He sees Conti handing me his no-limit credit card. What can I do but take it to the sales desk?

"He's purchased the nude, the one by my desk." My heart breaks knowing Angelo is taking the painting.

"Wonderful, and the gallery isn't even officially open." Mr. Manschild's face beams. He runs the card and doesn't look up.

Mr. Manschild walks over, introduces himself, and signs the bill of sale. He says, "Our current exhibition is over February 1, so anytime after that that works for you, I'll have River and my installer deliver the painting."

"Ahh, Tony might not be available," I say. "He's in the hospital. Someone attacked him last night. He's broken his leg."

Mr. Manchild turns to Angelo, "No worries, Mr. Conti. I'll hire a delivery service and an installer to accompany Ms. Rogers to your home. Why don't you take Mr. Conti out for coffee or brunch? It's the least we can do." Mr. Manchild hands me the company credit card.

"Umm, I still need to hang the new show."

"No worries. You have all this week."

"Wonderful," Angelo says, looking lustfully at me.

I can't think of any other way to get out of this. I can't tell him the truth, that Angelo is a Dom who once had an arrangement with my boyfriend to play in his dungeon. Conti reaches for my coat and helps me put it on. When we get outside, he becomes more aggressive. "Get in the car, River."

"I have to pick up my children."

"Not until three. Get in."

How does he know that? Once I'm in the car, he bends over me, fastens my seatbelt, and closes the door. My heart is beating out of my chest. The sounds of traffic going by, the horns, and the braking cars seem amplified.

"Calm down. We're only having something to eat. Have some water." Conti passes me a bottle and stares at me. I gulp the water down. "Shut up, Marco."

"Who's Marco?"

"The man in the back seat is my brother. Can't you see him?" I turn around, but there's no one there.

Within minutes, the world slows down and gets foggy. I stare down at the water bottle. Was there something in it that's making me tired? "Stay out of it, Marco," I hear Angelo say. He whispers to me, "Rest, River, I'll take care of everything," and he pats my knee. Music plays in the background. Time seems to stop, or I may have fallen asleep.

When I wake up, Conti's parking the car, and I'm swatting his hands away. He's touching me, pushing my clothing out of the way, and I don't like it. "Stop it. Leave me alone."

"Calm down. We're here. We can have something to eat and talk. Marco will stay in the car."

"I still don't see him. Where is he?"

"Don't worry about it," Angelo says. I try to get up, but my legs don't seem to work.

"Let me help you." Angelo's on my side of the car, on the sidewalk, bent over me, extending his hand. "Here, take my hand. I'll help you up to the door, and then we can have something to eat."

'I'm not hungry," I say as he drags me out of the car.

"You need to eat something. Could be low blood sugar. That could explain your tiredness." He leads me into the restaurant, and we sit down at the nearest booth. He squeezes in next to me, instead of across. He's way too close, and it's making me dizzy. I want to go home, but I say nothing. I look at another table and see other couples who seem happy to be together. I remember how it was with Cruz.

They bring menus, and Conti orders me a Mimosa. I don't touch it. Raised voices come from the next table. "I'll decide what and where I want to go," the woman says.

"Why can't you be like other women I've dated?" the man asks.

"If you prefer them, go back to them," the woman says.

"I like to call the shots."

"So do I," the woman says.

The man raises his eyebrows. "Can't you be more subtle about it?"

"You mean play games and beat around the bush?"

"It seems he might have his hands full next door. He's not lucky." Angelo jabs with his thumb. "The poor man doesn't have a nice, agreeable woman," and he points at me.

Cruz always said my niceness was my biggest asset and my biggest curse. At the moment, no words come.

13
BULLIES

RIVER

I wait in the rideshare car for Joy to come out of her school, as snow blows against the dead ivy hanging on aged gray stone.

I think back to the words they screamed at me.

"Look how fat she is!"

Cracks, smacks, and slaps come from all directions. Impossible to escape. They pinch my flesh too, leaving dark pink circles that turn into purple bruises. They shoved me onto the frozen dirt floor of the forest, dead leaves stuck to my hair, dragging me backward, tearing my clothes, exposing my belly, breasts, and thighs, while shoes slammed into me and laughter echoed through the trees.

The boys go further, touching my breasts. Some pick up sticks and poke and hit me wherever they can.

I always wondered if my parents figured out what was going on, and that's why we moved my freshman year, not just to a different town but a whole different country. To share all the details of these hurts with my child now feels impossible. After the harrowing day I had with Mr. Touchy-Feely, I'm really not up to having this conversation, but I can't put it off any longer, not if my daughter is going through the same things I did.

Joy climbs into the back of the car as I move over. "How was school today?" I ask.

"Fine."

"Are you sure?"

"Uh-huh. How come Alex isn't coming with us?"

"Alex is going to his friend's house to work on a project." I pause. "You know, when I was in school, and my mom and dad asked me how things were going, I told them everything was perfect, but they weren't."

"You lied?" My daughter's eyes grow wide in disbelief.

"Yes. I wanted to protect them. I didn't want them to worry or make it worse."

"How would they do that?" Joy's eyes narrow.

"If my father had gotten involved, he would've gone to the principal and informed him what was going on. The kids would be in trouble with their parents because the administrator would call them. Then they'd come after me because I got them in trouble, and maybe they would hurt me worse. I promise you I won't do that. My job is to listen and help you come up with a way to deal with the problem on your own. Do you want to tell me what's going on?"

Joy takes a big breath and looks at the floor of the car. "They don't like me here."

"Who doesn't?"

"Some of the girls and a few boys."

"I understand."

"They make fun of me and call me names. They think my name is stupid and that I'm ugly. When I'm outside with them, I'm frightened."

"Do they touch you?"

"Sometimes." I wait for her to say more. "What did they do to you, Mommy?"

"They called me fat. They pinched me. When I walked home, they would push me down on the ground and tear my clothes."

"Is that why you don't let Alex and me walk by ourselves?" Joy twists her fingers in her lap.

The things I'm telling Joy, I'd hoped never to share, ever. I want Joy to trust other people and love herself. "We live in the city. I'll never let that happen."

"What did you do, Mommy? How did you make them stop?"

"It only stopped because my parents moved. I never told my parents what was going on. You aren't to blame for any of this, Joy, just remember this. It's them, not you."

"Maybe I can change my name?" Joy touches my leg, looks me in the eye. "Smile less and dye my hair?"

"You could do all of that, but most likely it will still be the same. They'd find other things to tease you about. Your name is beautiful, and people should smile more, not less. Do you like Cruz's hair?"

"Yes, Mommy." She nods her head.

"Your hair and mine are the same color as Cruz's. Let's think of some ways to keep you safe."

"Like what?" She turns away and stares at her lap.

"Are other children being bothered by this same group that's bothering you? You can hang out with them. There's safety in numbers."

"I've seen them tease two girls and three boys. They call them nerds." Joy straightens up, and a small smile builds. "And there's a boy who never talks who they push around."

"If you all hung out together, that would make six of you against them. And who knows, you might find some other kids who might want to join you, because they also don't like what these kids are doing. Are there adults in the exercise yard during recess?"

"Yes, two of them."

"What if, while you are outside, you played by the monitors so they can see what's going on?"

"The bullies might not bother us because they wouldn't want trouble."

"True, they wouldn't. What else would make you feel safer?"

Joy leans in, wiggles in the car seat, and smiles. "If Cruz came and visited me at school again. They never came near me when Cruz was there. They were frightened of him."

"Yes, I'm sure he was a good deterrent. Do you want to try some of this before I ask Cruz to stop by again?"

"Yes," she smiles. "Thank you, Mommy." She reaches over and kisses my cheek. Cruz is right on both counts: I *can* do this, and you shouldn't just run, but fight back. He's right about another thing: you can either be a victim or choose not to be. I pick up my phone.

"Who are you calling, Mommy?"

"My attorney. Hello, yes, is Mr. Mello in?"

"No, this is Kathleen, Mr. Mello's office manager. He's in court. I can transfer you to his voicemail."

"No. I've already left several, and he doesn't call back. I'll leave my message with you, Kathleen. Please tell him to consider himself fired, unless I hear from him by the end of today. Thank you."

"I'll tell him."

I hang up, and Joy exclaims, "Wow, Mommy, are you really going to fire him?"

"Yes, sweetie, I am."

I'M AN IDIOT. Why did I think I could do this? Why am I even here? You need to stop cutting yourself. You need an outlet. Stop it. Stop thinking. Just put the colors out on the palette and turn your brain off. What if I make something awful and everyone makes fun of it? It's a watercolor class, not brain surgery...although you could benefit from that. I think the man in the front row is an actual surgeon. You could go talk to him about brain surgery. Whew...

I'm finally at the art class Cruz encouraged me to take, and the teachers are doing a demo. Gosh, hers is lovely. Of course it is; she's an instructor. She has an MFA and regularly exhibits her work.

I'm going to try this wet-on-wet technique she demoed. I don't like how my paper buckles. Why am I so critical of everything I do? Maybe it'll straighten out later, or I can rip it up as she suggested and make a collage out of it.

Why do I put black on everything? Obviously, because I like black, or because I'm depressed. Here she comes. What's she going to say? Will she like it? Why do you care what she thinks? Why do you always care what everyone thinks? *Because I'm a people-pleaser.*

"What do you think, River?" The instructor, Deborah, asks.

"Umm, I'm not sure. It's okay, I guess."

"What would make you like it better?"

"Should it be more realistic?"

"Should it?"

"I'm not sure. One part looks like a face. But if it's abstract, it shouldn't look like anything. Should it be neater?"

"You're not cleaning your house."

"True. Maybe I should be. My house is a wreck. Maybe this piece is okay the way it is, and I should start another."

"You're thinking like an artist now. It's beautiful the way it is, in its imperfection."

"I never thought of it that way. Things can be imperfect and beautiful...interesting."

The teacher's eyes light up, and then she moves on to talk to the next student.

CRUZ

"I'll have an espresso martini, Frank."

"Coming right up, Cruz."

"Earnings are up," Liam says next to me, finishing up his latest report. "Even the guys are doing well." He pauses, looking around. "Check her out. What do you think?" He points to a woman sitting across from us.

"No, too much of a Blacklight Barbie," I say, "Looks good in a bar situation, but bad everywhere else."

"How about the one who just walked in?"

"Not bad. She's got that buttoned-up conservative look some guys like."

"You mean that you like," Liam says. "If that pencil skirt was any tighter, she couldn't walk."

"I like the stilettos. They've got to be four inches."

"You think she's a working girl?" Liam's eyes narrow. "She's checking you out. You should try to recruit her."

"Either that or an attorney. They charge like working girls." I laugh.

Frank brings my drink and sets it down in front of me. "Frank, find out what the young lady in the suit is drinking and put it on my tab, thanks."

"Will do." Frank walks over to Ms. Buttoned Up, points to me, and takes her drink order. She smiles and orders. Once it's delivered, she sashays over and stands next to me with her drink. "Thanks," she says. "That was sweet of you. Yours looked so good, I got the same thing. What's your name?"

"Cruz. Yours?"

"Kate." She holds out her hand. We continue to make chit-chat for ten minutes, but the way she goes about it is off. She asks too many questions, and it feels like a set-up. I ask Frank for the check, then I signal Liam to call Cork to pick us up.

"You're leaving already?" Kate's eyebrows shoot upwards. "Can't you stay and have another? I'll buy."

"Maybe another time."

"Would you like my number?" Her smile disappears.

"Sure." I put it on my phone, but I have no intention of ever calling her. There's something not right about her.

Once Cork picks us up, I check my messages. There's one from Marjorie, saying that something's urgent, so I call her back. "River called today," she says. "I think you should know she's upset. It seems Angelo Conti dropped by the gallery."

"Where was the security team I'd hired?"

"It turns out they had an emergency and—"

"Fire them. Find a new one."

"Those were my thoughts too, and I already did."

"What did River say? What did Conti do?"

"He gave her a case of champagne and made a pass. She didn't provide all the details, but she felt threatened." I remember now she asked earlier if I had sent her champagne.

"I'll tear off his balls."

"Remember you're on a line that's not—"

"Got it. Fine. I had someone watching her, too. He hasn't called. Thank you for notifying me."

"No problem at all. Do you want me to try for a restraining order?"

"I don't want to involve the police. I'm sure many of them are in his pocket. I'll reach out to him first."

"As you wish."

"How is she?"

"Considering the circumstances, she's good. She asked about you."

"Me?"

"Yes. She wanted to check on your case. Maybe you could call and offer her some reassurance."

"Yes, of course. I'll do that after I contact Angelo."

"She also wanted to hire me to close out her husband's estate and settle the business end of things. I'm not sure if I'm the best person for that, but she insisted, so I agreed."

"Thank you, Marjorie."

"I like River, Cruz. I want to help her."

I end the call with my attorney and dial Angelo's number. He answers. "Avoiding my calls, Cruz?"

"If I were, would I call you, Angelo?" Asshole.

"Perhaps not. I have exciting news. I saw your slave."

"What are you talking about? I don't have one at the moment."

"I misspoke. I mean your ex-slave, River. I purchased a painting from her at her gallery. Would you believe I have a date with her?"

"She'd never agree to see you."

"On the contrary, I'm seeing her Tuesday," Angelo crows. "Would you like to share any tips on handling her? Any limits I should push her past?"

I slam the phone down just as Liam enters. I'd left River in order to protect her, believing that if she weren't my wife, I wouldn't expose her to Angelo. Was it all for nothing? If I put a contract out on him, I'd pay a heavy price. I chant a spell, one to protect River.

"What's up?" Liam's eyebrows draw together.

"Who was on security this morning at the gallery?"

"What happened?" Liam stands with one arm holding his elbow.

"Just answer the question. Who?"

"Eddie. What happened?"

"He didn't show."

"How do you know?"

"Because Angelo Conti stopped by and threatened her."

"Why would Conti do that?" Liam's eyebrows furrowed.

"About a year ago, she was running from her husband with her two children. I told her I would help her in exchange for her becoming my slave."

Liam's mouth falls open, and his upper lip curls back. Finally, he says, "That's rough, mate."

"Would you expect anything else from me? Unfortunately, I made the mistake of opening my mouth about it to Angelo Conti. We were planning to go into business together. He insisted on an exchange for one night, his wife for River, as a test of my loyalty. When it came time to do it, I..." I stop talking.

"You couldn't. Because inside all that exterior hardness, there's a big softie. You love River, mate."

"Love does that," Cork pipes in. "Makes you a better man."

"Yeah, I backed out. He never forgave the slight. When he heard about my engagement, he became more enraged and continued to call and threaten her. It became clear I needed to break off my engagement to protect River."

"So that's why you wouldn't marry her? It all makes sense now." Liam nods his head.

"His wife's leaving must have pushed him over the edge."

"What can we do to help?" Liam asks.

I'm touched by Liam's willingness to put himself out for me. "First thing, get rid of Eddie. He's a liability. How's the new guy, Joey, doing?"

"So far, so good. The girls like him. Minds his business, is reliable, shows up when he's supposed to, and keeps his hands to himself. Unless you tell him differently, of course. You know the notebook you gave him?"

"Yeah, the one I told him to keep notes in."

"He does it every day. He asks the girls questions. Nice and polite, and he writes everything down. Keeps tabs on their moods and all the rest."

"I want him to take over Eddie's shifts to monitor River and her children. Call Joey and explain his new assignment."

"Done," Liam says. "Now, what can we do about Angelo Conti?"

"That's something we're going to plan."

"We're here for you."

"We've got your back," Cork confirms, shaping his finger like a gun.

"It's River's back I'm worried about."

Liam's cell rings, and he says, "Hold on," taking it out and listening. "She's out front."

"Who is?"

"River. She just had words with Heidi. I guess she was asking for you, and Heidi asked what her business was, and I guess River took offense."

"Where is she now?"

"Hold on." He listens a bit more, then hangs up. "Blimey. By the sounds of things, they're still at it. In the lobby—here at Monsters."

I jump from my seat and Liam, and we head to the front of Monsters, where I see my hostess Heidi and River, poking each other with their fingers and raising their voices. The only reason you couldn't hear them was the blaring music and a group of people surrounding them.

"River." I go up and wrap my arms around her, soothing her.

That seems to shut Heidi down. "Oh, Mr. MacKenzie, I apologize. I didn't know she was somebody you knew." Her face turns red.

"I told you I was a friend," River says to Heidi. "Why didn't you believe me?"

Heidi backs away from River. "I apologize."

"Is it because you don't think I'm attractive enough for him, or young enough for him? Which one is it?"

"Stop it, River." I take River's arm and lead her towards the bar. "What's wrong?"

"You told me not to be a victim and to speak up. Now that I am, it's a problem?"

"Speaking up is one thing, rudeness another. Why are you here?"

"I had my first art class, and I wanted to share the experience with you. It looks like that was a mistake. I won't make the same one again."

"It wasn't a mistake. I want to see you, but you need to calm down and tell me what the problem is."

"Your hostess was rude and condescending. Like, I wasn't enough of a hipster for this place. And instead of defending me, you're blaming me."

"That isn't true, I just—"

"I'm going. I don't feel well. I have to get home."

I watch as she pulls away, staggering, unsure on her feet.

"Wait, stay here," I say. "Sit down, I'll get you some water." But there's no way I can stop her; she stumbles away, gone before I can say anything more.

I go to the bar where Liam's talking to the bartender. "Go in the back and load up the video from the front door when River and Heidi interacted. I need to find out exactly what happened."

"I'll get on it." Liam turns and goes. Minutes later, he texts me: "It's ready." *You won't like it.*

I head back to the office and watch it. The whole thing happens in the space of a minute. River hadn't overreacted or exaggerated. It was how River said it was. Heidi talked down to her.

"What are you going to do? Give Heidi a warning?"

"I have to fire her. If she treats other people like she treated River, it's going to cost me business. Even worse, she lied about it. She has to go. Go get her."

"Shouldn't you wait until Monsters closes for the night?"

"No, there's no sense in that. When I'm done with Heidi, I need to see River and apologize, so I might as well get all of this over with."

14
WORSHIPPED

RIVER

There's a tapping at the front door. It's too late for visitors, after eleven at night. I look through the peephole and see who it is, then open the door. Cruz's eyes display a sudden warmth as he walks in. "I've brought gifts," he says. After he enters, he turns away to collect himself.

"Umm, why did you come?" I walk down the short foyer, entering the living room, and remain standing.

Cruz follows me. "To apologize. Where are the children?"

"In bed, of course."

"I made a mistake. I never should've doubted you. I watched the video from Monsters. You were right. Heidi was rude and condescending to you. I let her go."

"I didn't ask you to do that, and I don't want to be responsible for someone losing their position."

"You aren't. Heidi didn't execute her duties properly. She's a hostess. She's supposed to greet people and assist them, not act like a bitch. She didn't perform her assignment as she should have. I could provide training for that, but the lying's the part I can't tolerate."

"Would you hire her back if I asked you to? What if she's a single mother and needs the money to support her kids?"

"She doesn't have children. And it isn't good for me to be seen as weak. But I'd do anything you asked, as long as it didn't harm you."

"Please, Cruz, give Heidi another chance. Maybe she was having a bad day, or someone yelled at her before I came in tonight."

"Is this what you want?"

"Yes, it is."

"Then I will, but she has you to thank for getting her job back. So what's going on? You looked pale at Monsters and now, too. I stopped on the way over at your favorite Korean place and got that dish with the crispy rice you like, dolsot bibimbap with beef and all the vegetables."

"Thanks, but I'm not hungry."

"The last time I was over here, you looked thin. Now you look thinner. What's going on?"

"Nothing."

"Tell me the truth. I warned you what would happen if you self-harmed."

"But I'm not."

"Not eating is self-harming too. Get on your knees." Cruz's face is turning red. His nostrils flare, and he thrusts out his chest too.

"Umm, please, Cruz, don't. You aren't my master."

"Get on your knees."

He's backed me up against the wall. I can't get away from him, but the truth is that he's never done anything I've never wanted, and I don't want to run away from him. I do what he demands because what he's doing is right for me.

He brings my collar out of his pocket, the one I used to wear. He wraps the black leather around my neck.

"I'll always be your master. You know this."

For the first time in a long time, I breathe freely. The smell of leather calms me. The opposite should happen, but giving up my control to Cruz allows my mind to rest. The clicking of the buckle fastening in my ear makes me stop worrying about everything. I give control to him.

Cruz removes his coat and places it on the chair. I hear the crinkling of the bag opening. He pulls out a large Styrofoam bowl and a cardboard cup, opening them both. Steam floats in the air. He drags another chair over to me, sits down, and puts the container and cup between his thighs. The smell of the crispy rice, vegetables, and beef drifts into the room.

"Open your mouth," he says. He scoops the rice, vegetable, and beef mixture up with the plastic spoon and brings it to my lips.

I hate this. Being fed like a child makes me feel uncomfortable. I remember the first time he fed me, the night he introduced me as his slave in the great room of The Palace in front of everyone; I sat on his knees, and he got angry when I didn't eat the tiramisu he ordered. I felt fat sitting on his lap and thought I was too heavy to consume any kind of dessert back then.

"Chew, River," Cruz says. The food gets caught in my throat. He brings the jasmine tea to my lips, and I take a little sip. "Your face is cherry red."

"This is humiliating, Cruz."

"We've discussed this before. You still not knowing the difference between being worshipped and being humiliated saddens me. Perhaps, when you've finished the meal, you'll understand that there's no one else in my life I cherish as much as you."

"It'd help if you were on your knees, too."

Cruz chuckles. "I'll do it if it helps you comprehend what you mean to me. Next time, don't forget 'Sir.' I'll let you slide because you're suffering from delirium from lack of sustenance." He stands slowly, careful not to knock over the food or drink, then drops to the floor and faces me.

I'm shocked he'd agree to my request. He's always been a rigid master. If I'd offered such a suggestion before, he'd most likely punish me. Is he softening or revealing another part of himself?

"Is this better?"

"Umm, yes, Sir."

"Good, then open your mouth." Cruz brings another spoonful of delish-ness to my lips. The crispy pieces of rice mix with the various textures of the vegetables and beef strips. After I've chewed and swallowed, he stares at me. "Now tell me about the class. I want to learn about your discovery."

Perhaps he's trying to get my mind off what's happening, so I'll do what he wants me to do: eat. Or is he showing me another part of himself again?

"It doesn't seem important now."

"Everything you do and think is important to me. That's why I came over here. Tell me." His eyes look at mine, his pupils large.

The joy I felt in the watercolor class has returned because Cruz wants to hear about it. "As I told you at the club, I had my first class at the art center and made a few paintings, but I learned an extraordinary thing. *Did you know art is beautiful in its imperfection? That art doesn't have to be perfect, and is more attractive because of it?*"

"I read once that Renaissance artists would include one deliberate mistake in their paintings on purpose, because people back then believed only God was perfect. They considered perfect art an insult to God. Here, take another bite." Cruz says.

"That's true." I open my mouth for him, chew, and swallow. "Can you eat some, too, Cruz? I'm full." My stomach must have shrunk. This dish is my favorite, but I can't eat any more.

"You can't be. You've only had a few bites." He shakes his head.

I changed the subject. "I met an artist from our gallery who makes his pieces out of recycled materials. Old things people throw away. He said, 'Beauty is a word that people can't agree on.'

"That's true," Cruz nods. "The most perfect things in the world can still not be beautiful. That's why plastic surgery often goes awry, because perfect isn't beautiful."

Cruz brings another spoonful to my mouth. I try not to choke after chewing and swallowing. I didn't tell him about the plastic surgery I'm planning. Did he use his extraordinary witch powers on me? I think about what he just said, and wonder if this could happen to me. By making myself better, will I become worse?

"Please, Cruz, I can't eat anymore."

"Alright, you can take the rest to work tomorrow for lunch. Why do you have all those pictures of your mother out?" Cruz points to the pile on the floor where I'd left them before class. "I thought you couldn't look at them without remembering how you found her."

"I'm trying to get beyond that. I want to remember how my mother was before her suicide or whatever happened to her. I took a few of the photos with me and used them as inspiration for my paintings."

"To paint a portrait?"

"Not that. Just to capture something—my mother's inner spirit. Would you like to see the watercolor I made, inspired by my mother?"

"I'd love to." Cruz stands, takes my hand, and helps me up.

I'd taken the pieces I made and placed them under some books, trying to flatten them. I find the one with the darker jewel-like colors and hold it up for him to see.

"They capture a mood for sure," he responds. "For someone

who just started doing this, it's quite amazing. You should create a frame for that."

"Next week is the anniversary of her death."

"I should have realized." Cruz pats my shoulder.

"I'm happy you're here now." I feel my pulse in my throat.

"I brought you two other gifts besides the food." Cruz hands me a set of watercolor pigments. "They're supposed to be the best ones. French. The women in the store insisted they were."

"Oh, Cruz, thank you. I love them. I saw them in the art supply store but didn't dare buy them. I bought the cheapest set I could because I was just getting started, and with the children's tuition due and buying new clothing for my job—"

"The receipt is in the bag. If you don't like them, you can take them back."

"I love them, plus they're from you. I'd never take them back. Every time I use them, I'll think of you."

"Hopefully, all will go well when you make art with them, or you'll curse my name."

"Never, Cruz." I take his hand.

"Here's the other thing I brought you. I made this one." Cruz takes it out of his pants pocket. I reach for it, imagining what it could be.

"A doll?" I wrap my fingers around her. The whole thing is hand-sewn with tiny stitches. He must have stayed up all night to make it for me.

"How observant," he chuckles. "It's a poppet I made out of muslin, stuffed with herbs and other things for their healing properties. I've brought a white ribbon to write on."

"Is it like a voodoo doll? What will it do?"

"It's going to keep you from hurting yourself. You'll write on the ribbon." He hands me a marker.

"What should I write?"

"Affirmations: *I am beautiful, I can and will stop harming myself,*

I am strong, I will eat three meals a day, I have two beautiful children, or anything else that's positive and will promote good thoughts."

"I can't think of anything else positive."

"I've got a skilled master," Cruz offers, smiling at me.

"You're funny."

"See? That's positive." Cruz waits until I'm done writing on the long white ribbon. "Now wind it around the poppet, but face the words inward. Tie a bow to hold it in place, then put the doll in a safe place and protect it as I protect you."

"I enjoy tying the doll up. Does that mean I should try bondage on you?"

"It means you need a good spanking, or maybe a dose of restraint yourself." He pulls me to him while I hold the doll. "I'd do anything for you. You mean everything to me. I knelt before you tonight. Do you know why?"

"I mean everything to you?"

"Now I know you're listening." He pulls back from me and looks at me. "I'd lay down my life for you, Joy and Alex, if I had to. You're my..." He trails off.

"Say the words, Cruz."

"You're my family. My whole world."

Cruz is feeding more than my physical body tonight. He's nourishing my heart and soul.

"Hmm, Mr. Manchild, it was my understanding that I got paid a commission on the paintings I sold. So far I've sold four paintings, and I don't see the commissions on my check." It's the next day, and I'm at the gallery, casting a dubious eye over my paycheck.

"I'm sorry if I didn't explain this adequately before, but

commissions only start after your three-month training period is done."

"Okay, thank you." I return to the front of the gallery.

"Did you ask him?" Tony climbs down from the ladder.

"He said trainees don't get commissions."

"That's bullshit. Let me see your contract." I fetch it from my desk drawer and give it to him. Tony looks at it for a minute and passes it back. "It says nothing about a training period. I've never heard of such a thing before, and I've been here two years. I think he's making it up."

Should I go back in and point that out to him?" Tony nods his head in agreement. I remember what I wrote on the ribbon and wrapped around the doll: *I am strong.*

"Go get him, tiger."

Knock, knock. "I hate to bother you, Mr. Manchild, but where does it say that in the contract?"

"I'm not sure it does."

"Don't you think it should? I don't want to complain, but that's a considerable amount of money, and I was counting on it to pay my children's tuition and purchase some new work clothes. I don't require training if I'm able to sell four paintings already."

"Fair enough. I'll have your commission check by Friday for the four paintings."

"Thank you, Mr. Manchild. I appreciate it. I have to leave a bit early. I have a doctor's appointment this afternoon."

"No problem." Mr. Manchild goes back to reading his reports.

"How did it go?" Tony asks when I come back out, stepping away from the painting he just hung on the wall.

"He'll have a commission check for me on Friday."

"Congratulations, well done," Tony says.

"I'm going out shopping during my lunch hour. I need a dress for receptions. Now I'll have some money to buy something."

I head a few blocks away. There are a few stores I've wanted to check out. They always have the nicest windows. I see a dress in one of them and think, *Oh my Lord, it's gorgeous.* It's perfect for exhibition openings. I can't move past the window. I stand there and stare at the dress. I hope they have it in my size. I force myself to go inside and check, but I'm so used to being disappointed.

I know I've made a mistake as soon as I enter the store. This is one of those expensive shops that only stocks items in subdued color palettes, displaying each piece on its own separate rack. "Can I help you?" someone asks. But it's said in such a way that you know the person doesn't want to. The woman is super skinny and wears a size double 0. She's dressed all in black with four-inch heels, and she's looking down on me like she wishes I would leave.

"Yes, the black dress in the window on the right, I was wondering—"

"I'm sorry, but we don't have that item in your size." She makes a point of emphasizing the word *your.* I'm mortified, turning red and slinking towards the door to leave.

"Evelyn, go to the back and bring out the new dresses," another woman says. I turn to look at her. She's almost six feet tall and busty. There's a black, white, and red scarf wrapped around her neck, and she's wearing large gold hoop earrings. Her skin is beautiful, makeup flawless, hair styled into a twist on top of her head, posture perfect, and she carries herself like a queen. I wish I could carry myself with as much confidence. She notices me. "How about I start pulling some things for you to try on? My name's Caroline. I'm the owner here."

"Umm, the dress in the window. I love it. But I have to ask, how much is it?"

"Let me check." She goes to the front, reaches in for the tag, and comes back. "Twelve hundred dollars and it's a size four, but I can order one in another size."

"That's more than I wanted to spend."

"I understand, but you'd get a lot of use out of it because it's black. Consider it an investment. Once you wear a designer dress, you'll never want to wear anything else."

"That's what I'm afraid of."

"Why don't I do this? I'll order it for you, and you can come back and give it a whirl. You don't need to decide until you see it on you. I can have it here by the middle of next week. What size? "

"It depends...sometimes a ten or twelve. My chest—"

"The dress runs large. I'll order in both, and you can try them and see which one works best for you."

"I'd need it for an art reception, on the seventh."

"I'll have it by then, for sure. Leave your number, and I'll call as soon as it arrives. If it needs alterations, I can put a rush on them. I'll pull a couple of other dresses too, just in case, and you can try them on as well."

"Oh, that would be wonderful, thank you." Caroline has so much confidence and poise. I realize as I leave that it has nothing to do with size. It's what you believe about yourself.

15

THE PROPOSITION

CRUZ

"See that tall guy with a goatee and ponytail, standing at the end of the bar? " Liam asks me. "He says his name is Dante, and that he knows you. He apparently has a proposition for you. Do you want me to get rid of him?"

I look past Liam and spot the man. Yes, it's Dante, alright. He and I used to run in the same circles. "Bring him over."

He carries his drink with him. I stand and shake his hand. "Dante. What's it been, three years?"

"At least that long." His face appears haggard, and his eyes are bloodshot. He seems nervous but tries to smile and pretends he's not. "You've done well for yourself, Cruz," and pretends to admire the surroundings.

"Take a seat." I point to a chair, and we both sit down.

"I feel foolish coming here, but I've got a big opportunity on my hands, and I require a partner. I need someone I can trust who has the capital, the smarts, and the infrastructure to help me. Of course, you were the first person I thought of."

"What kind of business? You're aware of my line of work."

"Not women this time, Cruz." Dante's eyes wander the bar. He's looking for law enforcement, like I would do if I were doing something shady.

"Then I'm not convinced I'm good for this." I shake my head.

"Hear me out." Dante holds his hands out like a politician. "You can make a lot of money. A one-and-done kind of thing." But if it's such a sure thing, why does he seem desperate?

"Be specific with the details."

"Drugs."

"What type?"

"Fentanyl—"

"Hold on." I put both hands in the air in front of me. "I don't need to hear more. Weed, I might consider. Almost every state is legalizing marijuana now. But fentanyl…"

"Why not?" He hunches over. "Let me explain." He brushes his dark hair away from his face and takes a sip from his glass of red wine, as if considering how he's going to convince me.

Before he can open his mouth, I say, "Fentanyl's too dangerous."

"The media makes it sound worse than it is. A couple of teenagers don't know how to handle their high, and suddenly it's a 'national crisis.'" He holds up air quotes as he says it, a look of derision on his face. "I possess a substantial amount and require help with distribution. With your network of brothels, you could be the one."

"No doubt about that, but I'm uncertain if I want to employ my people this way. This would be a significant new leap for me. How much money exactly are we talking about?"

"If you can move it at the current street price, my calculations add up to twelve million."

"That's hard to say no to outright. I'll give some serious

thought to it. Let's say for now that I'm theoretically interested. But I'd need three million upfront." I move closer to him.

Dante's eyes widen in disbelief. "I'm not in a position to agree to that. If I had that kind of money, I'd just distribute it myself."

"That's the only way I'd even consider such a deal. Drugs are a dirty business and not a typical one for me."

"Ah...let me text the man above me." Dante fumbles with his phone. "I'll relay your thoughts, and he'll decide." Dante sends a text, and then we wait, chat, and drink our beverages.

Minutes later, Dante looks at his phone and smiles. "If you commit to the deal and take delivery of the product, he'll pay you the money you ask for upfront, and then you'll pay us as you sell the goods. It's a great deal, yes?"

"Let me consider it." *Why would they give me money up front? No one does that.*

"Get back to me by the end of the week. You're my first choice, Cruz." Dante gets up and moves back to the bar.

"I heard the whole thing." Liam smiles and sits down. "Oh my God, mate, he's promising the motherlode. This will finance your entire project and then some. And who knows, this might work out as a regular new revenue stream. You might even gain more brothel customers from it."

"It could also bring me severe problems I don't need. More heat from law enforcement, maybe overdoses at the brothels, both customers and employees. That means more money spent on bribes, lawsuits, and legal bills. I could even end up in jail."

"But you'd make gobs of money if it worked out." Liam nods his head.

"It's nonsensical. Trying to go legit by doing something more corrupt than before."

"How much time do you have left before the whole restaurant deal falls apart?" Liam's expression is grave.

"Three weeks."

"This drug deal would give you the cash you're looking for." Liam leans back in his chair and takes a sip of his beer.

"There's a saying I use whenever making decisions that affect the house. 'Don't poison the cauldron.' If I bring this poison into the house, it'll be bad for the people in the house, and these people are like family."

He shrugs. "I hate to say it, but your witchy stuff makes sense, even though you're giving up the money you need."

"You need more respect for my beliefs."

"I'm Catholic, what can I say?" He crosses his arms and rolls his eyes.

"What does that have to do with anything? If I need to explain this to you, you need to go to church more and take the sacrament of confession."

"I'm just sayin', I'm Catholic so I can't believe in what you believe."

"River's Catholic, too. You can honor other religious beliefs without actually practicing the religion. If you take the time to listen and learn, you'll find a lot of common ground between religions. Basic things, like right and wrong, never change."

"When do you have to give Dante your answer?"

"By the end of the week." I shake my head. "What if we had it around The Palace and Joy or Alex got into it? How would I tell River I contributed to killing one of her children?"

"You've got a point."

"I need the money, but it's a rabbit hole I'm not sure I want to go down. My life was ruined by an addicted mother. I want those restaurants but not at the expense of ruining the only families I have—River, her children, and the people that work for me."

"It's a sweet deal," Liam says, his eyes gleaming. "Three million up front."

"Too sweet. Something isn't right. Why are they so willing to pay me in advance? Have you ever heard of a wholesaler doing that?"

"No, but could it be they really want you? What are you going to do about the money if you don't take the deal?" Liam bites his lip and taps his fingers on the table.

"I'm unsure. I'll pray to Plutus and figure out another way."

"We aren't acquainted, but—"

Suddenly, Liam stands up, blocking a woman in her late twenties who was trying to approach our table. She's wearing a low-cut blouse and sunglasses. Who wears sunglasses at night? Then I remember River wearing them too. Is this a new fashion trend I'm not hip to?

"Sorry, lass, but we're not looking for company," Liam says to her.

"Cruz will want to meet me. I can help him," the woman says.

"Well, you aren't talking to him until you talk to me. You tell me first, and I'll decide whether you get to talk to him, got it?"

"I'm a witness in the criminal case against him, the rape." She flings her hair back and removes her glasses, thrusting her chest out. Her eyes shift back and forth, looking around the bar. "I know he didn't do anything, and I can testify to that; it's my friend. All I need is some help to make it happen."

"What kind of help?" Liam asks.

"I'll explain it to him." Liam looks over at me. I motion them over to the table.

"Check her for weapons and recording equipment, first, Liam."

"You're afraid of little old me?" she says, smiling. Liam frisks her, running his hands down her body, and she says with a coo, "Ooh, that feels good. Keep going."

He takes her purse, removes her phone from it, then returns it to her. "You can pick your phone up when you leave," he says, sitting down next to her and rolling his cigarette as he drinks his beer.

"Now, what do you want to tell me?" I ask.

"For a hundred grand, I'll tell them you didn't do a thing."

"I didn't do a thing. I've never seen your friend before."

"She was right here in Monsters two weeks ago on a Friday night, and sat right across from you at the bar. She was pretty pissed because you didn't notice her. She thought you were hot."

"So she's doing all this because I didn't notice her?"

"Not exactly, but if you want the entire story, you're going to have to pay me."

"You got a number?"

"Sure, it's—"

"Give it to my colleague when he walks you to the door. Thank you, ah...?"

"Mary Beth."

"Thank you, Mary Beth."

"You're welcome."

Liam comes back scowling and shaking his head back and forth. "You'd better talk to your attorney about this." He hands me the woman's wallet, which he managed to pinch from her purse as he looked through it. Good ol' Liam.

"Marjorie would just tell me not to do it."

"And she'd be right, because it's risky. It makes you look guilty. Who is she, anyway?"

"You heard her," I say, looking over her driver's license. "Mary Beth." I pull out my cell phone and press Marjorie Dallas' number. When she answers, I say, "You're working late."

"Don't tell me you're already in trouble again."

"Not yet. A woman stopped by Monsters tonight, claimed she's a witness to my rape trial, and offered to change her testimony if I paid her a hundred K."

"Who was she?"

"Said her name was Mary Beth, but her license says Nancy Walsh."

"Too bad we don't have proof of the conversation," Marjorie says.

"Oh, but I do. I record every odd conversation I'm a part of."

I hear Marjorie chuckling. "Priceless. Email it to me tomorrow, and I'll have my paralegal transcribe it. Anything else?"

"She left her phone with us, too."

"If she comes back, tell her she can pick it up at your attorney's office. That should make her heart skip a beat. It'll be interesting to see what's on that phone."

"I'll send one of my men over with it in the morning," I say.

"You will not. You'll send one of your men tonight to my home."

"As you wish."

"Now you're learning to do things the right way. As long as I've got you, by the way, I have some other good news. I learned who owns AT LLC, the corporation that paid Malory Jenkins. It's your friend Angelo Conti."

"I knew someone like him was behind this. That's great news, Marjorie."

"Yes, when I connect the dots for the judge, I'm sure he's going to have questions for Malory about her sudden wealth and dismiss the rape case against you."

"Marjorie, while I have you on the phone, could I talk to you about another matter?"

"What is it? You aren't in other legal trouble, are you?"

"No, it's nothing like that. It is about a business matter."

"If we're going to officially go on the clock, I might as well come over to your place. That way I can pick up that phone too."

"Understood."

"I'll be there in twenty."

True to her word," Liam shows Marjorie Dallas into my small

office at Monsters exactly twenty minutes later. It has nothing but two folding metal chairs and an old wooden desk. I spent all my money just opening this place, and had little left for my office.

"There he is, the resplendent king on his throne," Marjorie teases.

"Sorry about the chair."

"It's fine. Tell me about the other matter."

"A couple of months ago, I attempted to get a loan to finance this restaurant idea I've told you about, but the bank turned me down. Turns out the husband of the loan manager is both one of my clients and a sex addict, and he blew his family's savings on one of my women."

Marjorie covers her mouth, attempting not to laugh. "That's some bad luck. Although now that I'm thinking about it, I'm certain that in your line of work, a significant number of influential people in this town avail themselves of your services. Maybe that could work in your favor sometimes. What you need is a group of investors. Send me the project, Cruz. If I like it, I'll invest. Even better, I'll host a party at home and invite friends with deep pockets. You ask some of yours, too, and we'll see what we can do. Have you checked out the Lakeview East Chamber of Commerce?"

"Not yet, but River mentioned it the other night."

"Every neighborhood in Chicago has one. They offer classes, too, and it's excellent for networking. You should join, Cruz. It's beneficial if you're starting a business. I'm also a member of a country club, and I could sponsor you at mine. They're looking for fresh blood. I do more business on the greens than you can imagine. It's wonderful for networking. We'll talk more about it tomorrow. Let me ask you a personal question: Who are you going legitimate for, you or River?"

"All of us. Alex and Joy, too."

"Makes sense," Marjorie says. "We can talk more about it tomorrow." She walks out of my office.

I removed the proposal from my backpack, where I had stuffed it. It needs to be rewritten to be more accessible to investors. It wouldn't hurt to take some courses or join the local Chamber of Commerce. Being a member will make me look better to investors, and I might even learn something.

"Cruz, we've got a problem," Cork says as he rushes into my office.

"What?"

"I was at the bar, and Clarissa went to the restroom and didn't come back. I went and checked it out. She was in a stall, passed out. This was in her arm." He passes me a hypodermic needle. "I had to break the stall open to get her out of there. I had to give her a shot of Narcan to save her. Thank God the bartender keeps the stuff handy. What do you want to do? I thought you should know about it."

I don't know what to say. Clarissa's been with me the longest of any of my women. She was the first person I hired myself without Gloria, the previous madame. Clarissa and I are the same age. I remember when I found her. Some asshole had beaten the hell out of her for not earning enough money and left her on the steps of the neighborhood public library in the middle of a snowstorm. I nursed her myself. I got her through some rough times, and she got me through some rough times. She was never afraid to tell me when I fucked up or the opposite, when I did a good job.

She brought River into my life after finding her at the bus station. I'll always be grateful to her for that. Was it something I did or didn't do that caused Clarissa to do this? I stare at the needle. What if Cork hadn't found her in time? I have a second chance to connect with Clarissa and find out what went wrong. Had I not been paying attention and let her down?

"Take her back to The Palace. I'm going with her. Bring the car around."

"You won't hurt her, will you?" Liam's face is full of concern.

"Of course not. I need to understand what happened. I can't find out what went wrong if she's afraid of me. This is another sign, don't you think, that we shouldn't involve ourselves with drugs?" I take my phone off the table and send a text to Dante: *TY 4 the offer, Dante. My answer is no.*

"What are you going to do about getting the money?" Liam asks.

"I'll have to find another way." There'd be an empty place in my heart if Clarissa had died tonight. Much worse than losing any restaurant deal.

16

PAPER DOLL

MONTEL MACKENZIE

He can't contain himself as he peers out the window with his binoculars at River's house. A man, dressed in black with a ski mask, is trying to take away what God had chosen for him. The man parked his dark blue sedan in front of Montel's house, walked across the street to River's brownstone, then circled around to her backyard. Her children's lights are out, asleep in bed by this time. Is the man breaking in, or is he waiting outside for River to take out her trash? Tomorrow morning is trash day. How long will he wait for River in the frigid cold?

Montel slips into his canvas hunting coat and knit hat, then slides the stun gun and zip ties into his pocket. He puts on his gloves, crosses the street, and hides behind the frozen bushes in the front yard of River's home. Hours seem to pass before he hears the back door slam and scuffling in the distance. Moments later, the masked figure appears, and he's carrying someone over his shoulder, most likely River. Montel waits until the man is almost to the car and runs, shooting him. When the man goes down, Montel catches River, who's draped over the man's shoulder, and places her on the frozen ground. He takes the man he shot and drags him towards their vehicle. He finds the keys in the man's coat pocket, puts him in the car, removes the attacker's mask to get a good look at him, zip-ties the attacker's hands to the steering wheel, inserts the key in the ignition, and starts it.

He has the urge to call the police, but he doesn't. It might bring the heat on him. Instead, he returns to River. The abductor has already prepared her. She's blindfolded, gagged, and her appendages zip-tied. It'd be easy for Montel to carry her back to his apartment across the street, but if he takes her now, he won't enjoy her. It's like when the meal arrives too early after ordering at a restaurant. River is wearing a denim jacket, a lace top, and suede boots with lambskin lining. She's shivering as she lies on the snow-covered ground. Montel sighs. He picks her up and heaves her over his shoulder. River flexes her torso back and forth as he carries her, making it harder for him.

"Stop it," he whispers. "I'm only warning you once. Remember, your children are asleep inside the house." She ceases moving. He arrives at the back of her home, enters the unlocked door, and lays her down on the kitchen table.

"Stay still," he says, locking the back door, lowering the overhead light, and walking to the knife block on the counter by the sink, finding the one he likes best. "Decisions, decisions. Should I cut you free or cut your flesh? If you move, I'll kill you, understand?"

River nods her head.

"I thought you'd be smart about things."

He removes the gag first, then cuts the plastic off her ankles and wrists. He leaves the blindfold on. Again, she stays perfectly still.

"Now be a good girl," he whispers in her ear. "Remember, if you scream or do anything I don't like, I'll hurt your children and then you." He brings the weapon down her throat, leaving a red line. "Hmmm. You have lovely skin."

He lights a cigarette and watches the tip turn a rich orange. He blows a cloud of smoke towards her, enjoying the taste, and stares at River.

She coughs once. "Are you going to kill me?"

"If I decide you'll die, you will."

"Let me go. I won't tell anyone."

"What's in it for me?"

"Are you kidding?"

"Do you see me laughing?"

"I can't see anything. I'm blindfolded."

"Best we keep it that way. If you see me. I'll have to kill you. I'm like your last boyfriend, Cruz. I don't joke. I don't have a sense of humor."

"You know him?"

"You could say that."

"You're wrong. Cruz is funny."

"You don't say. Get down off the table." He takes hold of her hand, helps her down, and then pushes the top of her head. Her knees buckle and hit the ground hard. He tips her head up. "I think I like you in this position. Women listen better when they're on their knees. Are you ready to start?"

"Start what?"

"You need to pay me back for saving you."

"I can't."

"Then I'll give you back to him. He's waiting in the car outside. Ready to take you away from this house and your children forever."

"Please, don't."

"I like it when women beg. That's a good first step. From now on, when I call you, you answer. No more hanging up. Whatever I ask you to do, you do. Understand?"

"It's you calling me?"

"I'm asking the questions. Whatever I ask you to do, you do. Do we understand each other?"

"Yes. "

"Now we're getting somewhere. I expect obedience."

Suddenly, there are two loud bangs, then a scraping noise. "What's that?" he asks.

"I'm not sure. It could be branches scraping the house," she says, "Or a loose shutter."

"I'm going outside to check. Don't move." Montel opens the door and steps outside. When he does, River climbs to her feet, races through the kitchen blindly into the hall and up the stairs to her bedroom, and closes and locks the door.

Montel goes into the living room and finds the release button for the bookcase, revealing the staircase behind it. He takes the stairs upward, reaches her bedroom, and looks through a peep-hole. He can barely make her out in the darkness, but finds River huddled in the corner, her head buried between her knees. He releases the panel to enter River's bedroom and then puts it back in place. "I didn't say you could move," he says.

River's head jerks up. "How did you get in here? I locked the door." She's still wearing the blindfold. Lucky for her.

"I've told you before, you answer my questions, I don't answer yours. You can't get away from me, and if you run again, you'll pay for it. I've just proved I can get to you, no matter where you are. You can thank me later for rescuing you from that other man. I don't think it would be wise to call the police. Your story will sound far-fetched. Think about it—two abduc-tors in one night. And again, whatever I ask you to do, next time you'll do. If you don't, I'll hurt your children. Count to a thou-sand, and then you can go to your children. Start counting." He needs to leave because he doesn't know who made the noise outside.

"1, 2, 3, 4, 5, 6—"

Montel leaves the room, walks down the staircase and through the kitchen, and sneaks out the back. As he thought would be the case, the blue sedan is gone. He praises God and celebrates by singing his favorite song, "Bringing in the Sheaves."

If Montel stayed any longer in River's house, he'd have to have her, and there'll be plenty of time for that later. Who was the man who tried to abduct River? Montel plans to find out, now that he has the license plate number. When he sees the car again, he'll talk to the driver. Was this River's new boyfriend, playing out a kidnapping scenario? River is about to get a big surprise if she's into that kind of thing.

Montel walks down the block and circles around before coming back to his apartment. When he returns, nothing is going on at River's house. It's as he suspected; River does not call the police.

JIMMY

"I enjoy flying first class," Tommy says.

"As long as it's on someone else's dime, sure, it's the only way," Jimmy says, looking at the server's ass as her skirt bunches up while she bends over to get more soda under the rolling cart.

"This should be an easy one," Tommy says.

"That's a great way to screw it up. There are no easy ones."

"You agree with Maxksim's angle on this?"

"Yeah. It's in a woman's biology to protect her young, so going after the children and using them is the natural way to go."

Jimmy doesn't like Maxksim, or Tommy either. Maxksim, his boss, is a snake, but Jimmy knows one thing: he had better please him. And his partner, Tommy, is so stupid that he has to monitor him at all times. But the job pays well. Unfortunately, his boss always pairs him up with Tommy.

Jimmy doesn't like hurting women, not one bit, under any circumstances. He didn't grow up with those values. His father drilled it into him: "Women are to be treated with respect and protected." So this assignment is already a bad one.

He remembers River, Pearson's wife, from before. He felt sorry for her back when Pearson was alive. Pearson was a real asshole. Used his wife and his children as punching bags. When Jimmy heard River had gotten away, he was relieved, but Pearson couldn't let her go, and now his boss had fallen into the same trap, and here Jimmy was, flying to Chicago. Doesn't make Jimmy look like he has any brains, either. It's going to be a long couple of days of worry, but as long as no one gets hurt and he gets River to cooperate, he'll count the job as a success. The only wild card is his partner Tommy, no brains.

Jimmy sends a text to his cat sitter. *How is Joker?* Jimmy hasn't had Joker long. Like many cats, the cat found him. Since Meredith, his wife, died last year, Jimmy hasn't been able to stand being home. Someone had always been there before, one of his three daughters or his wife. Now they're all gone. The girls had graduated from college, gotten good jobs, or married. The quiet, the sound of the clock ticking or the hum of the refrigerator, drove him to distraction. He'd been taking more jobs from Maxksim to avoid the quiet, and he shouldn't, because he didn't like the guy, and the jobs always involved something he didn't want to do.

Two weeks back, he watched the cat in his drive stalk a bird. It got down low, his belly scraping the black asphalt. It crept up the drive, its eyes focused on its prize, and pounced. Too late. The bird flew upward, and even though the cat jumped, it wasn't high enough to reach the bird. The gray-and-white cat had shown up two days earlier. Where it had come from, Jimmy didn't know. He noticed a gash under its neck. Later that night, he'd put a plate of leftover meatloaf on the stoop and called to it. The cat was friendly and came to clean the plate, but the cut on its throat looked worse. He thought about killing the cat to put it out of its misery. The other option was to catch it and take it to the vet.

The next morning, he found a cardboard box in the closet full of his dead wife's clothes he'd planned on donating. He emptied the contents of the box onto the floor. The cat was at the end of the drive. He walked outside with the plate and the box, put the plate inside the box, and waited. The cat didn't even wait a minute. It trotted up the sidewalk, climbed the steps, jumped into the box, and started eating. Jimmy closed the box and put it in the car. He went inside, grabbed his car keys, locked the house, and returned to the vehicle.

One $450 vet bill later, covering shots, stitches, and an official cardboard carrier, Jimmy was back in his car. He stopped on the way home and purchased cat food, a litter box, and other supplies. Jimmy was now a cat owner; or the cat was now the owner of Jimmy, depending on how you looked at things. All would agree that Jimmy was no longer alone.

His cat sitter hasn't gotten back to him, and Jimmy looks at the phone again. "How old's the kid we gotta take?" Tommy asks.

"Keep your voice down. She's eight."

"How ya know?"

"Cause the sheet Maxksim gave us says so." Jimmy waves it in Tommy's face.

"How are we going to grab the kid?"

"Easy, with this." Jimmy flashes his phony Chicago detective ID. "I'm going to the front desk of the school, tell them the mother has been in an accident, and we need the child, and that we'll be back later for the son."

"You don't think they'll be suspicious of us removing just one?" Tommy asks.

"No. Should I take the entire class to make it look less suspicious?"

Tommy says, "I guess not."

"Drink your soda, look out the window, and be quiet." Jimmy stares down at his phone. His cat sitter better not fuck up. Joker needs to be fed at five and likes to play with his mouse-on-a-stick toy. He needs the stimulation now that he doesn't go outside anymore. Jimmy doesn't want his cat to get depressed and start scratching up his furniture or peeing in the house.

RIVER

I glance at all the magazines on the table. What would I have said if I had called the police? *I got abducted while taking my trash bins to the curb. I don't know who did it. I was blindfolded. And then someone saved me from that abductor, just to abduct me again.*

When they ask what he did, what will I tell them? *Nothing.* They'll think I made the whole thing up. I can't even prove the other thing happened when he called back later. Should I contact Cruz?

The magazines all display women trying to look younger, smoother, thinner, and better, and I pick one up.

The man called himself my black knight. He said, "Seeing you spread out on your kitchen table and then on your knees tonight stimulated me. I had to use all my willpower not to use you the way you were meant to be. Especially when you were on your knees. I wanted your mouth, but I'll settle for something less." He made me put the phone on speaker mode. He said if I didn't do what he said, he'd come back and wake my children.

"Slide your fingers inside your pants. It will soothe you after your ordeal, or maybe you'd rather cut yourself. Which one would make it better, River? Both are wet, but blood is red, and cutting relieves the pressure, doesn't it? And it leaves beautiful marks on your body. If you don't choose one, I'm coming back over, and I'll choose one for you, or hurt your children." *He knows. He's watching. How? How does he know?*

He gave me more instructions. "Move, River. Get the vibrator out of the nightstand drawer. Don't make me say things twice. Put the phone on the small table next to the chair, the brocade one in the corner with the flowers on it, so you can hear me. Take your pants off. Sit in the chair and spread your legs...wider still. That's better. First, use your fingers, spread the folds, and show me your clit. Start nice and slow. Go in circles. Slow down...I want this to take a while. Don't rush this. If you come too fast, I'll make you do it over until you do it right. And I can tell if you're faking. You can't use the vibrator until I tell you to." The man knew everything about me, about my room, and where I kept things.

My fingers thumb through the magazine as a woman with white hair and a friendly face sits down. I glance up, and she smiles at me. "Hello, darling, are you alright? You look like you've seen a ghost. I hope it isn't me?" Her face is full of concern, and I notice the scars running down her face and neck.

"Umm, fine, thank you. No, it's not you. I just have a lot on my mind. How are you?"

"I'm wonderful." Her eyes sparkle. "I'm here to plan out my breast reconstruction surgery, and after that, I'm going to a tattoo artist to have them paint me some new nipples. It's unbelievable what they can do nowadays. The breasts are a gift for me, but the nipples are an eightieth birthday gift for my husband. I know he'll be surprised when he sees them. He was a rock when I went through my breast cancer treatment. The least I can do is let him have matching nipples." She laughs.

"How long have you been married?"

"Sixty-three years and counting. We've had our difficulties, but even when it's down, you don't remember how down it is. That's the beauty of it. You just remember the ups being brighter, you know? Are you married?"

"Not yet."

The nurse opens the door. "Mrs. Bradford," she calls.

"Oh, that's me. Good talking to you, dear." She touches my hand, "Whatever it is, talk it over with someone you love and trust, and they'll help you through it."

She's right; I need to tell Cruz what's happening.

"Good luck with everything," I say. She walks away, the nurse leading the way.

I go back to my magazine and listen to the office personnel behind the counter chat. I'm the last one in the reception area and perhaps they've forgotten I'm here. "Yes, what's this, her fifth bout with cancer?" one says.

"All that scarring on her face and neck, and now she's lost her breasts too? What's next? "

"She's old anyway, so it doesn't matter. Why is she even bothering with reconstruction at her age? "

"Some people don't know when to give up."

"She's got one foot in the grave and doesn't seem to know it." Both of them laugh.

I can't believe what I'm hearing. I jump from my seat and stalk to the counter." I don't think you should be talking about a patient like that, do you? Not only that, but Mrs. Bradford is a beautiful woman in all the ways that matter." Neither of the employees behind the counter says a word. They stare down at their desks instead.

I turn to go back to my seat when the door opens. "River Rogers," another nurse calls out, "the doctor is ready to see you." I follow her to the examination room. "Take everything off and change into this gown. It opens in the front. Doctor Bing will be just a few moments. He's going over your pictures." After I remove my clothing and slip into the gown, I'm cold, and I want to bolt. I realize I'm having second thoughts.

The door opens, and Doctor Bing steps into the room. "I've studied the pictures I took the last time you were here, and I've got a plan. If you stand up, I'll sketch it out on your body so you can see."

I get up from the table, but my feet don't seem to touch the floor. "Do you mind?" he says, taking out a black marker. When I shake my head no, he starts making a series of lines over my breasts and stomach. The whole thing is embarrassing. It seems to take forever, but when I look at the clock, I see that it hardly took him five minutes.

"Look in the mirror," Dr. Bing says. "The lines show where I'll make my cuts to take out the excess. It'll give you a slimmer, more modern look. I think this is what you're going for. I can move some of it to your rear. You know, women today like to have larger cabooses. What do you think?"

I appear more like a paper doll from one of those books I used to have as a child, but one that someone has decided isn't right and wants to remake. I didn't know what to say at first, but eventually the words flowed out of me.

"Do you think I can have some time to think about this, please?"

"Ms. Rogers, take all the time you need," Dr. Bing says.

"Umm. I'm sorry for wasting your time."

"I wish more people took their time and thought things through."

I get dressed and leave. My heart beats faster as I head to the reception area. "When do you want to come back?" the receptionist asks. "Next week or in a few days?"

"Sure, fine."

"Which one?"

"Oh, sorry, a couple of days."

"Friday, then. I'll give you his last appointment that day. Also, if you decide you want to proceed with the surgery, here's the folder with the cost. You'll need to cover the full cost of the surgery upfront. There are financing options available, of course."

I pick the folder up off the counter. "Thank you," I say, heading out the door. It's early, so I end up walking home instead of going to school to meet the children. The closer I get to my neighborhood, the more deserted the street becomes. The dog that ate my scarf growls at me. He's home from the vet, and I haven't heard from his owner, thankfully.

"River," another neighbor calls to me. She's walking her dog, a year-old Doberman. I want to go over and chat, but the dog scares the hell out of me. She crosses the street anyway, coming to me. *Don't come.*

"I was wondering if you or your son could watch my dog this weekend, let him out, feed and walk him," she continues. "I'll be gone all day Saturday and return Sunday evening. His name is Crypto, and he's very well-behaved."

The dog sniffs my coat and then my crotch. I pat the top of his head. His fur feels silky. He looks up at me. His eyes are dark brown. His eyes seem friendly. He licks my hand. For the first time, I connect with an animal. "Um. I don't know...I don't know too much about dogs."

"It's easy, I'll write it down for you. It'd really help me out if you could do it."

"I guess."

17
WINNER

ANGELO CONTI

Angelo pushes the woman's head between his legs. He'd only booked her for two hours.

"Suck harder."

He wanted River to hear her the other day, but River hung up, and the next time he called, he got River's voicemail. He hadn't planned to hire the whore, but after bolloxing up the abduction of River from her house, Angelo didn't have a choice. He needed the release.

Why this obsession with River? Even now, as a completely capable woman sucks his cock, all he can think of is River. Is it because she once belonged to Cruz MacKenzie, and because Cruz had denied him having a taste of her?

"This one has a similar appearance to River," his dead brother Marco says.

"Shut up."

Angelo imagines the woman between his thighs as River. The girl glances up. She thinks Angelo's talking to her.

"Keep your eyes down."

Angelo requested a woman with short hair, like River used to wear hers, and a woman with a fuller body like hers, too. Only this lady doesn't have River's pale skin or sprinkles of freckles. River's appearance had changed over the past several months. Her hair is longer now, and she's lost weight. He preferred the curvy figure she used to have.

"Why doesn't Cruz MacKenzie own River anymore?" Marco continues. "Which one called off the engagement? What caused them to separate?"

"Who can say? The heart is fickle. I almost had River the other day."

"How?"

"I threatened Cruz I'd take her if he didn't give her up, and since she didn't live with him, I went to her house to steal her. When she brought her trash out, I stunned her and then zip-tied, gagged, and blindfolded her. I was bringing her to my car. Next thing I knew, I found myself zip-tied to my steering wheel. I had to drive home that way. My men cut through them and let me loose."

"What happened to River?"

"She disappeared."

Marco laughs. "Why did you go there alone? You have soldiers who could've helped you take her, or they could have gone and brought her to you. Most likely, Cruz had men guarding her."

"I don't need help to take a woman."

"Obviously you do, or you wouldn't have been tied to the steering wheel of your car." His brother points down to his lap. 'This girl is a hard worker. Will River suck your cane like this one?"

"I can't say."

Angelo hopes River will consider an arrangement in which she'll agree to become his submissive. Of course, ultimately, it doesn't matter what she wants. In the end, she'll do what he demands. No one ever refuses him.

"This one's a professional. Unh, I'm close." Angelo grunts and pulls the woman's hair up and down faster.

He imagines it's River's pink lips sliding down on his dick, not this lady's painted crimson ones. The image of this in his head makes his cock erupt, and the woman drinks and swallows his cum.

"*Ben fatto*, well done," Angelo says, holding a small strand of her hair between his fingers. He notices the hair is just a wig, as a strand of ginger hair peeks from under it. She must have the hair-piece pinned or taped on tight, so it would not come off when he pulled.

"Thank y—"

"Don't talk," Angelo says.

The woman's voice is deeper than River's, and when she speaks, it ruins the illusion. She tries to move.

"Stay on your knees with your head on my lap. I'll tell you when to leave." He stares out the window as the snow falls.

The evening news said there'd be less than three inches of accumulation. He's forgotten the name of this one already. He should try to remember. Goldie? Gwen? She tried to please him, and she swallowed without spilling. If she doesn't talk again and spoil the mood, he'll offer her champagne along with a handsome tip. River likes bubbly. Angelo smiles, remembering how tipsy she got and the way she knocked her flute over at the dinner he'd had with her and Cruz.

Ring, ring. Angelo picks up his phone and sees the caller ID. "How'd it go, Dante? Did he bite?"

"He said no."

"What? How can that be? I offered him the money in advance."

"Cruz was suspicious. He's smart."

"The rape charge may not hold up. I need something else to use against him."

"You still owe me."

"Of course, Dante. You won't let me forget."

"I want The Palace, as you promised."

"First, we have to get rid of the present occupant." Angelo ends the call with Dante.

"Cruz is smarter than you planned on, dear brother."

"Shut up, Marco."

"Who's Marco?" the whore asks.

"No one. Here, take your money and this bottle of champagne and leave." His brother laughs.

Angelo calls the man he has working on the inside. "What happened?"

"I did what I could, mate. Cruz doesn't like drugs for a myriad of reasons. Then one of our girls overdosed in the restroom. It spooked him."

"Boss, there's a man at the door," Ricardo says, "Says his name's Eddie and that he works for you."

"I've got to go," Angelo says. "We'll talk later." The man hangs up. Angelo turns to talk to Ricardo. "He was supposed to be here twenty minutes ago. Show him in."

"Hey, Mr. Conti, good to see you," Eddie says as he walks in.

The whore exchanges glances with his worker, Eddie. Angelo doesn't like it.

"Antonio, show our guest out, please."

Eddie continues, "It pissed off Cruz beyond belief when you got in to visit River at the gallery. Cruz's people have been calling my cell, leaving messages, wanting to meet with me. There's no way I'm meeting them. I can't go back."

"You're on my payroll now. Follow Cruz and keep me informed. What he's doing, who he's seeing."

"Got it! Should I report on Cruz's woman, too? Cruz treated her like her pussy is magical."

"Quiet. She isn't his woman, she's mine."

"I didn't mean to insult you. It's interesting, both of you tied up over the same one."

"Boss," Ricardo waves.

"Hold on," Conti says to Eddie, pointing his finger at him. "What is it, Ricardo?"

"There's another man outside. Says he's Cruz's father. He wants a word with you."

"Show him in."

The man enters. "Mr. Conti, my name's Montel. Montel MacKenzie."

"Cruz has mentioned you. You look familiar. Have we met before? The pastor, right? Wait one moment while I finish some business with one of my employees. Eddie, take this. "He hands Eddie a burner phone. "I forgot to put a number in it. This is your contact. Her name's Kate. You will work in tandem with her. Put this number in right now: 312-772-3223. Text her. Don't contact me, understand? From now on, whatever information you find, give her."

"Got it."

"Here's payment. There'll be more if you continue to provide good intel." Conti passes an envelope to Eddie.

Eddie thumbs through the pile of crisp hundred-dollar bills, slides off the leather couch, and walks towards the atrium, eventually reaching the outside sidewalk.

He climbs into a cab and calls a number on his phone. "Did you hear the part about Cruz's father, G? He's in town." Eddie's starving, but it's not quite lunchtime yet.

"Yeah, I did. Wherever you put the microphone, it's picking up everything. Does he pay more than I do?"

"I aim to please and have no comment about that. However,

seeing you in the wig was interesting. You should wear it for me. I don't think Conti liked the way we exchanged glances with each other."

"I don't care what he likes. He's a pig, and when he's done paying me, I put all thoughts of him aside. I'll call you later."

Eddie hangs up after she does. If she knew how much Eddie had in the envelope, she'd want some. G has expensive tastes. Eddie laughs to himself. G hasn't figured out who he is. By the time she does, it'll be too late. He has to admit he enjoys sharing her bed, but he doesn't like sharing her with others, and he can't trust her. His brother did, and he ended up dead.

The snow's falling again. It'll take ten minutes for this cab to hit the main drag. Eddie wonders why Cruz's father was speaking to Conti and whether Cruz knows his father is in town. He spies a bar flashing an open sign advertising HOT ROAST BEEF. He's hungry for something bloody. "Let me out here," Eddie says to the driver and climbs out of the cab.

RIVER

All day I think about it. It's now or never. I have to make my decision today. Yes or no. There's no more putting it off. Should I call the doctor and cancel, or see him in person and tell him? It seems cowardly not to face Dr. Bing, so I keep the appointment.

The nurse leads me into the doctor's personal office. "The doctor said to bring you in here since you'll just be chatting." I nod my head.

As soon as I sit down, the doctor comes in, sits across from me, and smiles. "Have you mulled it over?"

"Yes, umm, I don't think surgery is right for me. I think it's too extreme and—"

"We could do less, or do it in two surgeries."

"I've changed my mind about things. There's more to me than just this." I wave my hands in front of my body. "I've learned to love myself." I wonder if what I said sounds stupid.

"I wish everyone felt like you." He laughs. "But if they did, I'd be out of a job! If you change your mind or need anything, come back." The doctor extends his hand to me. I shake hands with Dr. Bing and leave his office.

The entire way back to the gallery, I'm rehearsing what I'm going to say to Mr. Manchild. How will he take it? The truth is, I don't care. It's not worth keeping a position if you have to alter yourself to keep it. The bell on the door rings when I enter the gallery, and Mr. Manchild's head lifts from his desk. His eyes widen, and his face wears a look of surprise. "I didn't expect you back today," he says. "I thought you were going from your appointment to pick up your children."

"Yes, that was the plan, but I thought I'd come back here first to let you know that I'm not getting any plastic surgery. I like how I am. After taking art lessons down the street at the community center and selling art here, it occurred to me that there is no single variety of art or single form of beauty. It comes in all flavors and varieties; therefore, people do, too. If my job depends on having it, I'll resign. I wanted to tell you now, to allow you time to hire someone."

"Wait a minute—"

"My appearance should be my business, as long as I perform my duties and it doesn't affect the way I do it."

"I agree. I was only trying to help you out, give you a leg up. I think you misunderstood. I never meant to say you needed plastic surgery. I just said others who worked here had gotten it. I don't think you have a problem, now that you've changed your clothing and your hairstyle."

"Would you have done the same thing to a man? Suggest he improve his looks?"

"Ahh, I don't know. Perhaps I was out of line. I apologize. I want you to know you're doing an excellent job. I was going to suggest a pay increase based on your performance. I also heard from our sister gallery in Manhattan. They're going to be conducting a job search for a full-time manager in three months. If you're interested in a transfer, I'd be glad to recommend you." Mr. Manchild spins around, eager to get away from me, rising from his desk chair and ducking into the back room.

"What happened?" Tony asks when I pass him at his desk.

"I got a raise," I say with a bit of amazement.

"From that cheapskate? You must have something on him. What is it, sexual harassment?"

"Don't be so cynical."

"Did you get it in writing?

"No, but I recorded it on my phone."

"Yes, queen. Now you're learning."

CRUZ

"You look great, boss," Liam says.

"Bring the presentation boards into Marjorie's house, and my handouts, too."

"What handouts?"

"The handouts I made for people to look at. I gave them to you to put in the car, Liam."

"I'm sorry, Cruz. I must've forgotten them. I can go back and get them."

"Never mind."

"Are you nervous?"

"No. I want to get this over with. I've practiced this so many times, I can say it in my sleep."

"Since you don't ever do that, it should be easy," Liam quips.

I walk up the steps to her lovely stone-fronted townhouse. Marjorie answers the door, dressed in red. She's had the whole thing catered, and I see plates of cheese and fruit laid out on the counter. "Some of your clients are here already," she whispers.

"Looks great, boss," Liam says. "You won't need that bank at all."

"Yes, well, don't count your chickens until—"

"Alright, but I have faith in you, mate. Besides, can't you say 'abracadabra' and make it so? If you have the power, why not use it?"

"I did perform a few spells before I came here tonight."

"Have you ever left your body or turned into a wolf or anything like that?"

"Do you think I'd tell you if I had?"

"Where do your powers come from, anyway?"

"Inside of me. You have them too. Everyone does, if they choose to see and act on them. Most people don't want to acknowledge them. They're afraid, or they're too busy doing other mindless busy work—running their daily lives, answering their phones, distracting themselves too much to bother looking around and connecting with the real world, the trees, the birds, the insects, nature. Right now, all I've got is one investor, Marjorie Dallas, who's pledged 1 million. That'll cover construction and operating expenses for six months. I want to get at least five to ten million more and have some cushioning for the next year after that."

"How many people said they were attending?" Liam asks.

"Twenty-five people RSVPed, but who knows if they'll all show."

"Is River coming?"

"No, I asked her not to. I thought she'd make me nervous. But she's framed one of her watercolors, and we're going to do a raffle for it. One lucky winner will take it home. It's on the easel over there." I point to it.

"That's beautiful," Liam says.

"Marjorie saw her work and wanted to do it. She thought it'd make the night more festive."

By eight o'clock, everyone had arrived. Marjorie gathered everyone together, then turned the floor over to me. I began, "It's a pleasure to share my project with you tonight. For those who don't know me, my name is Cruz MacKenzie. I've lived in Chicago since I was twelve years old. I love the city, especially the architecture. I own The Palace. It used to be an old church. I also own the nightclub Monsters. I have a plan for the future. I want to build a chain of restaurants and bars throughout the city. I've already found the perfect sites for them, hired the architect, designed the buildings, and even hired a head chef to plan the menus. What I need are individuals willing to invest a minimum of $5,000 for a 5-year term. I'm asking you to be part of something, to watch something grow and be successful. I'm building five restaurants and bars this year. All the details are in the proposal."

Everyone starts talking amongst themselves, looking through the prospectus and business plan, pointing out the proposed locations I've identified on a map printout.

One of them comes up to me. "I'm Jeff Richardson," he says, shaking my hand. "I live here in the building. I'm in marketing. Marjorie gave me your proposal last week. I'm interested. I

184 • KAY FREEMAN

brought a check with me." He takes it out of his pocket and hands it to me. "She told me about the bank turning you down. I started my business the same way, with private investors. I didn't go to college either. Let me know when we break ground. It's exciting."

No sooner does one person hand over his check than it's like leaves falling from trees. One after another, they all come up, talk, and hand me money. I leave with eight checks and have to tell the others I'll keep them in mind for future projects. "I can't thank you enough, Marjorie. I can't."

"You're welcome. And I can't believe I even won the raffle for River's painting! We're all winners tonight." Marjorie slaps my back.

After we help Marjorie clean up and load the car, Liam says, "That Marjorie's a lucky one, winning River's painting. She clearly loved the work more than anyone else. River will be happy too."

"Yeah, it was easy for her to win when I only had one ticket in my pocket."

Liam chuckles. "You're not a legitimate businessperson, mate."

"I'm true to my most important investor, Marjorie Dallas, and my girlfriend, River. Case closed."

"You won't get an argument out of me."

18

THE UNIVERSE IS US

CRUZ

I'm in my car parked out front of River's brownstone, checking messages, when I reach one from Angelo.

I'm unable to comprehend what I'm seeing, images of River unclothed.

Why would River take off her clothes for Angelo Conti? Something isn't right about them. Her eyes are half-closed. Did he drug her?

> What did you do to her?

>> Nothing yet. No details, could be slave, sub, or just mistress

>> Concerns about her children

>> When she delivers the painting I've purchased, we'll work everything out, if not sooner

You'll have nothing to do with her, or
u pay

You're in no position to do anything

She doesn't belong to you, and I run this
town, not you

She doesn't belong to you either

Not yet, but soon. And she's not all that
will eventually belong to me

What does that mean?

You can't always trust the people around
you, Cruz

The cell goes dead. The bastard hung up on me. I shove the damn device in my pocket.

"What's wrong?" Liam asks.

"The same old crap...Conti. I'll call you later." I climb out of the car.

I pound on the door and announce my arrival, like she wants me to. River opens the front door. "Are you seeing Angelo Conti?" I immediately ask.

"What are you doing here?"

"Answer the question."

"Not exactly." River avoids meeting my eyes.

"What do these mean?" I bring the photos up on my phone.

She blushes and turns away. "Those are old. My boss made me take Angelo Conti out to lunch when I sold him a painting. It happened days ago. It's not how it appears."

"Half-undressed, sitting in the passenger seat of his car, is difficult to misinterpret."

She angrily responds, "Stop telling me what to do. You lost the right to tell me anything."

"Why, because I didn't marry you?"

"That's part of it. We don't match well."

"Did I say that?"

"No, I did."

"Is my business the problem?"

"Have you changed occupations?"

"No, but I'm giving it a go." Her scent floods my nose, and I move closer, wrapping my arms around her. My lips find hers.

"Why do you make this so hard for both of us?"

I don't answer and make sure she hears my footsteps leave and the door close. She thinks the room is empty. I hear her cry. A few moments later, I press a kiss on her cheek. She opens her eyes, but I've made myself invisible.

"I can make it so you don't see me."

"Can you make it so I don't remember you?"

"No, and even if I had that ability, I'd never put that spell on you. I brought you another gift. How is the other one working, the doll?"

"I'm eating, and I didn't make any fresh cuts."

I take the red string out of my pocket and wrap it around her left wrist.

"A red bracelet to ward off evil energy. Wear it and set an intention. Repeat to yourself, 'This bracelet brings protection, luck, and good fortune as long as I wear it.' If it falls off, don't worry about it. Leave it where it falls. Don't put it back on. I'll bring you a new one."

"Will it protect me?"

"If you believe it will, it will. I need you to believe. I also need to be close to you, River. Will you allow me that?"

"Yes." She holds her wrist up to her face and examines it.

"Let's go to your room." I take her hand and lead her up the stairs, down the hall, and into her room. "Do you have a preference on position?"

"No," she breathes.

"You're testing my patience, aren't you?"

"I thought we agreed we shouldn't see each other."

"I thought I could go without you, but I can't. Do you feel differently, River? If you do, I'll leave."

"I need you too, but I need to tell you the truth. Even though I've learned a lot being on my own, I've made some good decisions and bad ones."

"What are you trying to say?"

"I've fucked up. I..."

"Tell me the good decisions you've made first."

"I canceled my plastic surgery."

"Why the hell would you get plastic surgery?"

"For the gallery job. Mr. Manchild suggested it."

"He what? What a fucking moron. I'll kill him."

"No, you won't. It was a mistake."

"You bet it was."

"Mr. Manchild just said other managers had gotten it. He didn't mean I had to, but in my head, I thought something was wrong with my body."

"Of course you would. I've told you thousands of times your body is glorious, but you never listen."

"All I could hear were the children who tortured me when I was younger. Even though it was years ago, it's hard to forget. I thought if I got it, I'd rid myself of my big boobs and have a flatter tummy and wear a size four."

"Are you out of your mind?"

"Not anymore. I decided that I'm okay the way I am."

"You're more than okay, River."

"Yes, I'm good."

"You're perfect."

"Let's not get carried away. I'm not that. I made some mistakes, but there's more to me than just my outside."

"That's a positive realization, River."

"I did something else positive. I pet a dog."

"You touched an animal? What kind? How did it happen?"

"A Doberman. My neighbor asked me to dog-sit over the weekend. I had to walk it, let it out, and feed it."

"That's a large dog, River. You weren't afraid?"

Jesus Christ, I can't even imagine she would ever let an animal that big within twenty feet of her.

"At first, but his fur was soft, and his eyes were gentle. I walked him, and he didn't pull. His name's Crypto."

"That's nice, River." I realize she wants to tell me something I'm not going to like. Her eyes are wavering back and forth. "Did you sleep with Conti? Or is there someone else? If you did, I'm not mad at you." *Although I might have to murder the person.*

"No. Someone's blackmailing me. It's going to sound baffling, but it really happened this way. A week ago Sunday, while I was taking the trash out, someone came up behind me and tasered me. They tried to kidnap me, but someone else did something to them and caused them to fall, and then that second person kidnapped me instead. He kept me blindfolded and said I owed him because he saved me from being taken away by the other man. He threatened me and said that if I didn't do exactly what he told me to do, he'd hurt the children and me. He also found a way to get into my bedroom, even after I'd run away from him and locked myself in. I don't know how."

"I have the answer," I say, sighing. I should have told her a long time ago about the hidden passageway. "I'll show you how he did it." I show her the hidden button to open the panel on her bedroom wall. We go through the walkway, down the stairs, press the release, open the bookcase, and enter the living room.

"Oh my God," she says, amazed. "I never knew this was here. How did you know?"

"The real estate agent told me about it. A better question is, how did your kidnapper know about it?"

"I don't know, but later that night, he called me and made me..."

"What, River?"

"Umm...play with myself."

"Where was he?"

"I'm unsure. He wasn't in the house. He knew everything I was doing, though. He was watching me."

River becomes more upset, and I do, too. I clench my fists. "He's got cameras in the house somewhere. We're going to find them right now."

"If I take them down, he'll hurt the children or me."

"You can't be a victim and bow down to this bully. Come, let's search the bedroom." I check the alarm clock, a common place to hide cameras, and sure enough, I see the tiny lens in the divot where the big and small hands of the clock meet at the center of the face. I throw the whole thing on the floor and stomp on it. "Where did he make you do the deed?"

"In the chair in the corner."

I sit in the chair and gaze forward to where a camera might be placed to see it all. Sure enough, there's a hole in the painting on the opposite wall, and I find a second camera there. I crush it with the heel of my shoe. "There might be more," I say, "but it looks like these two were light-activated. If you're in doubt in the future, just keep the lights off."

"I'm sorry, Cruz."

"You did nothing wrong. Now let's get back to the real reason I came. You're not the only one who's screwed up. You've asked me why I postponed our wedding, so I'll tell you." River's eyes widened. "Angelo and I had that arrangement you knew about, where he and I were supposed to exchange partners for a night. When I didn't follow through, he started threatening to take you by force, then, when we became engaged, he ramped up his threats even more. I thought if I canceled the wedding, he'd back off. It seemed to work for a while, until his wife left him."

River's eyes never leave me as I continue, "And it gets worse. I tried to give up the brothels for you, but I couldn't secure financing for my restaurants. One of the loan managers told me my brothels had destroyed her family's life. I decided then I wasn't good enough for you.

You did the right thing by giving back my ring. You need to marry someone from your world. I'm not. I've always believed that what I do is a victimless crime. After all, I don't force anyone to have sex. But after this woman called me out and said her husband had spent all their savings on the brothel, how could I pretend that what I do doesn't harm others? It's made me reconsider. You need to marry someone who can support you and your children through legitimate means, who isn't running an illegal business, who can't get arrested at the drop of a hat."

"Cruz, I had someone like that, but I never knew when the next beating would come."

"It's all a smokescreen anyway. I've come to realize that the real reason I broke things off is that I was afraid. Having you and your children in The Palace was a reminder of the danger I faced if I made you my family and loved you. It made me vulnerable. I was fearful I'd lose control. I loved you and them too much. What if I hurt you, or someone else did? I couldn't live like that. I had to get rid of you. Just like my father needed to dump me so he could do every depraved act he was compelled to do. If I hadn't run away from Ithaca, he would have beaten me to death. Don't you understand? I'm like him. I'm a monster, a devil. There's no help for him or me."

"Don't say that. You're a good person. You're nothing like him."

"You want to believe that, but wake up. I'm the devil."

"If you are the devil, then you're the devil I love." She grabs hold of my shirt. Our eyes connect, and her lips brush mine.

"Look at what I do for a living. I'm a pimp. Look what I did to you. I almost traded you to Angelo Conti."

"But you didn't. That's the important part. You didn't go through with it."

I pause. "Perhaps. There was something else I couldn't go through with last week, too. I had a chance to secure financing by distributing fentanyl, and I turned it down."

"I'm proud of you, Cruz."

"Are you?"

"Yes, I am. Not just because of that, but because you're confiding your feelings."

"I wanted the money, but the idea of destroying other people's lives, like my mother destroyed hers...or the idea of Joy or Alex getting hold of it...I couldn't be a party to that."

I bring River close to me and wrap my arms around her. The smell of oranges and jasmine hits me.

"I want you in my life. I may never be good enough for someone like you, but I'll try to make myself worthy. Will you wear my collar again?"

"Yes, Sir." River sinks to her knees.

"Good girl." I pull the leather collar from my pocket, strap it around her neck, and buckle it. "Hands in the air. Keep them there." I grasp the bottom of her blouse, pull it over her head, and lay it on the bed. I unsnap the back of her bra, bring it from her, and lay it on top of the shirt. I get the handcuffs out next and attach them to her wrists. "Do you remember the rules?"

I unbutton my shirt, then unbuckle my belt and slide it off my pants. I make sure she hears it.

"Yes, Sir. To address you as 'sir' and not to cum until you give me permission."

"Good girl." I pull her to her feet and walk her to the bed. "Bend over." I push her yoga pants and panties down around her ankles and help her step out of them. "Where are the children?"

"Over at sleepovers."

"Aren't we lucky?"

I push one hand on the flat of her back, and use the other one to knead the perfect skin on her ass.

"You own me, River, not the other way around. I'll always be your slave. I'm a slave to your every desire and wish." I bring my palm down on her ass with a slap.

"Oh, Cruz."

"How does it feel?"

"So good, Cruz."

I give her a few more gentle ones, warming her skin. Her pale skin becomes pinker. I bring a harder one down, and this time she jumps. "Ouch."

"Too much? Remember, the safety word is 'Gothic.'"

"I'm fine, Cruz."

"Are you?"

"Of course."

I bring down another one, and now her ass is turning red. "You're forgetting the rules." I wait.

"Please, please, Sir,"

"Good girl." I rain more smacks down on her sweet ass, each one getting harder. She's beginning to move.

"Stay still, or I'll have to restrain you."

River will like the threat of that. By this point, she's got to be wet. Between the handcuffs and the spanking, she's in need. I flip her over and spread her thighs, running my finger over her swollen clit. Her juices are flowing. I rub her clit in small circles, and she groans and moves against my finger.

"Stop moving." I bring my hand up to her nipples and pinch them, and she moans.

I drop my face between her legs, lick her swollen clit, then begin alternating between licking and sucking so she doesn't know what I'm going to do next. She's arching her back and crying out. I slide my finger into her pussy. She's sopping wet, and I laugh.

"Someone wants to get fucked." I slide another finger in with the first and start fucking her with them. I can tell she's already close to coming.

I issue the command, "Don't cum."

"Cruz, I can't stop it."

I pull my fingers out, bring my fingers to her nipples, pinch them hard, and flip her to her stomach again. I take my belt and use it on her, giving her ass one brutal hit. The sound of the cracking leather whipping through the air, the pain, and my words distract her enough to throw off her orgasm.

"I warned you, don't cum."

"Cruz, fuck me, please. I need to cum."

"Do you? Put your ass higher in the air."

River does what I ask, and I stand over her and make her wait.

"Tell me again what you want me to do to you."

"Fuck me, please."

"How?"

"You know."

"Provide instructions."

"Please, Sir, fuck me hard."

"Hmm. You do make it look and sound appealing."

I make her wait a minute. I enter her, teasing her at first, just giving her the head of my cock. She's trying to take more.

"Stop it. You've forgotten your manners. I'm in charge, not you." I slap her ass with my folded-up belt. She settles down and stops moving, and I go back to work, driving deep into her pussy until my balls are slapping her ass. "Do you still want me to continue with the belt or my hand?"

"The belt, please, Sir."

I unfold the belt and bring it down on her ass as I continue to fuck her, but I notice her ass is getting too red. I don't want to give her too many more hits and break the skin, harming her. "Cum now, River."

No sooner do I say the words than River's pussy clenches around my cock.

She screams, "Cruuuuzzz, the universe is us!"

Her body shudders. I can't hold off anymore, either. My cock's buried deep inside of her, and I spill my heat into River. It seems like I cum forever, because it's been so long since I've been inside of her, or any of my other women, either. I've wanted no one but her. I've stopped fucking my workers when they've asked for my attention. Joey's been handling those duties. It's working out so far.

I remove the handcuffs from River's wrists, pull her into me, and wrap her in my arms. We haven't been intimate in this way since she gave back the ring. She hasn't allowed me to penetrate her until tonight. I know now I can never part from River.

"Please," she says as she places her hands on my shoulders. Then she slides them to my ass as we lie together. It's winter, but our bodies are hot and sweaty. I run my fingers through her hair, keeping her close to me. Everything is as peaceful as it should be when we are together.

"I've left something for you on the dresser." I motion towards it.

"What are they?"

"Bags of protection powder. Hang them on the doorknobs around the property when I leave. You can even carry one. It'll protect you from evil when I'm not here."

"What's in it?"

"Very simple ingredients: ground-up sea salt, black peppercorn, and some whole black-eyed peas."

I say a chant to Bisu, the ancient Egyptian deity. He protects households, mothers, and children from the enemy. My enemies will come after them, for sure. I bring River closer and imagine the four of us as a family: me, River, Joy, and Alex...

"I need to tell you something else, River. There's another way to get out of the house in an emergency. It's in the cellar. I'll show it to you before I leave. Angelo also gave me a warning on the phone tonight. He said, 'You can't always trust the people around you.' Who do you think he meant?"

"It has to be a person you depend on, and you'd never suspect has betrayed you. The only person who comes to mind is Liam."

"I can't just accuse him, River. I need proof."

"Bug his phone."

"Do you think Cork is in on it?"

"I don't know. It sounds unbelievable that Angelo could get to both of them."

"Why would Liam betray me? There must be a reason."

"Maybe he was promised something...The Palace, perhaps. You mentioned you brought in a new guy. Perhaps he felt threatened."

The other possibility is that River's betrayed me, but doesn't know it.

19

OBSERVE & OBSCURE

RIVER

"Good morning, Mr. Manchild."

"Don't come in today, River. Work from home until you deliver the painting. That will make things easier. You can meet the delivery people at Conti's house."

"I was thinking with the weather, maybe we could postpone it. I mean, it's snowing, and we don't want to damage the work. And with the opening reception tonight…"

"It's not snowing that hard, and the work's wrapped. The delivery people are already scheduled to pick up the painting. I don't want to disappoint Mr. Conti."

"Mr. Manchild, could someone else go and hang the painting? I don't want to go to the house without Tony. I don't feel comfortable with Angelo Conti. I'm sorry."

"Alright. I'll go myself."

"Thank you." Mr. Manchild ends the call, but then it almost immediately, the phone starts ringing again. Is he calling back? "Hello?" I say.

"It's Angelo. Make sure you come today. Don't send someone else in your place. You wouldn't want what happened to Tony to happen to them."

"Excuse me?"

"You heard me. And if I have to, I'll send someone to the gallery to collect you anyway. Best for you to come yourself and not involve anyone else." The call ends. What should I do? Did Angelo Conti really hurt Tony? Would he harm Mr. Manchild if I don't go?

I call Mr. Manchild back. "Umm, Mr. Manchild, I realized I'm being silly. I'd like to deliver the painting this afternoon if it's okay with you?"

"Are you sure?"

"I'm sure it'll be fine."

"I don't want to force you to do anything you aren't comfortable doing. If you want, I can ask the installers to make sure they don't leave before you leave."

"No. I'll be fine. Thank you, Mr. Manchild."

I don't want to go, but he could hurt my boss or go after one of my children if I don't. Should I call Cruz? Why can't I handle things by myself for a change? What kind of message am I sending to Mr. Manchild when I need help handling an uncomplicated delivery?

CRUZ

Joey stands in front of me. Observe and obscure; you don't want to reveal everything about yourself. One of the rules of being a witch.

In a roundabout way I've taught this to Joey. People will look at him and think he's muscle with not much going on upstairs. They'll be wrong. If I hadn't had him keep the notebook on the people in the house, I would've made the same mistake and never discovered that his observational skills surpass mine.

I try to hire people who bring skills to the table I don't have. Cork, my driver, can outdrive any vehicle on the road. Liam, my right-hand man, assists me in seeing things from every angle and keeps me from making snap decisions. In Joey's case, I've brought in someone who has skills I do have, although I have to admit that his are even better than my own. Even the women who work for me are beginning to bond with him.

"Yeah, so I follow your girl to a fancy house," Joey says. "She arrives by a ride service. It turns out the mansion on Astor Street belongs to Conti. She's there from 12:25 to 2:00. I couldn't get close to it at first because there's guards front and back, and they never leave their posts." He shifts nervously back and forth between his feet. I'm filled with rage. What is River doing? It's one thing for Angelo to go to her, but why is she willingly going to him?

"Anything else?" I'd love to flee and be anywhere else right now and not hear Joey's report.

"At about 12:45, a van and two delivery guys show up in an unmarked van and carry in a large bubble-wrapped flat item."

"A painting?"

"It seemed like that; it took two of them to bring it in. The two men in white are there for half an hour, then they come out with just the wrapping paper and leave. Then it's quiet until she comes out at 2:00. She doesn't look good. Conti and his driver accompany her. Conti gets in the back seat with River. Her face is pale, her cheeks are red, and her eyes stone cold. I got closer, because his guards are busy, opening his door and talking to him. She looks like she may have been crying."

"What did her clothes look like?"

"What do you mean?"

"Don't play dumb, Joey. You know exactly what I mean. Were they rumpled, messy, straight, orderly? Tell me the truth."

"Please don't raise your voice. You're making me nervous. Messy, but she looked scared, like she was afraid of him or something. She wasn't standing close to Conti. That's my take."

"Did I ask for your take? I just want you to report the facts. Now get out." I point to the door. I'm worthless. I didn't protect her. Life is meaningless. I pick up the bust of Athena and throw it across the room, where she breaks in pieces. I hold my head in my hands and wonder what will happen next.

Ring, ring. I answer it. "Cruz, it's Alex."

"Alex, how are you? How's school?"

"I'm not sure. My sister Joy disappeared today. Two detectives picked her up from school, saying my mother was in an accident, but at the end of the day my mother came as usual and picked me up. She was very upset and even though I kept asking questions, she doesn't seem to know where Joy is and wouldn't call the police or let me do it. She went back to work, at the gallery for some kind of opening. I didn't know what to do, so I snuck her phone out of her purse before she went back to the gallery, and I'm calling you."

"You did the right thing. I'll come over."

"What if they're watching the house or something?"

"You're right, Alex. You're very smart; good call. I'll sneak over, but later tonight, after your mother gets home. Don't worry, Alex. everything is going to be fine."

RIVER

"I should be happy; it's my first opening reception. But instead, I'm distraught because my mind keeps drifting back to this afternoon when I received the news that Joy's been kidnapped. As I scan the room, I spot Lia in the corner. Despite the turmoil in my mind, I manage to greet her with a smile. "Hello! I'm glad you received my invitation and came." I pretend that everything is wonderful.

"I'm glad you invited me. You look fantastic. That dress looks great on you," Lia touches my shoulder.

"Yes. I bit the bullet. It's new." Suddenly I see Maxksim Oberlin. "Yes, umm...I'm sorry, I have to go. There's a man over there who looks interested in that piece, and it's my job to convince him to buy it."

"Definitely go. You're doing a great job, River, really." Lia smiles at me. "We can chat another time. Thank you for keeping in touch with me."

Maxksim Oberlin sneers once I reach him. "Aren't you going to offer me a glass a wine?"

My hand trembles. "White or red?"

"Red." He takes the glass and smiles. I notice a woman and a man having words in a heated argument at a painting near us and I crane my neck to listen. "*I told you before I'm not going along with this. If you want to do it, be my guest, but I'll not be a party to it. Now leave me alone.*" The woman stalks away.

Oberlin snaps his fingers at me. "Pay attention. Since so much time has passed and you've made me wait so long, I think I need to be compensated. I know you wanted fifty percent of our holdings and earlier we agreed to thirty-five percent, but now I think fifteen percent reflects the current climate. It's more than fair. You're getting something far more valuable in addition to these assets, don't you agree?"

"But I need the money for my children."

"You have a suitor in the wings who's more than willing to take care of all your financial needs. Conti runs Chicago. I should commend you. You do have a way of landing men with deep pockets. I suggest you work out something with him. My attorney mailed our agreement here to your place of employment. You should receive it in the morning. Sign it, call the number on it, and he'll send someone to pick it up. Just so you know I'm serious, I'm sending you a video. You'll get that in the morning too, in case you're unsure about these new terms."

"Please, don't. I believe you. Don't hurt Joy. I'll sign." I reach towards him, but Oberlin snatches his arm away and marches towards the door as the throng of people block my way and keep me from following. By the time I reach the sidewalk, a limo is pulling down the street. What am I going to do?

CRUZ

Cork, "Here's the plan for tonight. Drop me off two blocks over from River's brownstone. I'll text you when I'm ready to get picked up. And don't tell Liam about any of this."

"Why the espionage?" Cork asks.

"I'll explain later, when I know more." I climb out of the SUV. I head through her neighbor's yard and hope they don't have dogs. I reach River's back door and see her sitting at the kitchen table crying. I push the door open and walk in. "You don't lock your doors anymore?"

"I, I forgot." River's eyes are red.

I can immediately tell something's wrong by her shaky voice. "What's going on?"

"Nothing. Why are you here?"

"To talk to you about Angelo Conti."

"Don't talk too loud. I don't want to wake up Alex. He finally went to bed."

"Is it true? Are you considering signing a contract with him to be his sub?"

"Where did you hear that?"

"What does it matter? You will not go with him. Do you understand? Does he have something on you? Where's Joy?"

"Upstairs."

"I'm going up to see her."

"No, you can't. She's, she's asleep."

"You've turned into a liar, and a bad one. Where is she?"

River starts crying and puts her head down on the table. "A motel somewhere. I'll get her back tomorrow. I just have to sign some paperwork agreeing to settle the estate with Maxksim Oberlin and they'll return her."

"And if you don't?"

"We didn't discuss that part."

"Who's we?"

"Me and Conti."

I pinch my nose. "Of course he's involved. I'll protect you...us. Understand? You stay away from him. "

"I can't. I need my daughter back. Whatever I have to do, I'm going to do. "

"Is that part of the arrangement too, doing what Conti wants?"

"What choice do I have? I can't call the police."

"No. You're right, you can't." I've failed River in the worst way possible. I've lost one of her children. "I'm going to her room. I need to feel Joy's energy and control the outcome."

I start climbing the steps, but then stop. There's a photograph of Joy and me together hanging in a gold frame. Both of us are smiling. I remember the day River took the picture. Joy's sitting on my shoulders and her hands are cradling either side of my head, her legs draped around my neck and hanging down my torso. That's the first day I thought River, Joy, Alex and I could be a family. But the thing I've feared has happened—one of them has been taken. I feel my throat tightening and my eyes getting wet. What's wrong with me? I haven't cried since I was a child. I'm being torn apart.

I reach Joy's room. Her bed is unmade. I go to it and lay my head on her pillow, smelling strawberries and bubblegum, Joy's smell. The pillow moves slightly and a piece of paper sticks out. I move swiftly and reach for it. It's the unicorn card. I move the pillow out of the way and find the amulet there, too. I hold it in my hand and chant, rocking back and forth, asking the deities to keep Joy safe. River comes into the room and kneels beside the bed, praying to her own god. We're united in our love for Joy. *What has become of my family?*

JIMMY

Brring, Brring. "Hi Jimmy. It's Maxksim. I just saw the mother. How's the kid?"

"Which one?"

"Funny."

"Let me step outside. She's sleeping."

"I hate to ask you to do this, Jimmy and I know we agreed

there'd be no rough stuff, but I'm getting some pushback from the mother, and I need to show River I'm serious."

"I'm not hurting a child. I didn't sign on for that."

"Fine. Put Tommy on the phone."

"He's not here. I sent him out for food."

"Okay. When Tommy gets back, have him call. I'll work something out with him."

Jimmy shoves the phone in his pocket, walks back into the room, sits down, and watches as Tommy flips through the stations with the remote. He thinks back to earlier, when they had first checked in.

"How do we check into a motel with a kid? Tommy asked when they first grabbed Joy. "Two grown guys with a little girl? Makes us look like pervs."

"Easy," Jimmy told him. "I purchased a large suitcase. It's in the trunk. I'm going to pull under the bridge over there, and you're going to put her in it."

"I'm not doing that," Tommy said, a look of shock crossing his face.

"You are. Then five minutes later we'll unpack her in the motel room, call the boss, and tell him we've done our job."

"What if something happens?"

"It won't, I've made sure. I've punctured the suitcase so she can breathe. But she's only going to be in there a few minutes, anyway." He had to convince Tommy. Tommy's face had turned white, but he did as he was told, and sure enough, a half-hour later, the suitcase was lying on the bed unzipped and Joy Pearson was sleeping next to it.

Jimmy needs to make sure Tommy doesn't talk to Maxksim and get talked into anything.

T<small>HE FOLLOWING DAY</small>, Joy is giving Jimmy problems. "I want to go home. I want my mommy."

"I know you do. Grab your coat. We have to make one stop first."

"Where?"

"We have to go find someone."

"Tommy?"

"Yes, him." Fuck; if the little girl knows Tommy's name, she undoubtedly knows Jimmy's name too. It'd been so easy to drug Tommy last night; all he had to do was triple the girl's dosage and put it in Tommy's soda. The salty chips made Tommy thirsty.

"Can I sit in the front seat?" the little girl asks.

"Sure."

"My mommy doesn't ever let me sit in the front seat, because she says I'm too short."

"Well, then, maybe you actually should be in the back seat this trip."

"Shoot," Joy says, slamming the door, opening the rear door instead, and climbing in.

"Don't forget your seatbelt." When Tommy had asked the night before who had called, Jimmy had already decided he wasn't going to tell him. Jimmy wasn't going to let dummy Tommy get talked into anything by Maxksim. Tommy had faded fast after he drank the soda, and it had been nothing to drag him into the car, find a hardware store, buy a few supplies, and an abandoned house. He'd duct-taped Tommy's mouth and zip-tied his hands and feet. He chained his hands to a secure post and left a bucket near him in a basement. Even though Tommy would have to struggle, he'd be able to pull his pants down if he tried. Jimmy left Tommy plenty of blankets from the hotel so he wouldn't get too cold. He's probably going to be mad, but once Jimmy explains the situation, he'll see Jimmy only had two choices, and the other choice wouldn't have been a good one. There's no way in hell Jimmy would let Joy get hurt. No way. He doesn't care what Maxksim Oberlin thinks of it. Fuck him. Hurting little girls is crossing the line.

"These houses look ugly," the little girl says.

"No one lives in them. People buy them and then make them pretty." Jimmy says. He pulls in the drive at the house where he left Jimmy.

"Why are we at this one if no one lives here?"

"That's a great question. Tommy is here temporarily. He's playing a game." Jimmy didn't want to bring Joy in, but it's dangerous to leave a child alone in a car.

"He is? I want to play too."

"Good. He's hiding inside. You can help me find him."

20

DISAPPEARING ACT

ANGELO CONTI

"We had a deal." Angelo Conti's eyes grow angry.

"What's the problem?" Maxksim falls into the chair. "We still do."

"River called me this morning and said you demanded more money, threatened to hurt her child. Chicago is my town. I don't do business this way. You have one hour to produce Joy, or you're a dead man."

"Don't threaten me."

"Be quiet. You aren't leaving here until I see her."

"I'm having an issue. My men have disappeared, and they have her."

"Well, then it seems you have a problem."

"But if you eliminate me, you won't be able to contact my men." He gives a triumphant smile.

"Of course I will. I have your cell." He reaches over and plucks it out of Maxksim's hand.

"But if you kill me, you won't have me," Maxksim says, "and you need me to open my phone."

"I only require your face. The phone doesn't care if you're dead or alive." Maxksim blanches, and Angelo continues, "Put this asshole in the dungeon." His two soldiers take the man away. He texts River:

Where are u?

On my way

RIVER

One of Angelo's men escorts me into his home. "You're finally here," he says when he sees me, moving forward and attempting to hug me.

"Where's my daughter?" I push him away.

"You help me, and you'll see her. That's how this works, River."

My eyes land on the Boudicca painting. I wish I had the strength of Boudicca.

"Have you ever been with another woman before?" He asks.

"No, never. Why are you asking me this? I can't think of that right now with Joy gone."

"Haven't you ever wanted to try it?"

"I don't want to do this. Please, Angelo."

"You're so much more conservative than I imagined. I thought you'd be more adventurous, being with Cruz."

"Now that you realize I'm not, you can find someone more your style."

"He must have seen something in you."

"Whatever he saw, he stopped seeing it since he dumped me."

"You're so funny and honest. I like that about you. Refreshing."

"I just want my daughter back."

"I'm working on that. I promise you." *Buzz. Buzz.* Angelo looks down at his cell. "Ahh, the woman I asked to join us is at the door. You're going to like this if you'll just relax. Plus, it'll get your mind off things."

"I don't want my mind off things. I want my daughter."

Seconds later, one of his men escorts a woman into the room. It's clear she's attempting to disguise herself. She's wearing a wig and heavy makeup, eyeliner, eyeshadow, even fake eyelashes.

"Goldie, this is River," Angelo says.

"Nice to meet you, River." Goldie smiles at me.

"You, too."

"You girls get acquainted, or not. You'll get to know each other really well later." Angelo chuckles. "I'm going to bathe, unless you two want to join me. Do you?"

"No, I've had a bath," Goldie says.

"How about you, River? Your name has to do with water. Would you like to shower with me?"

"No, thank you."

Goldie reaches for a bottle of champagne. "We'll be drinking while you get ready. I love your champagne."

"Of course you like my champagne." Angelo hands Goldie three glasses. "It's five hundred dollars a bottle, but I want to keep you happy. It's like having twins here." He looks back and forth at us, noting that our hair is almost exactly the same style and color.

"I'll open the champagne." Goldie moves to the bar and twists the top of the bottle. The cork shoots across the room to Goldie's delight, and the bubble foams out of the neck of the bottle. Goldie pours some into the flutes and returns one to Angelo. He drinks it as he carries it to the shower.

"Here, River, have some." She passes me a glass.

"I'm not sure..." I don't like this woman.

"Do you remember me?" she whispers, staring into my eyes. But I'm distracted by something else, the ruby choker she's wearing. Cruz once had me try one that looked something like it. He told me it was one of Gina's pieces, the madame who owned The Palace before Cruz. My eyes return to the woman wearing it now. The way the gold slithers around her neck...oh my God...

"What are you doing here, Gia?"

"Helping you escape."

"Why? The last time we met, you tried to kill Cruz and me."

"I was sick. My psychiatrist wants me to make amends for my actions."

"Thanks for the offer, but I can't leave here, not without my daughter."

"Angelo doesn't have her anymore. Check your phone."

I do as she says, and there's a text message from Cruz, along with a picture of Joy sitting on the couch in my house. Four words: *Joy's safe. Come home.*

"How did you know?" I ask.

"My girlfriend and I are in communication with some people. You need to go while Angelo's in the shower," she says.

"I can't leave you alone. What if he does something to you?"

"I can handle him. My girlfriend's on the way. She'll help me. Go, River."

"I'll go when she arrives." I text Cruz: *Gia's here. I can't leave her alone with Angelo.*

CRUZ

"Something isn't right. There are always two men standing guard at Angelo Conti's house. Now no one's here, and all the windows are dark. Liam, you stay in the car with Cork."

"No way, mate. I'm coming in with you."

"Are you sure you want to?"

"Why wouldn't I?"

"Because you take money from Angelo Conti, that's why."

"What?"

"You heard what I said. I'm not sure if I can trust you when it comes to you having my back." I step out of the car.

Liam gets out, too. "You don't understand, mate. I needed the money, so I took what he offered, but I never betrayed you. I would never do that. Conti simply asked me to talk to you about the drug deal when it was offered. That's as far as things went."

"We'll talk later, but when I hired you, I wasn't hiring a subcontractor."

"You've changed, Cruz. A month ago, you would have shot me; as soon as you found out, there would be no questions," Liam says.

"Then why would you do this if you knew that?" I ask.

"I had to. I still have family in Ireland."

I tap on the window, and Cork rolls it down. "Cork, if any of Conti's men come, warn us."

"Will do, Cruz."

We approach the home. As usual for this time of year, it's freezing, the sky gray and threatening snow again. The front steps are slick with ice, and no one has salted them in the last few hours. The wind howls, shaking Christmas lights that have broken free and are blowing against the house. There are two droopy wreaths hanging on the door that no one's bothered to remove. We try the door, and it's unlocked. Once inside, we cross a pond with a bridge, koi fish, and plants, but the plants seem like they're dying. This place isn't the way I remember it, vibrant and luxurious.

Music plays in the distance, and there's a tapping noise. "Are you picking up on that?" Liam asks. I nod my head. We head towards it. We enter the massive living room with couches, a fireplace, and large pieces of art. The fireplace hasn't been cleaned of old ashes, and there isn't any new wood stacked there. We keep moving, following the music as it leads down a long hallway. There's an iron odor, and I recognize that smell...blood. Other disagreeable smells hit me too. The odor of urine and feces becomes stronger. Liam and I move cautiously. I consider drawing my gun, but I don't want to set Gia off if she has a weapon too.

We reach an open doorway where jazz sounds echo. There's a mammoth bed, unmade, but no one's on it. We creep towards a closed door.

"I think this is the main bath," but there's no sound of running water.

"Should we go in?" Liam's eyes pierce mine.

I nod.

Liam touches the door with his foot, and it opens with a creaking sound. It's a huge bathroom with walk-in closets and a dressing area. At first, we see nothing out of the ordinary, but after passing the walk-in closet and rounding the corner, we reach a horrendous scene. There's blood everywhere, splattered on the walls and the ceiling. It resembles some sort of Expressionist painting. There's a large tub in one corner, and that's where we find Angelo, inside of it with one leg slung over the side, nude and lying face-up in the blood pooled there. His eyes stare up at us, empty. Someone's carved "MARCO" into his belly, dried blood crusting around each letter. When we move closer, I see several other stab wounds, one near his heart and two in his jugular vein.

"Whoa," Liam asks. "Did Gia do that?"

"I don't know."

"Who's Marco?" Liam asks.

"I think that was his brother's name. Angelo told me he died years ago."

"Do you think someone's still in the house?" Liam crouches low. "Maybe they left, and River went with them."

"But River would message me."

"If she could," Liam says.

"Let's search the whole place. Let's start with the dungeon."

I lead Liam back towards the living room and to the basement door, but it's padlocked. "Stand clear," I say, pulling out my gun. *Bang.* The lock explodes, and pieces of metal fly free, chipping the door. I remove what's left of it, and we both proceed down the steps. I listen for anyone else who might be waiting for us.

When we get down there, we find a woman chained to the wall, dead. Her bloody blond hair covers her face. I stumble down the stairs in shock and hurry to her, praying it's not River.

"Gia?" I ask as I lift her head, but it's not her. "Do you know who this is?" I ask Liam, but he simply shrugs. There's another person chained next to her, an older man, also over sixty, with a bullet hole on the side of his head. Who is he? Where's River?

"River! River!" I call. Light thumping and bumping start from somewhere, but I don't know where. I head towards one play-room and open it, but she isn't there. I try the bathroom door, but it's locked. Frustrated, I kick it in. There's a man lying on the bath-room floor. He's dead too. I listen and hear a tapping sound again.

"It's coming from the other side of the wall," Liam says.

"He must have a safe room. Look for a release button or something." I run my hands along the stone wall. I feel one stone that's loose, so I pull it free, and when I do, a door opens, one that had been blended in perfectly with the wall.

River peeks out. I grab hold and hug her.

"There were shots and screaming," she says. "Then it was completely quiet, until your voice."

"Who locked you in there, River?"

"Some older couple. They knocked on the door, and Gia answered it while Angelo was in the shower. They pulled a gun on the two of us, brought us down here, and locked me in the bathroom. I'm not sure where they put Gia."

"Was Joanna here?"

"Who?"

"Conti's ex-wife."

"I didn't see any other woman. Where's Gia?" River asks.

Liam and I look at one another. "I don't know."

River runs out of the safe room and stands by the wall, looking at the bodies of the two people who'd been shot. "This is the older couple who locked Gia and me down here. Who did this to them? Where's Angelo?"

"In his bathroom upstairs, but he's deceased as well."

"Did you kill him?

"No, we found him that way. How about you? Did you hear anything else while you were in there?"

"Like I said, screaming. Something about 'you have to pay,' and 'no, no,' and then shots."

"Do you know who the man in the bathroom is?" Liam asks.

River walks to the restroom door and looks in. "That's my husband's partner, Maxksim Oberlin, from New York. You're sure Joy is okay? she asks, turning to me.

"Yes, she's fine. Two men...they said they worked for him, your husband's partner, returned her. They said they quit and wanted Joy to come home safely."

Liam gets a notification on his phone and looks at it. "Well, mate, we're in deep shit now. Cork just sent a message. Three carloads of men just pulled up outside. What are we going to do, Cruz?"

"Search for an exit." But there didn't appear to be one down here. A few minutes later, we detect a few footsteps on the floor above us. We're trapped in a house with four dead bodies.

"Should we hide?" River asks.

"They're going to think we did this," I say. Liam and I both draw our weapons. We notice more and heavier footsteps above us moving about, then the squeak of the basement door opening. We're frozen in place as the sound of footsteps on the stone steps echoes, and multiple sets of feet appear.

Four armed men face us, staring at the scene of the people chained to the wall and shot dead. They stare back at us. One of them says, "We're here to clean up, but we only expected one body."

"We didn't do it. We came to provide a ride, to my...girlfriend."

The man takes out his cell and makes a call. "Yes, Don Farello, there's a problem. There are four bodies here, not one, plus three live ones. The main gentleman is..." He looks at me as if expecting my name.

"Cruz MacKenzie."

"Cruz MacKenzie. He says he discovered the bodies." He pauses, listening to the other side of the conversation. "No, Don Farello, your daughter isn't here. And Angelo's parents are dead, along with Angelo and another man, too." He pauses again, then turns to us. "Don Farello is coming and wishes to speak to you when he arrives. I must ask that you turn over your weapons." Liam and I exchange looks. I nod my head, and we present our guns.

Minutes later, Don Farello shows up, surrounded by body-guards. He's an older man, about five feet three, wearing a black fedora and a camel-colored wool coat. He removes his hat to reveal white and thinning hair. His eyes appear dark brown, almost black, and his face seems drawn. It's difficult to say how old he is. He stands in front of me, holding his hat.

"I've checked you out, Mr. MacKenzie. You have a solid reputation. Do you know where my daughter Joanna is?"

"I don't."

"What happened here?"

"I wish I could tell you, but we only arrived a few minutes before your men did. I'm here to rescue my fiancé, River."

"You're real?" the don exclaims, looking River up and down. "There actually is a real River? I thought you were a figment of my ex-son-in-law's imagination." He comes closer to her. "Did you hear or see anything else?"

"I listened to an altercation of some sort, but I couldn't see it because I was locked in a room. Someone said, 'Stop, don't do it, Eddie, please don't.'"

I turn to River. "Did you say, Eddie? That's the name of an employee I fired the other week." Is it possible I underestimated Eddie? Is his dumb act just that, all an act?

Don Farello bows his head. "Whoever he is, I'm putting a contract out on him for killing my in-laws. The killing of Angelo, my son-in-law, was not his doing. That was his parents' doing, with my daughter's help and my blessing." He must have seen the shock on our faces, because he continued, "Angelo sinned against his family. Killed his own brother, turned his back on my daughter, and his children. His parents took retribution. Now I must take retribution against this Eddie person for killing my in-laws. Where has he taken my daughter? Where is this man, Eddie?"

CRUZ

Eddie wraps himself in the plushness of Cruz's black lambskin jacket as he paces outside of Conti's huge home. He never returned the jacket Cruz lent him. When Cruz first gave it to him, he looked the brand up on his phone. The coat costs two grand. It's too large for Eddie, but he liked it too much to return it. He pushed Cruz to the breaking point that night with his complaining and dissing River.

Eddie looks at the heavens and points. "For you, Bones. I did this for you." He meant to kill G, too, but when it came time to do it, he didn't. She talked him out of it. He let her and her girlfriend waltz out the door. He knew he could change his mind later. Right now, he's intent on taking out Cruz MacKenzie.

Why his brother ever left New Orleans, he'll never understand. Chicago is too windy, too cold, too gray, too everything.

Bones could've worked for various criminal enterprises in New Orleans, so why come to Chicago? He'd apparently seen too many mobster movies. New Orleans is full of color and parties, not to mention Mardi Gras. There's no Mardi Gras here. Eddie had come to Chicago for one reason: to make anyone associated with his brother's death pay. Cruz had something to do with it. The last time he'd communicated with Bones was in a text. His brother crowed about some get-rich scheme. Bones said he had a partner named Gia, that they were going to meet River's husband at some hotel, and that when he was done, he'd be rich and the boss. Then no word until an acquaintance of Eddie's mailed him a newspaper article about the discovery of River's husband's body, with cash, drugs, and the corpse of another unidentified male who was missing his hands. Eddie thought the unidentified man was his brother, but he couldn't call the law. Eddie was wanted for outstanding warrants. But months passed, and he never heard from his brother again. He decided rather than get the legal system involved, he'd do his own investigation and dispense his own justice. After checking Cruz and Gia out, he concluded they were the guilty parties; they killed Bones.

The irony is that Gia found him. Once she discovered Eddie worked for Cruz MacKenzie, Gia approached him.

"I need you to keep tabs on him, report to me." After she got him to do that, she seduced Eddie into her bed and asked for more, "Could you get hired by Angelo Conti and watch him too?" Gia was an operator, and he found her fascinating. There's no stopping her, and neither did he want to, not yet, anyway. Eddie had plans for her.

It startled Eddie to find Angelo being stabbed to death by his own parents when he first entered the house. What parents kill their own child? When they finished with their son, he walked the couple into the basement to shoot them, surprised to discover it was a dungeon, and that's where he found Gia chained to the wall. Eddie let her loose and killed the couple, even though Gia tried to talk him out of it. He found another man already dead in the basement bathroom. Eddie had no idea who killed him, and Gia claimed she didn't know him.

If Eddie had seen River, he would have taken her out, too. Eddie had nothing personal against her, but he knew his brother Bones had had a thing for her, and that one way to hurt Cruz was to hurt River or one of her children. It wasn't until he saw River walking out of Conti's that he'd realized she had been inside with the others the entire time, and Gia hadn't said a word. Where had River been hiding?

"It isn't too late," he mutters. Eddie steps away from his car and starts firing at River and Cruz.

Cruz pushes River down behind the car, then comes up firing. Cruz's two men are already firing rounds at Eddie, too, but Angelo's men are scattering like roaches at night when you turn on a light. Cruz is on the offensive, and he's coming after him. Eddie's hit, but he's unsure how many times. There's little pain, only a flood of warmth. There's nothing now as Eddie floats towards the ground. It's white. Is it the snow? Shadows, then a startling bright light. His brother is waving at him. How's he doing that? How did Bones get here? He's got his hands back. He's smiling. The light is so bright until it's not.

"He's still breathing," Liam whispers. "I've got his wallet."

"Should we call an ambulance?" I ask.

"No. He isn't going to make it," Liam says. "He's got a few minutes, five if he's really lucky. He's bleeding out."

Liam passes Eddie's wallet to me. Besides his Illinois license, he has a license from New Orleans, with a different name. Eddie never discussed New Orleans. Eddie's got a picture tucked in with his cash, and it stops me dead. I show it to the others.

"Who's this?" Liam asks, pointing to the other man in the photo.

"It's Bones. He used to have your job before he got killed." My hand shakes as I hold the picture.

"People who work for you don't last long," Liam chuckles.

"It appears Bones and Eddie were brothers. That's why Eddie was unhappy with me. He held me responsible for Bones' death."

"Were you, mate?" Liam asks.

"No. Gia stabbed him, but I helped Gia get away. So perhaps Eddie blamed me."

"So Eddie's behind some of this?"

"Seems that way," I say.

21

PROMISE

RIVER

The Boudicca painting hangs over our bed now. I didn't know how Cruz arranged it, but he got it for me. One phone call to Don Farello made it happen. Cruz says I've become Boudicca, strong and brave.

"Are you ready to submit?"

"Let me think about it."

He wraps my collar around my neck and buckles it. I smell the leather.

"There will be no more thinking on your end. Get on your knees." I slip down and gaze up.

"Eyes down. You like to be dominated, don't you? Admit it. You don't have to be ashamed." My cheeks heat. "Come on, how difficult is it? You're being stubborn." He's got his hands on either side of my head. I don't feel controlled but comforted. "I'll give you something easier to admit to. Do you want to serve your master?"

"Yes, Sir."

"Open your mouth." He unzips himself.

I open my mouth for him, and he slides his cock in. Should I be ashamed? My mouth stretches wide to accommodate him. He's not all the way in. I'm aware he's holding back, allowing me to set the pace. I'm taking him in and out of my mouth. Once in a while, I stop and lick around the crown, then come down and lick his shaft. I can tell I'm driving him to the brink because he's holding his breath. I bring my hand to my pussy.

"No, River. You don't get to do that until I say." Damn, he's such a control freak, and I love that about him.

He pushes my hand away, fucking my mouth harder and pulling my head closer.

"Get ready, River, it's going to be soon, and I'm going to give you all my cum. Don't miss any of my essence. Drink it all."

I nod my head. He thrusts faster, and my face gets hotter. He yells out, "You're beautiful!" and spills into my mouth.

I can't keep up and don't swallow all he shoots into me. Will he say something? I look up at him to see if he's noticed. He wipes a few drops off my lips.

"Did I do well enough, sir?"

He pulls me up in his arms. "Of course you did. Your turn. I'm going to give it to you like you like—hard." He spins me around and bends me over the dresser, lifting my skirt. "No panties?" He slides his hands between my legs and finds my clit. I'm wet and swollen. "Someone's in serious need." He brings his hands out and gives me a hard swat on my ass. "For not wearing any panties, like a little slut."

"Ouch!" I scream out. "I forgot to do laundry."

He swats me again. "For not doing laundry." Then again. "For not saying 'Sir.' Anything else you want to confess to?"

"I let some of your sperm go on the floor, sir."

"You're a bad girl. You'll get three more hits for wasting my essence." Slap, slap, slap. "You're nice and red now." He strokes my clit again, and this time I'm soaking. "I love this." He pinches my clit.

"Ouch!"

"Did you like the pain?"

"Yes, I liked it, sir."

"Do you want more pain?"

"Yes, more, please, sir."

Cruz reaches up onto the dresser for a leather bag. "I've got your nipple clamps."

"Oh, yes."

"Turn around." Cruz takes the silver jewelry and attaches them to each nipple, tightening the screws. The heat radiates from my nipple down to my pussy, making me even more needy for Cruz. "Bend over the bed. I'll spank you some more." Even the sheet touching my nipples or brushing against my pussy makes me want to cum.

"Cruz, I need you. I can't take much more of this."

"Not yet, River. Not until I give you permission."

"I'm begging you, please, please."

"Say the magic word, River."

"Please, sir."

"Good girl." He grabs my shoulder and flips me on my back. "You are a goddess." Cruz spreads my legs and draws me forward, bringing me to him, then drives his cock into me hard. I'm so wet there's no resistance. He's buried deep inside me, the base of his cock hitting my clit with every thrust. His hand brushes against my nipples on purpose, knocking into the nipple clamps, sending waves of pain through them. "Too much?" he asks, reading my eyes.

"Overwhelming...gothic."

Cruz backs off. "I'll remove them." He pulls himself out of me and unscrews them a bit at a time until he can take them off of me. "Better?"

"I'm sorry, it's been a while."

"Don't apologize. If something's too much, always say something. It's about your pleasure." Cruz holds his cock and enters me again, beginning to fuck me in a fast rhythm. He brings his fingers to my clit, rubbing in a circle.

"Oh, Cruz, yes."

"Tell me what you want."

"Umm, I want..."

"What do you want?"

"Take me from behind?"

"Fuck your ass?"

"No, no. Just fuck me from behind."

"Turn over." Cruz helps me up.

I lie on my tummy with my ass in the air, and he stands behind me.

"You look delectable. Would you enjoy a butt plug, River?"

"Um, I'm not sure. I don't usually like them."

He walks over to his black bag and rummages around until he finds what he's looking for. "This one will fit you and might make you think differently. You've never tried one with me."

"That's true. Alright."

"Breathe, River, and relax. Like you do in yoga. That's a girl. Another push and I'll have it in. One more inhale. How's it feel, River?"

"Umm, fantastic, Cruz."

"Wait until I fill your pussy." Cruz drives into me, and he's right, having both holes filled is unbelievable. He slides his hand underneath me and rubs my clit again. "I should get the vibrator out."

"No," I don't need it." I'm close to cumming. Is Cruz trying to torture me by making me wait?

Cruz whispers in my ear, "I want to fuck your ass so bad, River," and an orgasm rips through me, as my pussy squeezes his cock. He holds on to my hips and rides it out. I can feel him having his own orgasm, with his cum spilling into me.

"Wow, that was something," he whispers in my hair. He sinks down next to me. "What do you think?"

"About what?"

"Don't play dumb."

"I'm not sure. There's a difference between a butt plug and a man's cock, and your cock is super big, and my ass is small."

Cruz laughs. "All true. But my lady does like pain."

"In small doses."

"You already know I'm good at getting people through anal sex."

"I realize that. I saw you with Melinda when—"

"Right, we'll revisit the topic again another time. No pressure. It's not something I need from you."

Should I be happy that Cruz can go elsewhere for anal sex? I put the idea aside and told him about the phone call. "I have exciting news, Cruz."

"You won the Mega Millions?"

"Not all good news has to do with money."

"Most of it does. You're pregnant?"

"You suppose that would be good news?"

"If it came from your lips, it would be."

"You're sweet. I heard from Gia. She and Joanna are safe. The reason they didn't hang around is that Joanna doesn't want to be a Mafia princess anymore, and her father could never accept her in a relationship with a woman. She thought he'd force her into a marriage with some Italian stallion, so she took the children, and she and Gia are lying low."

"I'm glad it worked out and that Gia's not mad at you anymore. Maybe in time she'll soften her views towards me."

"She has. She didn't try to kill you this time around. You know, Cruz, I never knew Jo-Jo, the mother from St. Cloud, and

Joanna, Conti's ex-wife, were one and the same person until Gia told me."

"Don't feel bad. I never made the connection either," Cruz says. "I have some news too, and I hope you like it. I picked the space at Belmont and the lake to open my restaurant."

"Oh, good. That was my favorite choice too, because it's within walking distance to The Palace."

"I changed the plans with the architect somewhat."

"Why? I thought they were all going to be the same."

"I had the architect add a small gallery, enough to hold about a dozen two-dimensional works and a few sculptures. It also has a smaller room in the back with a transept window to let in light, which you can use as a studio. I attached the gallery to the restaurant, so you'll have traffic flow from there as well."

"Oh, Cruz, you've considered every detail."

"If you don't want to quit Protean, you can stay, and the other gallery can be part-time, only open certain evenings a week. Thoughts?" His eyes study me.

"I love it, Cruz, I do. I can't believe you included me in your project." I hug him.

CRUZ

"Don't you trust me? It's not a trick question, Cruz." River's blue eyes swim with concern, and the afternoon-setting spring sun warms our bed. Joy's adopted three-legged cat, Venus, likes the sun too. She's curled up at the end of the mattress. The cat's named after Joy's favorite sports idol.

"Of course I do," I say.

River's eyes are the same color as the girl in my father's basement. Children's laughter drifts in from the open window from the garden below, reminding me of a childhood I never had.

"At least as much as you can." River traces the lines inside the palm of my hand, and it relaxes me.

"I'm ready to talk about my past."

"Is it the beatings from your father?" She touches my shoulder, encouraging me to go on.

"I wish that was all it was."

"You can tell me anything. I'll never judge you. You're everything to me."

I take a long pause. "My father took a girl. It happened when I was a kid."

"What?"

"Yes, it sounds preposterous. Normal people don't do those kinds of things, but there was nothing normal about my father or what I saw. Although I'm sure you'd agree, I'm not normal either. You're aware already that I'm different, and the truth is, I hold back with everyone. If I let myself go, well..."

"It's okay, Cruz. Everyone's different." She touches my head.

"Not like me. You know that better than anyone. You've seen the other side of me."

"Cruz, you don't scare me."

"I should. Why didn't I figure out what my father was doing in the basement? He wasn't human, and there's a good chance I'm not either."

I get up and try to leave, but she's holding on to me. "Cruz, you're wrong. Stay. If you don't want to talk about him, we won't. Let's talk about your truth."

My truth. "You don't want something broken like me, River."

"I want you, Cruz, however you are."

"The world is a cruel place filled with evil people."

"Sometimes it has good people, and beauty too."

"I can't deny it when you're in my arms, or when I'm in the woods with nature." I hold River and feel her heart beating against mine.

She pushes me away, takes my hand, leads me to the bed, and sits down next to me. "Everything's going to be fine. I'm not going anywhere. Whatever you tell me, I'm here to listen." She holds my hand.

"You won't let this go, will you?"

"I can't. Whatever you saw, we can tell someone else, and then they can deal with it, and you won't have to carry it alone anymore."

I wonder if I can. "It was right before I came to Chicago to be with my drug-addict mom. That morning, my father beat me with his Bible. The spine of it broke. All the pages blew around my room. My father said it was an omen, and it spooked him. 'You're going to turn out like me,' he yelled."

"But you didn't. You don't beat children." She clutches my hand.

"Maybe not, but that doesn't make me a good person. You were my slave. You know the truth about me. I've done bad things."

"Deep down, you're a good person, and everyone has done some bad things." She hugs me. "God will forgive you if you ask him. Tell me the rest." Her Catholic faith allows forgiveness if one repents, but I'm not a Catholic. I'm a Wiccan, which makes me a witch. There's nothing evil about my religion, but me? That's a different story. Witches have a deep trust in nature, the cycle of the seasons, and magic. We are of the opinion that there isn't a sole god, but a multitude of gods and goddesses. In fact, I know fully that the devil and evil exist without a doubt. The irony here is that my father is a pastor, the epitome of a churchgoing, God-fearing man, but none of that matters; he was evil to the core. And

I'm deeply afraid I've inherited my father's genes, traits, and ways.

I continue telling my story to River. "You need to know the truth. Don't be a flamingo."

"What do you mean?" Her forehead wrinkles and her eyebrows pull together, a mask of confusion covering her face.

"Flamingos are showy birds that bury their heads under water. They are also women unwilling to see their partners for what they are—criminals. Having a flamingo girlfriend is dangerous because you can never be sure she won't one day turn on you and call the cops." I turn away from her, button my shirt, and sit on the bed.

"Do you think I'd do that to you? "

"If I do something terrible, I hope you will. What if..."

"What if what?"

"I turn out like my father?"

"You aren't. You won't."

"You don't know that."

"I do. I know you won't."

I touch her hair. It shocks me that anyone believes in me so much. It makes me well up inside. I want to give her the rest of the story and tell her everything.

"It was later in the afternoon that I came into the kitchen to get some soda. We usually didn't have that kind of thing because my mother spent her money on drugs, but she had gotten a welfare check that day, and my father took it from her. He went to the grocery store and bought stuff. When I came down from my room, I found the basement door ajar, though it was never normally left open. I heard groans and crying coming from below. I should have kept away, but I didn't. I had to check it out. I snuck down the steps, taking them one at a time, keeping close to the wall, holding onto the banister to see who or what was making the noise. At first, I saw nothing because the basement was dark and there weren't any lights on, but as my eyes grew accustomed to the darkness, I saw her...a girl chained to the wall, unclothed, hair matted, head bent, and she was crying, huddled on the floor. My father hovered over her, holding his folded brown leather belt. I recognized her because she lived down the street from us and had disappeared weeks earlier. She'd appeared on the front page of the papers, local and national ones, too. My father turned around and sneered, 'I beat her or you. Pick.' I tore up the stairs and never returned. Before I ran away, he told me it was our secret. I never did anything or told anyone. It still haunts me."

"You need to see someone. Please, Cruz." River's eyes search mine for agreement.

"I can't forgive myself for not helping her escape or going to the police."

"You were an abused twelve-year-old boy. You couldn't take on that kind of responsibility at that age. Is your father still alive?" River reaches for my hand and holds it.

"Most likely."

"What do you want to do?"

"Forget, but I can't. None of my spells work anymore. I've tried everything from my Book of Shadows."

"You need to see someone. Please, Cruz, go to a professional. Get counseling. You need help."

"Can you still love me after everything I've told you?"

"It doesn't change my heart or anything else."

"Will you wear my ring again?"

"Yes, but you must promise to help yourself and talk with someone, anyone."

"I promise." I slip the butterfly skull ring over her head on the silver chain and bring her close.

That night, from my office at Monsters, I keep my promise. I make the call anonymously. I drop a dime on my father, Montel MacKenzie. For the first time I can remember, I sleep peacefully.

22

SITCOM

CRUZ

"I realize it's not the way you imagine it, River, and it's not the way society portrays the ideal family, but it's only temporary. If you can wait until the restaurants are producing, then...." I'm trying to convince River to move back in with me. My women aren't helping me as they sashay down each step, scantily dressed. They ask for her opinion on their new dresses.

"Ahh, they're nice." River looks back at me with an *I told you so* look. "You know I love everyone in the house, but I don't think having my son surrounded by women dressed like this is—"

"Alex is smart, and he's got a good sense of right and wrong. Living here won't alter that." I button the top button of my shirt and put on my tie. River likes it when I wear a tie, and her eyes dance as I wrap it around my neck. Does she pretend I work on Wall Street instead of doing what I do? Soon I'll be the owner of MacKenzie's Bar & Bistro, but until then...

"Alex is going to realize I'm not leading him in the right direction. And that reminds me, I need to go back to the brownstone. Alex has to work on a school project with a friend who lives on our street, and I want to pick up a few things."

"Fine, I'll drop you off, but can you take a ride service back? I've got a lot going on at Monsters."

"Does money always need to be the top priority? You have a family now."

"Come on, River, money keeps a roof over our head. And you're wrong about Alex. Alex knows I'm a good guy who loves you and wants what's best for you and them."

"If that's true, you wouldn't want us to rely on a ride service to pick us up late at night."

"As I said, I've got quotas I have to meet. You should understand. Speaking of which, I got a call from Marjorie today. Good news. The case against me got dismissed. Marjorie presented the phones as evidence, and they charged the woman with blackmail. It's a class D felony, so she could end up serving three to seven years if she's convicted. I thought of filing a civil case against her, but she doesn't own much, even if I win."

"I'm thankful it's over, and the truth came out."

"Thanks for your faith in me." I wrap my arms around her from behind, while she breaks free and checks her phone.

"Oh, my God. Oberlin's family's going to give me fifty percent. Marjorie said a check should arrive next week. I can't believe it."

"I told you it'd be better with her handling your case. Oh, did she tell you she's getting married?"

"No, she didn't mention it. Who to?"

"The judge in my case."

"You're kidding."

"No, I'm not."

Alex walks into the room, and River asks, "Where's your sister?"

"Joy joined the chess club, don't you remember? She's taking the bus home. What's for dinner?"

"Whatever you two are making," I say. I try to leave when Cruz leaps over the couch, making a grab for me. He pulls me into his arms and kisses me as my son Alex yells, "Luuuucy, I'm hoooome!"

"What?" Cruz asks.

EPILOGUE—FBI

CRUZ

"Are you two kissing again?" Joy smirks, walking through the front door of The Palace, a backpack slung over her shoulder.

Two men follow her in but stop short in the vestibule. Why are they tailing Joy?

I rush towards the foyer in protective mode, ready to draw my gun. My eyes land on their dark suits and shiny black shoes, and I holster my weapon, realizing these guys are law enforcement.

"Cruz MacKenzie?" one of them asks.

"Yes." I lower my gaze to the shorter man and walk towards them as River, Joy, and Alex study them.

"I'm Special Agent Mark Malroy, FBI," the shorter man says, "and this is my partner, Pete Fratglo." He points back at Pete. They both hold out their IDs in clear plastic sleeves for me to examine. "Could we have a moment of your time?"

The odor of the dank, moldy basement and sweat, and the

sound of crying and pleading, come back to me from that day. *Fuck.*

"That depends. What's this about?" My hands shake, and I stuff them in my jacket so they can't see. My stomach heaves and my head throbs. I get myself under control.

"It's about your father, Montel MacKenzie. We're investigating several unsolved missing person cases and two murders in Ithaca and Syracuse."

I grit my teeth. Why did it take them this long?

River gasps, and she brings her hands to her mouth, spinning and taking the children's shoulders as she moves them towards the kitchen.

I only reported one.

"I have nothing to say. If you have questions, contact my attorney." I pull out my wallet and hand them Marjorie's business card. No way am I letting them interview me with my people in the house and without Marjorie present.

Malroy's body tenses when he takes the card. "Please don't be this way, Mr. MacKenzie. We just—"

"Call my attorney. I know what you want." I rub my eyes with the bottom of my palms, pushing the tips of my fingers into my eye sockets. Waves of nausea flood through me, and my muscles weaken. I slump down into the large leather chair nearest to me as the two FBI agents watch me.

The thing I've most feared has happened, and I made it happen. River begged me to do this. I never left my name, but they came anyway. The room spins. It's all over. Or is it all beginning?

RIVER

It's strange to be back in the brownstone. I make a cup of chai and take a sip, swirling it in my mouth. The clove and cinnamon warm me. I climb the stairs, holding the tea with one hand and the banister with the other. The house is quiet without the children here. It's like the last time I entered my bedroom and sensed something wrong. It doesn't have a pleasant aroma, and I explain it away as being because I haven't been here for a while, and the house has been closed up. It's the same smell as previously, like a pair of smelly sneakers or dirty laundry. I made my bed a week ago before I left, and now I see that someone has rumpled the covers and put a dent in the pillow.

I notice all my dresser drawers are open, and it's not because I've moved my things to Cruz's. I move closer to the empty top drawer of my dresser and look down. I'm dizzy, and my stomach churns. I run my hand inside, feeling the paper liner and the empty drawer. The dresser is lit by the moon, and all my underwear is gone. Who took them? The house has a security system. How did they get in? The only ones who could—

Is it the creep that's threatening me? Or would Cruz do this? I sit on the bed and ponder. I even considered calling Cruz, but changed my mind. I don't want him to think I'm coming up with reasons to call to make him pick me up, and he has enough on his mind after the visit from the FBI agents about his father. I don't want to appear like a needy middle-aged woman. Did Cruz take them? I doubt it; if he wanted a pair, he'd just ask for them from me. Should I contact the police? Would they come out to investigate stolen underwear? Not.

Knock, knock.

MONTEL

"Please let me go. I won't tell anyone." Montel memorized the phone number Angelo gave to his employee, Eddie, when he was in Conti's home. After that, it got even easier. Montel called Kate and told her that Angelo had instructed him to call. They were supposed to meet and work together to follow Cruz MacKenzie. She believed him, came over, and met Montel in his apartment.

Montel found Kate attractive and, like many women, too trusting and easy to subdue. He overpowered her using his trusted stun gun. She tried to fight back, but she was no match for him. He bound her hands and feet. Kate had skin you could peel off, but it's much too soft and prone to tearing. They'd made Little Mouse of tougher stuff.

Having Kate takes the edge off of things and allows him to slow down with Little Mouse. He plays with Kate for two days. She continues to whimper and beg throughout the second day. He tired of her cries and had to finish her off. He records everything and watches the video over and over whenever he needs a fix.

Montel hasn't seen or spoken to his son, Cruz, in over twenty years. Cruz won't be happy to see him. When you rear a God-fearing child, it can go one of two ways. Either they become obedient soldiers, willing to comply and follow God's commands as interpreted by you, or they rebel and hold everything you did against you. Cruz is one of the second kind.

Montel's obsession with River hasn't diminished. In fact, it grew the whole time she wasn't visiting her brownstone. He's broken in many times, and he's installed new cameras. It's his destiny to have River, tonight. He calls out to Little Mouse, "I'm going to get you a different friend, the woman from across the street. The other one didn't work out.

Here, watch." He brings the laptop and sits down next to Little

Mouse. They watch River looking down at the open, empty drawer of her dresser. The camera captures her confusion first, then panic spreads across her face as she realizes all her panties are missing.

"I've got them all right there." Little Mouse's face transforms from fear while looking at the screen to horror when Montel points to the heap of lingerie now on the floor. The panties are white and rose-colored. Montel imagines what they'll appear like against River's pale skin and grows excited. "Would you like to wear some of her underwear? Maybe later you can try some on." He picks up the computer, walks towards the pile of underwear, and finds the special pair, the white lace ones with a tiny pink ribbon on the front. He found them in River's hamper in the bathroom. River hasn't discovered they're gone yet. He returns to the living room and brings the panties to his nose, inhaling. River's scent is intoxicating, a faint rose fragrance and something else... her. He licks his tongue along the crotch of River's panties. She's delicious. Montel can't wait to sample the real thing.

Montel's dick pushes against his zipper. He unzips his pants and runs the white lace panties over his throbbing cock. He uses one of the leg holes to lasso it, then tightens the panty over it, imagining the fabric is River's tight cunt. He fantasizes about having River pinned to the floor, restrained and naked. Her wrists are chained with red welts on them, and she's unable to move, arms stretched wide, knees pulled back, her pussy lips exposed for him. He tightens the fabric more, bringing it back and forth around his cock, keeping himself on edge by changing the tempo. Near the end, he squeezes more tightly, letting the lace saw and cut into his cock, making his body shake. A hot flood of cum spurts out, dripping all over River's white panties with some drops spilling onto the hardwood floor. He takes the underwear, now covered with his sperm, and holds them up to the dimming light and roars. "You'll feel the pain the next time I cum," he vows.

Montel brings the panties to his mouth and tears the ribbon off with his teeth. The tiny piece of pink satin sails over his tongue, leaving a strawberry flavor, and slides down his throat. Will her pussy also have the flavor of strawberries? Montel laughs.

"It's destiny that River be the one," he says out loud. "My name, like hers, comes from nature. 'Montel' means 'mountain.' Rivers flow underneath and through mountains. I will penetrate her with my body, my mind, and my knives. She enjoys cutting herself, so she'll enjoy me decorating her."

What tools will he choose? He lays out his scalpels, silver and shiny. River has pale flesh, and he imagines what her skin will look like when he decorates it with cuts, both shallow and deep, straight and curved. River will like some of it. How long will he be able to keep her alive? Hopefully, for months before the cuts are too numerous or he makes them too deep. Sometimes his obsession gets away from him before he's finished having fun. Perhaps this time it will be different.

Little Mouse is in the other room. He can keep both of them. Little Mouse has lasted longer than the others. He's even developed some kind of feelings for her. He's not sure what they are, but he doesn't want Little Mouse to die. This is something he hasn't experienced before. Perhaps Montel will develop feelings for River, too. In the early days, he tortured his victims mentally to break them down, to stop them from trying to escape, and to make them follow his orders. Some were a pile of jelly in a week, and others took months. The red-headed neighbor girl was his first kill. He didn't let her live after Cruz saw her, and once he tasted blood, there was no going back. He should thank Cruz for turning him into a successful serial killer.

Montel had doubted he had the patience to break them down mentally anymore. until Little Mouse. It's what's inside their bodies, under their skin, the blood and bones, that fascinate him now. The problem with exploring the insides of his victims is that they seldom survive more than a week or two from the physical demands he places on them.

Little Mouse is the first one who has lasted longer than that. Has he held back with her? If he has, it could be that he's maturing. However, he finds his interest in the mental aspect of his work reignited. Torturing River through phone calls and stalking, while not laying a hand on her, has proven to be fun.

If Cruz were an obedient son, Montel could command Cruz to sacrifice River to his hunger, and that would be that. But since Cruz is stubborn, he'll have to do this without his permission or help. He reflects on his early years rearing Cruz. Perhaps Montel's biggest mistake was the name he gave, a powerful one, derived from the Latin word *crux*, meaning "cross." He should've given Cruz one of the apostles' names: James, Peter, Matthew, John, Simon, or Andrew. With a name like that, his son would do his bidding.

During Cruz's formative years, he fed the child the word of God and reinforced the truths of the gospel through discipline. He thought he understood what Cruz needed, but he accomplished nothing. Cruz continued to defy him, like Montel had defied his father, always disobeying. The day he broke his Bible on Cruz in anger was the final straw. Later that day, he made another mistake by failing to lock the basement door. Had he wanted Cruz to discover his addiction? He didn't expect the boy to keep the secret all these years. Montel assumed Cruz would inform the police, and they would come, but they never did.

If it wasn't for the one girl who got away nine months ago, no one would've suspected Montel of anything. In the beginning, they were skeptical of her claims, dismissing her as a drug-addled prostitute, but they gradually took her words seriously. That's what forced him to leave Syracuse, come to Chicago, with plans to visit his son.

Montel's hungry again. River will satiate him, no doubt. The idea of touching his son's conquest thrills him even more. He'll ask her which of them she prefers and, of course, River will pick him.

He lines up his tools on the couch and places the stun gun on the milk crate by the door. He opens the door and heads down the stairs as tiny snowflakes drop and caress the sidewalk as he crosses it, moving towards River's house. The aroma of burning wood lingers in the air. Someone has a fire somewhere.

"Cruz has done well for himself," Angelo had said to him. "He lives and owns a place called The Palace. He has money, multiple cars, bars and nightclubs, and many employees. Your son is in the sex business." Montel was afraid Cruz would turn out like him, with dark tendencies. The fact that he did must be part of God's plan, proof that Cruz would help Montel get away. He could give him money, secure a passport, help him leave the country, and start over. Getting rid of River will help Cruz concentrate.

Montel opens the gate, climbs the steps to her large front porch, and rings the doorbell. When she opens the door, the intensity of her cornflower blue eyes makes him lose his train of thought. He never saw them the night he placed her on the kitchen table. Angelo had covered them with a blindfold. Montel wonders if they'll stay that color when she's crying and screaming in pain.

"Hi," he says, pushing his voice down an octave. "I just moved in across the street. My name's Montel. Could I use your phone? Mine isn't working."

"Umm, sure, come on in. Let me get it." *Too trusting.* She walks into the kitchen area and comes back, handing him her cell. "Here you go." The house is quiet. If the children are there, they must be upstairs.

"Thanks. I don't know what's wrong with mine. I'm having a

hell of a time getting some boxes moved into the bedroom, so I'm calling someone over to see if they can assist me. Your son wouldn't happen to be interested, do you think? I saw him outside once or twice. A strapping young man." Montel smiles.

"No, unfortunately, he's at friends', but I could help you."

"You? You're such a little thing. I don't—"

"I'm stronger than I look. I go to the gym. I'm sure we could do it together. How many boxes?"

"Three." All you have to do is suggest a woman isn't strong enough these days, and they'll jump at the chance to prove you wrong. He'd had them demand to go back to his house numerous times to move refrigerators, freezers, breakfronts, and other heavy things that never existed, only to be subdued, raped, tortured, and killed as soon as he got them through the front door.

"Let's go. I'm sure we could do it." River puts on her jacket and brushes her hair from inside it, popping her phone in her pocket.

"I appreciate it. Thank you." Her eyes are extraordinary.

River opens the door, and Montel follows, but they're both brought to a dead halt. A towering, menacing male figure blocks Montel's path. It's like looking into a mirror and going back in time.

"What are you doing here?" his son Cruz asks. "And where do you think you're taking her?"

"It's good to see you," Montel smiles.

Cruz turns to River. "If I hadn't stopped back here to get you myself, can you imagine what he'd have done to you?"

"Who?" River asks, staring at Cruz and back at Montel, her eyes full of surprise.

"Him." Cruz points at Montel. "My psychopath serial-killer father."

"Serial killer is such an ugly label," he says.

But no sooner does Cruz demand that Montel tell him where he plans to take River than a black SUV pulls up nearby, and

Montel's favorite FBI agents, the same ones who questioned him in Syracuse, jump out.

"Crap." Montel backs up, glancing around quickly, considering which way to run.

The End

ABOUT KAY

Kay Freeman spent the early part of her career as a professional artist. She's shown her work throughout the United States under her professional name, Kay A. Klotzbach. Kay was a full-time art professor in South Jersey for over 23 years and was awarded a Princeton Mid-Career Fellowship for her teaching and community-based service-learning projects.

Kay decided to pursue her passion for writing after her manuscript, *Truth Moon*, was selected by Romance Writers of America's RAMP program in 2021, which led to the publication of her debut novel, *Truth Moon*, by The Wild Rose Press. Kay has since self-published nine other novels.

Kay has won several awards for her writing. In 2022, Hitman's Honey won third place in the Mid Atlantic Author Society's Romance Contest, and in 2024, her novel *Leather Man* was a finalist in Passionate Ink's Passionate Plume Contemporary Short Category. Her novel *The Flower Queen* topped Amazon's Best Seller List in June 2023 in the Historical Romance 20th Century category. In 2025, her novel *Other Worlds* won a Stiletto in the speculative category. Kay is celebrated for crafting hard-won happily-ever-afters that involve spiritual journeys and transformations for her characters.

For the past four years, she has also written a publication for romance authors, *What Do Romance Authors Think About,* a free Substack newsletter.

Besides her passion for art, reading, and writing, she loves the blues, tequila, baking bread, and her husband, Barry. Kay lives in Wilmington, DE. You can learn more and sign up for her newsletter for readers on KaylaaFreeman.com.